PINEAPPLE

LIES

A Pineapple Port Mystery: Book One

Amy Vansant

Vansant Creations, LLC / Amy Vansant
Annapolis, MD
http://www.AmyVansant.com
http://www.PineapplePort.com

Cover art by Stephen Novak
   Copy editing by Carolyn Steele

DEDICATION

To the real Pineapple Ports. Y'all are nuts.

CHAPTER ONE

"Whachy'all doin'?"

Charlotte jumped, her paintbrush flinging a flurry of black paint droplets across her face. She shuddered and placed her free hand over her heart.

"Darla, you scared me to death."

"Sorry, Sweetpea, your door was open."

"Sorry," echoed Mariska, following close on Darla's heels.

Charlotte added another stroke of black to her wall and balanced her brush on the edge of the paint can. Standing, her knees cracked a twenty-one-gun salute. She was only twenty-six years old but had always suffered bad knees. She didn't mind. Growing up in a fifty-five-plus retirement community, her creaky joints provided something to complain about when the locals swapped war stories about pacemakers and hip replacements. Nobody liked to miss out on that kind of fun.

Charlotte wiped the paint from her forehead with the back of her hand.

"Unlocked and open are not the same thing, ladies. What if I had a gentleman caller?"

Darla burst into laughter, the gold chain dangling from her hot-pink-rimmed glasses swinging. She sobered beneath the weight of Charlotte's unamused glare. Another pair of plastic-rimmed glasses sat perched like a baby bird on her head, tucked into a nest of champagne-blonde curls.

"Did you lose your other glasses again?" asked Charlotte.

"I did. They'll turn up."

Charlotte nodded and tapped the top of her head. "I'm sure."

Darla's hand shot to her head.

"Oh, there you go. See? I told you they'd show up."

Mariska moved closer, nudging Darla out of the way. She threw out her arms, her breezy cotton tunic draping like aqua butterfly wings.

"Morning hug," she demanded.

Charlotte rolled her eyes and relented. Mariska wrapped her in a bear hug, and she sank into the woman's snuggly, Polish-grandmother's body. It was like sitting on a favorite old sofa, rife with missing springs, and then being eaten by it.

"Okay. Can't breathe," said Charlotte.

"I'm wearing the top you bought me for Christmas," Mariska mumbled in Charlotte's ear as she rocked her back and forth.

"I saw that."

"It's very comfortable."

"This isn't. *I can't breathe.* Did I mention that? We're good. Okay there…"

Mariska released Charlotte and stepped back, her face awash with satisfaction. She turned and looked at the wall, scratching her cheek with flowered, enameled nails as she studied Charlotte's painting project.

"What are you doing there? Painting your wall black? Are you depressed?"

Charlotte sighed. Darla and Mariska were inseparable; if one wasn't offering an opinion, the other was picking up the slack.

"You're not turning into one of those dopey Goth kids now, are you?" asked Darla.

"No, it has nothing to do with my mood. It's chalkboard paint. I'm making this strip of wall into a giant chalkboard."

"Why?" Darla asked, her thick, Kentucky accent adding syllables to places the word *why* had never considered having them. Her mouth twisted and her brow lowered. Charlotte couldn't tell if she disapproved, was confused, or suffering a sharp gas pain. Not one guess was more likely than any other.

"Because I think I figured out my problem," she said.

Darla cackled. "Oh, this oughta be good. You have any coffee left?"

"In the kitchen."

Darla and Mariska lined up and waddled toward the kitchen like a pair of baby ducks following their mama. Mariska inspected several mugs in the cabinet above the coffee machine and, finding one, put it aside. She handed Darla another. Mariska's mug of choice was the one she'd given Charlotte after a trip to Colorado's Pikes Peak. She'd bought the mug for herself, but after Charlotte laughed and explained the double entendre of the slogan emblazoned on the side, *I Got High on Pikes Peak*, she'd thrust it at her, horrified. Mariska remained proud of her fourteen thousand foot spiraling drive to the peak, so she clandestinely drank from the offending mug whenever she visited.

Charlotte watched as she read the side of the mug, expelled a deep sigh, and poured her coffee. That heartbreaking look was why she hadn't broached the subject of Mariska's *I Got Baked in Florida* t-shirt.

The open-plan home allowed the two older women to watch Charlotte as she returned to painting the wall between her pantry door and living area.

"So are you pregnant?" Darla asked. "And after this, you're painting the nursery?"

"Ah, no. That's not even funny."

"You're the youngest woman in Pineapple Port. You're our only hope for a baby. How can you toss aside the hopes and dreams of three hundred enthusiastic, if rickety, babysitters?"

"I don't think I'm the youngest woman here anymore. I think Charlie Collins is taking his wife to the prom next week."

Darla laughed before punctuating her cackle with a grunt of disapproval.

"Stupid men," she muttered.

Charlotte whisked away the last spot of neutral cream paint with her brush, completing her wall. She turned to find Mariska staring, her thin, over-plucked eyebrows sitting high on her forehead as she awaited the answer to the mystery of the chalkboard wall.

"So you're going to keep your grocery list on the wall?" asked Mariska. "That's very clever."

"Not exactly. Lately, I've been asking myself, what's missing from my life?"

Darla tilted her head. "A man. *Duh.*"

"Yeah, yeah. Anyway, last week it hit me."

Darla paused mug nearly to her lips, waiting for Charlotte to continue.

"What hit you? A chalkboard wall?" asked Mariska.

Charlotte shook her head. "No, a *purpose.* I need to figure out what I want to *be.* My life is missing *purpose.*"

Darla rolled her eyes. "Oh, is that all? I think they had that on sale at Target last weekend. Probably still is."

Charlotte chuckled and busied herself resealing the paint can.

Mariska inspected Charlotte's handiwork. "So you're going to take up painting? I'll take a chalkboard wall. I can write Bob messages and make lists…"

"I'll paint your wall if you like, but starting a painting business isn't my *purpose.* The wall is so I can make a to-do list."

Darla sighed. "I have a to-do list, but it only has one thing on it: *Keep breathing.*"

Mariska giggled.

"I'm going to make goals and write them here," said Charlotte, gesturing like a game show hostess to best display her wall. "When I accomplish something, I get to cross it off. See? I already completed one project; that's how I know it works."

There was a knock on the door and Charlotte's gaze swiveled to the front of the house. Her soft-coated wheaten terrier, Abby, burst out of the bedroom and stood behind the door, barking.

"You forgot to open your blinds this morning," said Mariska.

"Death Squad," mumbled Darla.

The Death Squad patrolled the Pineapple Port retirement community every morning. If the six-woman troop passed a home showing no activity by ten a.m., they knocked on the door and demanded proof of life. They pretended to visit concerning other business, asking if the homeowner would be attending this meeting or that bake sale, but everyone knew the Squad was there to check if someone died overnight. Odds were slim that Charlotte wouldn't make it through an evening, but the Squad didn't make exceptions.

Charlotte held Abby's collar and opened the door.

"Oh, hi, Charlotte," said a small woman in a purple t-shirt. "We were just—"

"I'm alive, Ginny. Have a good walk."

Charlotte closed the door. She opened her blinds and peeked out. Several of the Death Squad ladies waved to her as they resumed their march. Abby stood on the sofa and thrust her head through the blinds, her nub of a tail waving back at them at high speed.

Mariska turned and dumped her remaining coffee into the sink, rinsed the purple mug, and with one last longing glance at the Pikes Peak logo, put it in the dishwasher. She placed her hands on her ample hips and faced Charlotte.

"Do you have chalk?"

"No."

She'd been annoyed at herself all morning for forgetting chalk and resented having it brought to her attention. "I forgot it."

Darla motioned to the black wall. "Well, there's your first item. *Buy chalk.* Write that down."

"With what?"

"Oh. Good point."

"Anyhow, shopping lists don't count," said Charlotte.

Darla chuckled. "Oh, there are *rules*. The chalkboard has rules, Mariska."

Mariska pursed her lips and nodded. "Very serious."

"Well, I may not have a chalkboard, but I have a wonderful sense of purpose," said Darla putting her mug in the dishwasher.

"Oh yes? What's that?"

"I've got to pick up Frank's special ED pills."

She stepped over the plastic drop cloth beneath the painted

wall and headed for the door.

"ED?" Charlotte blushed. "You mean for his—"

"Erectile Dysfunction. Pooped Peepee. Droopy D—"

"Got it," said Charlotte, cutting her short.

"Fine. But these pills are special. Want to know why?"

"Not in the least."

Mariska began to giggle and Darla grinned.

"She's horrible," Mariska whispered as she walked by Charlotte.

Darla reached into her pocketbook and pulled out a small plastic bottle. She handed it to Charlotte.

"Read the label."

Charlotte looked at the side of the pill bottle. The label held the usual array of medical information, but the date was two years past due.

"He only gets them once every two years?"

"Nope. He only got them *once*. Ever since then I've been refilling the bottle with little blue sleeping pills. Any time he gets the urge, he takes one, and an hour later, he's sound asleep. When he wakes up, I tell him everything was wonderful."

Charlotte's jaw dropped. "That's terrible."

Darla dismissed her with a wave and put the bottle back in her purse.

"Nah," she said, opening the front door. "I don't have time for that nonsense. If I'm in the mood, I give him one from the original prescription."

Darla and Mariska patted Abby on the head, waved goodbye, and stepped into the Florida sun.

Charlotte shut the door behind them and balled her drop cloth of sliced trash bags. She rinsed her brush and carried the paint can to the work shed in her backyard. On her way back to the house, she surveyed her neglected yard. A large pile of broken concrete sat in the corner awaiting pickup. As part of her new *life with purpose* policy, Charlotte had hired a company to jackhammer part of her concrete patio to provide room for a garden. The original paved yard left little room for plants. With the patio removed, Charlotte could add *grow a garden* to her chalkboard wall. Maybe she was supposed to be a gardener or work with the earth. She didn't feel particularly *earthy*, but who knew?

She huffed, mentally kicking herself again for forgetting to buy chalk.

Her rocky new patch of sand didn't inspire confidence. It didn't resembled the dark, healthy soil she saw in her neighbors' more successful gardens. Charlotte returned to the shed to grab a spade and cushion for her knees, before kneeling at the corner of her new strip of dirt. It was cool outside; the perfect time of day to pluck the stray bits of concrete from the ground before the Florida sun became unbearable. She knew she didn't like sweating, so gardening was probably not her calling. Still, she was determined to give everything a chance. She'd clean her new garden, shower, and then run out to buy topsoil, plants, and chalk.

"Tomatoes, cucumbers..." Charlotte mumbled to herself, mentally making a list of plants she needed to buy. *Or seeds? Should I buy seeds or plants?* Plants. Less chance of failure starting with mature plants; though if they died, that would be even *more* embarrassing.

Charlotte's spade struck a large stone and she removed it, tossing it toward the pile of broken concrete. A scratching noise caught her attention and she looked up to find her neighbor's Cairn terrier, Katie, furiously digging beside her. Part of the fence had been broken or chewed, and stocky little Katie visited whenever life in her backyard became too tedious.

Charlotte watched the dirt fly: "Katie, you're making a mess. If you want to help, pick up stones and move them out of the garden."

Katie stopped digging long enough to stare with her large brown eyes. At least Charlotte *thought* the dog was staring at her. She had a lazy eye that made it difficult to tell.

"Move the rocks," Charlotte repeated, demonstrating the process with her spade. "Stop making a mess or I'll let Abby out and then you'll be in trouble."

Katie ignored her and resumed digging, sand arcing behind

her, piling against the fence.

"You better watch it, missy, or the next item on the list will be to *fix the fence.*"

Katie eyeballed her again, her crooked bottom teeth jutting from her mouth. She looked like a furry can opener.

"Fix your face."

Katie snorted a spray of snot and returned to digging.

Charlotte removed several bits of concrete and then shifted her kneepad a few feet closer to Katie. She saw a flash of white and felt something settle against her hand. Katie sat beside her, tail wagging, tongue lolling from the left side of her mouth. Between the dog and her hand sat the prize Katie had been so determined to unearth.

Charlotte froze, one word repeating in her mind, picking up pace until it was an unintelligible crescendo of nonsense.

Skull. Skull skull skullskullskullskuuuuulllll...

She blinked, certain that when she opened her eyes the object would have taken its proper shape as a rock or pile of sand.

Nope.

The eye sockets stared back at her.

Hi. Nice to meet you. I'm human skull. What's up, girl?

The lower jaw was missing. The cranium was nearly as large as Katie and had similar off-white coloring, though the skull had better teeth.

Charlotte realized the forehead of this boney intruder rested against her pinky. She whipped her hand away. The skull rocked toward her, as if in pursuit, and she scrambled back as it rolled in her direction, slow and relentless as a movie mummy. Katie ran after the skull and pounced on it, stopping its progress.

Charlotte put her hand on her chest, breathing heavily.

"Thank you."

Her brain raced to process the meaning of a human head in her backyard.

It has to be a joke... maybe some weird dog toy...

Charlotte gently tapped the skull with her shovel. It didn't feel like cloth or rawhide. It made a sharp-yet-thuddy noise, just the sort of sound she suspected a human skull might make. If she had to compare the tone to something, it would be the sound of a girl about to freak out, tapping a metal shovel on a human skull.

"Oh, Katie. What did you find?"

The question increased Katie's rate of tail wag. She yipped and ran back to the hole she'd dug, retrieving the lower jaw.

"Oh no... Stop that. You sick little—"

Katie stood, human jawbone clenched in her teeth, tail wagging so furiously that Charlotte thought she might lift off like a chubby little helicopter. The terrier spun and skittered through the fence back to her yard, dragging her prize in tow. The jawbone stuck in the fence for a moment, but Katie wrestled it through and disappeared into her yard.

"Katie no," said Charlotte, reaching toward the retreating dog. "Katie—I'm pretty sure that has to stay with the head."

She leaned forward and nearly touched the jawless skull before yanking away her hand.

Whose head is in my garden?

She felt her eyes grow wider—like pancake batter poured into a pan.

Hold the phone.

Heads usually come attached to bodies.

Were there more bones?

What was worse? Finding a whole skeleton or finding *only* a head?

Charlotte hoped the rest of the body lay nearby and then shook her head at the oddity of the wish.

She glanced around her plot of dirt and realized she might be kneeling in a *whole graveyard*. More bones. More *heads*. She scrambled to her feet and dropped her shovel.

Charlotte glanced at her house, back to where her chalkboard wall waited patiently.

She *really* needed some chalk.

CHAPTER TWO

The Sheriff's deputies allowed Charlotte to stay in her home while they oversaw the removal of human remains from her garden; the garden she now lovingly referred to as *The Garden Never to be Touched Again.* It wasn't as catchy as *The Garden of Eatin'*; the nickname one couple in Pineapple Port had dubbed their screened-in porch area, but it would have to do. It was still better than *lanai.* Everyone in Pineapple Port had a *lanai.* Outside of Hawaii, calling a porch a lanai smacked of Sun Belt snobbery. As if Florida sun porches were more exotic than those in Maryland or Vermont. *Maybe they are.* Her fellow Floridians could grow palm trees and dwarf fruit trees in their southern porches. Maybe it was okay to call a porch a lanai. *I mean if it makes everyone happy...*

Charlotte rubbed her eyes.

No wonder I never get anything done. I spend time thinking about the dumbest things. A human head was sitting in her garden and all she could think about was whether she had the right to call a porch a lanai.

Priorities, Charlotte, priorities.

Outside, two young deputies stood in drab tan uniforms watching the dig with little interest. Frank Marshall, Darla's husband, and the Manatee County Sheriff, stood beside the diggers, clearly wishing he could be anywhere but standing in the Florida sun watching nerds excavate a body one brushstroke at a time. Whenever Charlotte trotted water to the crowd in her backyard, Frank released an exasperated sigh that conveyed his deep preference for ice-cold beer. When she offered him a bottle, he glanced at his young companions and declined.

"I couldn't possibly have a *bottle* on duty Charlotte," he said, retrieving a handkerchief to swab his sweaty forehead. "Not a *bottle* this early."

"A can?"

Frank tilted his head and peered at her from beneath his brow, encouraging a second guess.

Charlotte considered the emphasis Frank had put on the word *bottle*.

"Aaah…"

She popped back into the house, poured the bottle of beer into a coffee mug, and returned.

"How about coffee?" she asked, handing Frank the mug.

"Oh, sure," he said, glancing at the younger officers. "I would love some *coffee*."

"It's good, I grind the beans myself."

"Do you, now?"

"They have a nutty, almost hoppy taste, don't you think?"

Frank glared at her. "Mm," he grunted, taking a sip. "You should probably go back in. I don't want you contaminating the scene."

She grinned and went back inside. Abby barked as she entered and ran toward the front of the house. Charlotte followed her.

"What is it, girl? Is Timmy down the well?"

The police had stretched a length of yellow crime tape across Charlotte's front gate and a line of chattering neighbors stretched from one side to the other. The police might as well have sat in the front yard with a bullhorn screaming, "Scene of the crime! Come see the scene of the crime!" Like sharks to blood, the people of Pineapple Port smelled gossip fodder from miles away.

Charlotte wasn't only the youngest resident of Pineapple Port, she was the most famous. Growing up in a retirement community made her the local oddity. If she purchased a different brand of coffee, within two hours, the whole neighborhood knew. Crime tape was overkill.

She'd moved to Pineapple Port with her grandmother, Estelle, at age eleven, following her mother's death. Estelle died nine months later. Mariska and Darla were her grandmother's best friends, and they conspired with Darla's husband Sherriff Frank, and Pineapple Port's founders, Penny and George Sambrooke, to allow Charlotte to remain in her grandmother's home. She spent most of her time at Mariska's, until her teens when she officially moved back into her grandmother's home. Though she lived alone, she had everyone in the community as foster parents, with Mariska and Bob, who lived directly across the street, as primary caregivers.

Growing up in a fifty-five-plus community had pros and cons. The con was having endless other nosey grandmothers watching her every move. The pro was access to golf carts. Everyone in the neighborhood had a cart, some quite fancy. Access to souped-up golf carts was a child's fantasy, and as a child, she'd dreamed of becoming a professional golf cart racer. She'd been horrified to discover there was no such thing. All other career options paled in comparison.

As an adult, the pros and cons of living in the Port shifted. The neighborhood scrutiny contributed to her lackluster love life. That was a *huge* con. The one time a man spent the evening at her home, she'd been greeted by winks or scowls by nearly everyone in the neighborhood the following day. In retrospect, she wished she'd worn a t-shirt that said, *He got to second base and then slept on the sofa.*

On the pro side, she never wanted for jams, jellies, or crocheted items of any kind. People without an endless supply of homemade jelly didn't know what they were missing.

Charlotte returned to her kitchen and watched them dig, drinking the rest of Frank's beer from her coffee mug to calm her nerves. The Sheriff wasn't the only one trying to avoid scrutiny. Frank looked through the window and she held up her mug in cheer. He reciprocated.

As they enjoyed their beers, the forensic team removed and labeled each part of a skeleton. Charlotte watched a tech dust and place what looked like a toe bone into a baggie. She took another sip from her mug.

"I'm her mother."

Charlotte's head swiveled toward her front door. She heard arguing. She recognized one voice as that of the female officer guarding her front door. The woman had a terrible demeanor, and her sharp bark was undeniable. The other voices sounded more familiar, particularly the one claiming to be her mother.

She drained her mug.

Charlotte walked to the front door to find Darla and Mariska on her porch, their faces twisted in agitation. From the conversation, she deduced the two were attempting to gain entry by claiming to be her mother and grandmother, but they'd forgotten to agree upon who would play which role, and neither wanted to be the grandmother.

"So, you're *both* her mother?" asked the officer. "Or you're both her grandmother?"

Charlotte opened her door just as two other neighbors, Penny and Bettie, joined Mariska and Darla on her stoop.

"Charlotte, dear," said Mariska. "I was so worried for you. What's going on? Tell Mama."

Darla glared at Mariska.

"What's going on?" asked Penny. "I demand to know what's going on."

Charlotte knew she'd have to tell Penny everything. Pineapple Port's matriarch ruled all the important committees and planned all the events worth attending. Those who disappointed her were doomed to a lifetime of weak bridge partners.

"Your *grandmother* and I are very worried," said Darla, stepping on Mariska's toe.

"Hi, Charlotte."

Behind the three louder women stood five-foot-nothing Bettie "Bettie Giraffe" Dahl, adorned in her trademark giraffe-print blouse.

"Hi Bettie, you're back," Charlotte said, unsurprised to see her. Bettie had no permanent place of residence. She visited friends until it was time to hop to the next host home, and appeared in Pineapple Port two or three times a year.

Bettie waved. "You look beautiful, Charlotte."

Bettie never had a bad word to say about anyone, didn't mind if other people did all the talking and her obsession with giraffes made holiday shopping for her a breeze. Her collection of friends was no mystery.

The officer turned to Charlotte, her thumbs hooked in her belt and her demeanor hovering somewhere between annoyed and simmering volcano. She was a woman of many moods, all of them variations of cranky.

"Two of your mothers are here," said the officer. "Should I be on the lookout for any more?"

Charlotte shook her head and stepped outside, leading her four visitors away from the door and toward the crime-taped gate.

"What's going on?" asked Mariska, as Charlotte half-beckoned, half-dragged her away from her front door. She herded the three instigators until they arrived on the edge of her property, as far from the officer as possible. Bettie, Charlotte knew, would follow wherever the others went.

"Are you okay?" asked Darla. "There's tape everywhere. We thought you were murdered."

"I'm fine. I was going to call you, but they showed up so fast I didn't get a chance. Did you read the tape?" Charlotte pointed to the yellow strips draped across her gate. "It says, *Do Not Cross*."

"It's on the fence," said Penny, punctuating her comment with a sniff. She had a sniff for every emotion, from a level one *Not Really Listening to You* to a level ten *Fury*. This was a about a two: *Don't Waste my Time*. "They didn't go across your door with it. It's a mixed message at best and a fine symbol of their infinite incompetence."

Charlotte paused, waiting for a level five *Why is Everyone so Stupid?* but Penny instead chose a well-timed hair flip, which, according to the body-language thesaurus, landed somewhere between a sniff and an eye-roll.

"We didn't cross the tape," said Darla.

"We didn't cross it," echoed Penny.

"I didn't cross it," said Bettie. She looked at Charlotte with large brown eyes. "I didn't, did I?"

Charlotte smiled and patted Bettie on the shoulder.

"No, you didn't cross it, Bettie. None of you did. But we need to disperse this crowd. You'd think Justin Bieber was throwing a concert in my backyard."

"Who?" asked Penny.

"Oh, he's that awful Canadian kid," said Darla. "Needs a good kick in the pants."

"But what's going *on*?" asked Mariska again.

Charlotte looked around to be sure no one but her immediate crowd stood within hearing distance.

"After you two left this morning I went to work on my garden and found bones."

Charlotte said *found bones* in a dramatic whisper. She didn't mean to; the word *bones* just inspired drama.

Mariska's eyes grew wide as silver dollar pancakes (one of the dollar-fifty specials at the local diner, half-price on John F. Kennedy's birthday.) Charlotte knew all the deals in town. She didn't mean to; she just naturally absorbed that sort of information living in the Port. Coupons, promotions, and deals made up twenty percent of local small talk. Fifty percent was medical related; the remaining thirty was a mixture of bragging about grandkids, disapproval, gossip, and recipes.

"Whaddya mean, *bones*?" asked Darla.

"Dog bones?" asked Bettie.

Bless her heart.

"Well, it was Franny's Cairn who did the actual finding, but no, *human* bones. Definitely human bones. A skull, to be exact."

All four women put their hands to their mouths, except Penny, who put her hands on her hips and cocked her head hard enough to send her short bob haircut swinging.

"That's ridiculous."

Charlotte shrugged. "It's true."

"There was a body in your yard?" asked Bettie. "A whole body?"

"No skin or clothes, just bones, but yes. When they removed the concrete for my garden, the bones were underneath. They're old. The police and some forensic guys are back there processing the scene."

"Ooh, is Frank there?" asked Darla. "I'll get the whole story from him."

"He's there. He isn't happy about it, but he's there with two other officers."

"Two policemen?" asked Bettie, touching her hair. Bettie was an incorrigible flirt.

"Did they bag and tag him yet?" asked Darla.

Darla watched an inordinate number of crime shows. Charlotte could see she was giddy at the opportunity to use her crime slang. Telling food store employees to bag and tag a sack of potatoes just wasn't as satisfying.

"Are you a person of interest?" asked Penny.

"What? *No.*"

Charlotte realized the local gossip mill would have her labeled as an escaped convict/serial killer before *Jeopardy!* aired that evening. Even sharing what facts she could would spare her little in the imaginations of bored retirees.

"From what I've overheard, the bones are at least ten years old," Charlotte said, taking a moment to make eye contact with each of the women, except Bettie, who had already lost interest and was watching a Blue Jay hop around the azalea bushes.

"And I can promise you they're at least fifteen years old because that cement has been there since my grandmother moved in. *When I was eleven.* I didn't kill anyone and tunnel them under my grandmother's porch like some kind of psychotic *Lord of the Rings* dwarf."

Penny squinted at her, her expression cold. "You were always a precocious child."

"Is it a man or a woman? What age?" asked Darla.

"I hope it isn't a child," said Mariska.

"I think I heard one of the nerds say the bones were female, but to be honest, I'm not sure. I can tell you the skull was normal adult size."

"Oh, that's good," said Mariska. "I mean, not *good*, but better."

"Do you think we *all* have bodies in our yards?" asked Darla, glancing down the street toward her own house as if it were a party guest she'd just found lurking near her good jewelry.

"Don't be ridiculous," said Penny. "This land was nothing but swamp when George and I expanded Pineapple Port, not a gravesite."

"I told you not to build this place on an Indian burial ground," said Charlotte.

Mariska gasped. "What? It was?"

"I'm just *kidding*. *Poltergeist* reference."

The women stared at her with blank expressions.

"You know... Little girl gets sucked into the TV? Their house was built on an Indian—"

"Precocious," muttered Penny.

Charlotte sighed. "Look, never mind. Bottom line is I don't know much yet, but I'll tell you everything when I find out. You all go home and let me do the snooping. Maybe if you leave, some of these others will wander off."

Charlotte watched a woman slowly pass her house, Dachshund in tow. It was the tenth time she'd passed by and the stubby-legged dog looked tired. One more circle and the poor thing would be dragging behind her like a deflated party balloon.

None of the women moved.

"Hello?" said Charlotte. "Did any of you hear me?"

Darla and Penny remained planted on the sidewalk just outside Charlotte's gate, trapped in a contest to see who could purse their lips more tightly. Bettie's attention wandered down the block, and Charlotte followed her gaze to find a tall, athletic-built man headed in their direction. He had dark hair; not shaggy, but long enough that Charlotte suspected it took real effort to keep it so perfectly in place. As he neared, his mouth curled into the sort of charming grin that could melt the icing off the ladies' best church bazaar cupcakes.

He made eye contact with each woman, spending no more or less time on each, and then glanced at the yellow tape half-heartedly hugging Charlotte's picket fence.

"This must be the place," he said.

The four women watched, silent, as the young man slipped past them and walked toward the stoop. The grim keeper of Charlotte's doorstep turned toward him as he approached, preparing for battle.

Good luck with her.

After a short conversation, the officer stepped aside and allowed the tall stranger to enter her home, her dour puss replaced by two rows of teeth arranged in the shape of a genuine smile.

She giggled as he passed.

Giggled.

Charlotte would have bet money the woman had never giggled in her life.

Noticing eight eyes upon her, the officer's face collapsed like window blinds, shifting back to her usual mask of disapproval. She crossed her arms over her chest. Charlotte wondered if the officer had just given her home to the dark-haired man and now planned to keep her out while he redecorated.

"Who the hell was that?" Charlotte said aloud, not expecting an answer.

Darla, Penny, and Mariska all answered in unison.

"Declan."

CHAPTER THREE

Charlotte passed the disapproving gaze of the officer at her door without turning to stone and reentered her home. She found the handsome stranger in her living room, bent over, scratching Abby behind her ears. Abby stretched and groaned, shifting her butt toward the man to offer him more spots for attention. He apparently had a mystical power over all women, regardless of species.

She glared at Abby, who remained oblivious to her failings as a watchdog.

Charlotte rolled the man's name over in her mind. She'd heard it before. He was the one who swept in and bought all the best things at the estate sales Mariska and Darla loved to peruse. She'd heard Mariska lament that she missed all the good stuff because 'Declan had already picked it over.' She'd pictured him older.

"Declan?"

Declan looked up, gave the dog one last pat, and straightened. He scratched his nose, and Charlotte saw he had large hands; each of his long, elegant fingers ending in perfectly clipped, buffed nails. She wondered if Declan had a woman in his life who worked at one of the four hundred nail salons in the area. He wore no wedding ring. If he were married to a nail technician, she probably would have told him to do his own damn nails by now, so that didn't make sense…

"Hellooo…?"

Declan's face was suddenly very close to hers, his bemused smile working the laugh lines on either side of his mouth to maximum visibility. He peered into her eyes and used the hand attached to those elegant fingers to wave as if she were a window and some small child stood on the opposite side of her skull.

Charlotte took a step back to better focus. Declan smelled like mint and expensive aftershave. It was not unpleasant.

"What are you doing?" she asked.

"You called me. Then you sort of phased out."

Watching him approach outside, she'd guessed Declan to be about six feet tall. Now, to scale with the other things in her home, including herself, she decided he might be closer to six-three. She wondered if he liked being that tall or if it made life difficult. Sitting in plane seats was probably uncomfortable, his knees pressed against the seat in front of him; but on the other hand, he had full access to high cabinet shelves, where most people could keep things only rarely used...

"You did it again," said Declan.

Charlotte refocused.

"What? I did what? Called you or phased out?"

"Phased out."

"I did not."

"Did not, *what*? Call me or phase out?"

"Either."

"Yes, you did. Both. The phasing bit you did twice."

"No, I didn't."

Declan opened his mouth and then shut it. He took a deep breath.

"Let's take this from the top. You just came in the front door, right?"

Charlotte looked back at her front door and then crossed her arms across her chest. She added a slight head tilt and twisted her lips, adopting what she would call "the disapproving parent" stare. This con man was not about to convince her that *she* had called him to her house. Who did he think he was? Who did he think *she* was, that she would fall for such a scam?

"What are you doing here?" she asked.

"Answer me first. You just walked in, right?"

She thought about her answer, concerned it was a trap. She couldn't find the harm in responding.

"Yes."

"And you said 'Declan' right?"

Charlotte's scowl released like a spring trap, her mouth forming into a small 'o.'

"Oh, you mean I *called* you..."

"*You called me.* Right. By name. See? Unless I'm not Declan anymore and, well, I can check my driver's license..." He twisted his body, pretending to reach for his wallet.

"No, no. I see what you're saying. I did say your name."

"Told you."

"I thought you were saying I *called* you to this house. Like on the phone."

He stopped pantomiming the move for his wallet and grinned.

"No worries," he said, leaning forward and lightly tapping her shoulder.

She instinctively jerked away from his touch. Declan registered her flinch and pulled back his hand, smile failing for a nanosecond. He ran his shoulder-tapping hand through his hair.

"How did you get in here?" she asked.

"What do you mean?"

"I mean why did the officer let you in here?"

"I told her I was a consultant."

"A consultant of what?"

"She didn't ask."

Charlotte scowled, remembering the officer's giggle. Abby wasn't the only crappy watchdog.

"Anyway..." he said, drawing out the word to fill the awkward silence. "I know you didn't call me here. This was a false alarm. I figured when I saw the crime tape, but I thought I'd double-check."

"False alarm?"

"Oh, sorry." He held out his hand to shake. "I'm Declan, as you know. I own the Hock o'Bell Pawnshop in town."

Charlotte shook his hand.

"Did you say the *Hock* o'Bell?"

Declan adopted a serious countenance, so serious, it bordered on sadness.

"It's named after my dear, departed mother, the Belle of Swansea."

Charlotte squinted. "Really?"

"No. Just kidding. It's a play on the restaurant. I just moved the shop to an abandoned Taco Bell."

Declan pulled his wallet from his back pocket and retrieved a business card. He handed it to her.

She studied it and then put it on her counter, mumbling, "Make a run for the hoarder."

She smiled at the look of surprise that leaped to his face. It was as if he'd just noticed her standing there. She felt like she'd been in a movie starring Declan until she'd diverted him from his scripted lines. He seemed lost.

"That's funny," he said. "*Make a run for the hoarder.* Can I steal that?"

She shrugged. "I'm not sure it's *me* you need to clear it with."

Declan replaced his wallet and thrust his hands into his pockets, still grinning and staring at her. Charlotte found it unnerving. Her eyes darted to Abby, who lay at his feet, her chin resting on his toes.

Traitor.

"Anyway, false alarm," said Declan. "I come around when the, uh, residents… you know… *move on*. But this fellow passed a long time ago. Just as well."

"What do you mean, just as well?"

Declan made a sweeping gesture with his hand. "There isn't anything of value here. It's practically barren. It looks like a dorm room. Like some kind of crazy professor off his meds lives here."

"Hm," said Charlotte, following his gaze as it swept her home. She'd never noticed how empty it was. Stacks of books leaned against the walls and each other. Two short sofas with different patterns, a table, and a rickety dining room chair were the only pieces of furniture. She made a mental note to write *decorate* on her chalkboard wall.

She looked at the strapping gentleman insulting her abode. She could feel a scowl creeping down her forehead, but was powerless to stop it.

"So you swoop in when old people die to buy their worldly possessions for your shop."

Declan winced. "I'm sorry. I didn't mean to be insensitive. I pay good money for good items. There are vultures around here who *do* try to steal what they can, but I always try to be fair. That's why they call me Fair Declan."

"They do?"

"No. But they *could.*"

"But they wouldn't because it isn't very catchy."

"No, not really."

He stared at her again. His head tilted to the right.

"Wait. How did *you* get in here? Are you visiting your grandparents? Oh no… is this their house?"

Charlotte shook her head.

"Whew," he said, putting his hand on his chest. "Thought I might have put my foot in my mouth there for a second."

She said nothing as he awaited his answer.

"So… What *are* you doing here?" he asked.

"I live here."

"In the area?"

"*In the house,*" she said sweeping her arm toward the living room. "Home, sweet dorm room."

Declan screwed his eyes shut as if in pain.

"You live *here?* You can't possibly be over fifty-five."

"No, I grew up here. I've been grandfathered in, so to speak."

"Are you a professor?"

"No. I just like to read."

"Are you off your meds?"

Charlotte glowered at him.

"Sorry. *Kidding.* Jeeze. I am sorry. I didn't—I mean, it's a nice house. Uncluttered. Furniture is over-rated."

"Uh-huh."

"I apologize for any misunderstandings," he said, clapping his hands together. "I feel as though I've overstayed my welcome and I'll be on my way."

He thrust out his hand to shake again. "Nice to meet you."

Charlotte was trying to decide whether to shake his hand or flip him off when one of the officers from the backyard dig entered and allowed her to keep her lady-like air.

"Hey Declan, you're still here," said the deputy, smiling and wiping his sweaty brow on his sleeve. He gave his belt a hard yank to pull it over his belly.

"Yeah, Daniel, I was just heading out."

Charlotte looked at the deputy and then back at Declan, her hand now enveloped in his. Everyone seemed to know the handsome pawnbroker. Maybe Deputy Daniel tipped him about deaths in the neighborhood. Declan probably had dinner with the ambulance drivers every Thursday. He was a *ghoul*. He made his living from the death of her friends.

"We were just saying we had something for you," said the deputy, holding aloft a plastic evidence bag.

"Oh yeah?"

He gave Charlotte's hand one last short shake before releasing.

"I mean if it wasn't evidence," said Daniel. "We pulled a necklace from the bone pile."

The officer held up the bag for Declan to see. Inside, Charlotte saw a sunflower, attached to a gold chain. Even with dirt caked to the delicate petals, the bright yellow and orange enamel glowed in the sun streaming through her front window.

"Think it's worth anything?" asked Daniel.

Charlotte's lip curled.

"Daniel, *really*," she said, but the deputy didn't acknowledge her statement. He didn't shift his stare from Declan.

"What is it?" he asked. "Declan? Are you okay?"

Charlotte followed his gaze and saw the blood had drained from the pawnbroker's face. Declan swallowed and took a step forward, his hand lifting to touch the bottom of the evidence bag. Daniel released the sealed bag into his open palm. Declan stood, staring at the necklace, his thumb moving the bag against the flower to remove more dirt from the petals inside.

Pale, he looked at the deputy.

"I know who she is," he said.

"You recognize the necklace?" Charlotte asked.

Declan nodded, his eyes never leaving the bag.

"I gave it to her."

CHAPTER FOUR

"You look like you're going to fall over," said Charlotte.

"I have to see," Declan said, pushing past the deputy and walking toward the back of the house. She followed, with Daniel close behind.

Declan opened the backdoor and the three of them filed out onto the screened-in porch.

"Whoa whoa," said another deputy. "Declan, I told you, you can't come down here. You'll contaminate the area."

"Dick, I think that's my mother," said Declan.

Charlotte gasped.

"They said the bones were ten years old," said Charlotte. "Your mother died when you were…"

"Twelve. Fifteen years ago. And she didn't die. She disappeared. We never knew what happened."

"Well, you can't come down here right now, Declan," said the officer. "I'm sorry. There's nothing to identify, just bones. You'll have to go to the station and then you can tell us everything you know. What makes you think it's your mom?"

"The necklace," he said, holding up the bag. "I gave my mother this necklace for her birthday, not long before she went missing."

"What are you doing with the bag?" Dick shot Daniel a dirty look and snatched the bag from Declan.

"Sorry," said Daniel. "I had to give it to him. He looked like he'd seen a ghost."

"Where is Sheriff Marshall?" asked Charlotte.

She hoped Frank might let Declan closer to the body if she asked. After all, she'd given him a coffee mug of beer *and* mowed his tiny patch of lawn for years as a teen. Without her, who would have pointed out that *Sherriff Marshall* was ridiculous and *clearly* he should have become *Marshal Marshall*? He'd stolen from her the boundless joy of greeting him with "Marshal Marshall *Marshall*" in her best Jan Brady imitation. He owed her a favor or two.

"He left, ma'am, and I'm in charge," said the reedy officer. He had a humorless disposition. Charlotte wondered if the female officer in her front yard was his sister.

Standing on the porch, Declan craned his neck to see, doing his best to gain a bird's eye view of the excavation. Most of the bones still lay half-buried in the dirt. The body lay flat on its back, head missing. Nearby, the skull sat in a clear plastic bag. The jawbone was in the bag as well. Katie had lost all her trophies.

Dick opened the door to the porch and ushered Declan and Charlotte back into the house. Daniel followed them.

"I want them out of the house," said Dick to his partner. He looked at Charlotte and Declan. "Go get a cup of coffee or something."

"It's *my* house," said Charlotte, feeling Dick was trying too hard to live up to his name. She'd met him when he was a brand new deputy, green as the sexiest M&M. She'd watched him drop his gun while trying to spin it on his finger like a gunfighter. He had a lot of nerve pretending he was large and in charge now.

"This house wasn't even built when she was buried. There aren't any clues in here."

"Yeah, well, I don't want to have to keep an eye out for you."

"Fine, Deputy *Dick*," said Charlotte. "We'll go. Just don't try and do any fancy tricks with your gun while we're gone. I don't want holes in my walls."

Dick pressed his lips into a hard white line and pointed toward her front door.

That's right. You remember now. I saw.

Declan's face was still ashen; his eyes seemed vacant.

"Declan," she said, softly touching his arm. "Let's go. We can go to Mariska's. She's like my mother. Okay?"

Declan nodded and allowed himself to be led from the house. Charlotte paused to clip a leash on Abby and then navigated them past the female officer. She wasn't surprised to find the ladies still gathered near her gate. Charlotte caught Mariska's eye and motioned to her. Mariska nodded and waddled in fourth gear to catch up to them. She had bad legs, so at that pace, she looked like a hyperkinetic penguin racing after the last mackerel.

"They kicked you out, dear?" asked Mariska as she grew near. "I don't know who they think they are. Was it Dick? He's not the sharpest cheese in the refrigerator, that one. They don't think you have something to do with the body, do they?"

"No, nothing like that. They just want the house clear while they finish up."

"You didn't kill that lady who cut your car off the other day, did you?" asked Darla, chuckling as she, too, arrived at Charlotte's side.

Declan looked at her.

"I think it's my mother."

"Oh," said Darla, covering her mouth with her hand. "Oh, my. Oh, I am *so* sorry. I should know better than to joke about something like this. Oh, I feel terrible."

"Declan, this is Mariska and Darla," said Charlotte stopping to point to each in turn.

He shook their hands. "Declan Bingham."

"Is your door unlocked?" Charlotte asked. "I think he should sit down for a bit."

"Yes, yes," said Mariska hurrying to open the door.

They went inside. Mariska's pound mutt, Izzy, ran up to greet them and Charlotte had to scramble to unclip Abby's leash before they all became entangled and fell to the ground like hog-tied calves. Released, the two dogs raced around the house together, narrowly missing furniture and knees. Part Dalmatian, part rat terrier, and part wildly over-fed, Izzy looked like a black-speckled body pillow with radar dishes for ears.

Charlotte walked past the kitchen counter to the living room and motioned for Declan to sit in a large, cushy La-Z-Boy chair. Every house in Pineapple Port had running water, electricity, and a La-Z-Boy with the shape of the man of the house worn into it.

"Can I get you something, Declan?" asked Mariska, tight on their heels. "Water? Milk? Soda? Tea?"

"No, thank you," he said.

"Juice?"

"No."

"Do you have any coffee left?" asked Darla.

"I do. Let me brew you a fresh pot. Declan, I have coffee and some milk. It's two percent... or creamer... I have hazelnut creamer."

"No, thank you."

"What about a donut? I have donuts. Oh, I have some wonderful muffins from Publix. Do you want a muffin? Blueberry?"

"Have you tried their pineapple coconut muffins?'" asked Darla. "They are to die. Simply to die."

"I haven't. I'll have to get some. That sounds wonderful."

"No, nothing, thank you," said Declan.

"Or corn muffins... I might have corn. No... No, I think Bob ate the corn muffins with the chili last night... Cinnamon apple? I do have a cinnamon apple..."

"No, thank you."

"I could cut a banana. Or I—"

"Mariska," said Charlotte. "He doesn't want anything."

"Okay." Mariska looked around her kitchen. "I have some leftover chicken..."

Charlotte shot her a look and she shrugged.

"Well, I *do*," she mumbled.

Mariska went to the coffee pot and dumped that morning's remains into the sink to start afresh. She didn't like to drink coffee more than three minutes old, and she didn't expect her guests to have to put up with nonsense like that either.

Charlotte removed a fake cat from a nearby chair and sat down. The cat was black and white and curled in a ball as if sleeping. Declan looked at the cat as she set it on the floor.

"That is terrifying," he mumbled.

"I know. I can't tell you how long I've begged her to get rid of it. Used to give me nightmares."

Declan offered a half-smile and rubbed his face with his hands.

"I'm sorry," he said. "I'm acting crazy. It was just a shock."

"I can't imagine. Did you—never mind."

Charlotte shook her head and waved her hands to say she was dropping the question.

"What?"

"Nothing, I... I was going to ask if you'd *thought* she was still alive. Before today."

Declan sighed. "I don't know. I guess part of me thought she was. Honestly, now I'm not sure if this is better or worse. It hurt to think she ran out on us. Now I know she didn't leave on purpose, but she's dead. Part of me hoped she was living a happy life somewhere."

Mariska slipped a small plate on the table next to Declan's chair.

"It's sharp cheese and pepperoni and crackers," she whispered.

Charlotte growled.

"They're Pepperidge Farm," said Mariska in a huff. She turned and disappeared to the back of the house.

Darla walked by and took one of everything on the plate.

"Darla," said Charlotte. "You're just encouraging her."

"Why wouldn't I encourage people to feed me?"

"Sorry," she said to Declan. "She means well."

Declan laughed. "Oh gosh, don't apologize," he said, taking a cracker and a slice of pepperoni. "I talk to old—er..."

Declan glanced at Darla, who arched an eyebrow.

"Tread lightly, mister."

Declan cleared his throat. "I mean, I talk to *mature* ladies all day long. They invite me to their houses to look at their antiques and they're always trying to feed me. I'm used to it."

"I bet they do," mumbled Charlotte.

"Well, you're so skinny. Both of you need to eat."

"I eat plenty. Don't you worry," said Declan.

"And I live across the street from Mariska, so you know I'm not going to starve any time soon."

Charlotte saw Declan's five o'clock shadow already showing. His hair was dark but his skin was pale for a Florida boy.

"Black Irish?" she asked.

"What's that?"

"Your name, your hair... I'm guessing you're Irish?"

"My father was from Dublin. Right off the boat."

"Was your mother from Ireland as well?"

"My mother was just a plain old American. But Irish and German, I think. I got my height from her side."

"You *are* tall," said Charlotte. Declan looked at her and she looked away, embarrassed.

You are tall. What a stupid thing to say.

"I mean, I'm tall so I notice when other people are," she added.

"What was her name, your mother?" asked Darla.

"Erin."

"That's a pretty name."

The room fell silent, but for the sound of Darla crunching on crackers.

"I should probably go," said Declan after a minute.

He tried to stand, but it took several rocks back and forth to dislodge himself from the deep cushions of the chair.

"Are you sure?" asked Charlotte, standing with him. "Do you feel okay to drive?"

"I'm fine. Thank you. I appreciate you taking care of me. This just isn't what I expected to find when I came to your house."

"No, you expected to find *me* dead," said Charlotte.

"No—well, yes, I guess I did," he said, the left side of his mouth hooking into a tiny smile.

He looked at her and she noticed his eyes were a brilliant green with brown edges around the iris.

How did I not see those gems earlier?

She suddenly felt very aware of herself and rushed to squash the uncomfortable silence.

"So, for me, the day turned out better than expected. I'm alive."

Charlotte raised her hand to cover her mouth, realizing how tactless her statement had been.

"That didn't come out the way I meant it. I meant—"

"I know what you meant," said Declan with a chuckle, letting her off the hook. He put out his hand and she shook it, eyes locked on her toes.

"Nice to meet you. Hope to see you again soon," he said.

"You, too."

"Nice to meet you, Darla."

"Nice to meet you," said Darla, popping another cracker in her mouth. As he headed for the door she met eyes with Charlotte and smiled, waggling her eyebrows suggestively.

Charlotte wrinkled her nose and waved her away.

As Declan passed the hallway that led to the back of the house he called out to Mariska.

"I'm leaving. Thank you for everything."

Mariska burst out of the bedroom with the dogs exploding forward on either side of her. They raced down the hall and Declan jumped to his right to avoid being trampled.

"Oh, my pleasure, dear. You take care of yourself. Do you want a muffin to take home with you?"

"No, thank you."

Declan offered a last wave to everyone before leaving.

From the door, Charlotte watched him walk down the street to his car.

"He has nice posture," she said. "I mean, for a tall guy."

"He has nice a lot of things," said Darla. "I can tell you his posture wasn't the first thing I noticed."

"Darla!"

"What? I meant his *face*. Now, who has the dirty mind? Didn't you think he was handsome?"

"I guess. Why didn't any of you ever tell me about him?"

Darla and Mariska exchanged a look.

"Oh, honey. We all thought he was gay."

CHAPTER FIVE

Charlotte grabbed her towel and headed to water aerobics at the Pineapple Port pool. It wasn't so much *aerobics* as it was swinging limbs back and forth, but it served as the epicenter of some of the best community gossip. She stopped in front of her chalkboard wall and picked up the chalk she'd purchased the day before. It had taken the police until eight p.m. to finish removing Erin Bingham's bones from her yard, and she'd gone shopping to kill time. She didn't buy seedlings. It would be a while before she'd consider gardening again. She could officially remove gardener and archeologist from her potential career list.

Charlotte wrote *find Erin's killer* on her wall. It seemed dramatic, so she erased it and replaced it with *solve mystery*. The statement was vague enough that if someone saw it, they wouldn't jump to the conclusion that she was nuts. She could say the mystery was the location of a missing earring or the clicking noise her dishwasher made.

Speaking of which...

She added *fix clicking* to the board.

It had been twenty-four hours since she'd found a skeleton in her backyard, and while life went on, as usual, she felt strange in her own home. She fought a persistent urge to peek out her back window. A tingling feeling on the back of her neck made her suspect that at any moment, she'd find Erin Bingham standing in her lanai.

But in what state? Would she look like she did when she was alive? Or a zombie? Or would she find a skeleton with a broken mandible tapping on her door?

She couldn't stop thinking about the poor woman or her handsome son. She felt terrible for Declan. She'd lost her mother at a young age, so she empathized. To relive his loss through such a gruesome discovery; she could only imagine what impact that might have on the enterprising pawnbroker.

Maybe the body wasn't his mother's? It would be a while before the officials identified the remains, but the appearance of the necklace didn't bode well. Maybe, the necklace wasn't unique. He'd only been a child when he bought it for her, surely, it wasn't very expensive. Maybe a local store had sold hundreds of them.

Her mind was still racing through the possibilities of both necklace sales and hauntings when she found Mariska and Darla waiting outside in their swimsuits and floral cover-ups. Mariska sat behind the wheel of her light blue golf cart, Darla in the passenger seat, her nose slathered in bright yellow sunblock. Charlotte hopped on the rear seat and set her towel beside her.

"Any news on your bones?" asked Darla.

"No. Any details from Frank?"

"Oh, you know that man. Getting him to talk is like pulling teeth. I told him about Declan's mother and he just grunted at me and asked what was for dinner."

"He's our only hope," said Charlotte. "I don't think the police are required to share information with the person who found the body. That would be Katie, anyway."

"It's just so awful," said Mariska. "You never think this sort of thing is going to happen in your neighborhood. The next thing you know we'll have the *Dateline* people lurking around."

"Ooh, I hope so," said Darla. "I like that Keith Morrison. He's like sexy old saddle leather."

Charlotte turned to look at Darla. "I don't even know what that means, but I do *not* want an explanation."

"Do you think this will lower our property values?" asked Mariska as she stomped on the pedal.

"Yes," said Charlotte, grabbing the cart to keep from flying off the back. "I think our homes will plunge tens of dollars."

She closed her eyes and enjoyed the artificial breeze created by the moving golf cart until they reached the community center. The pool was to the right of the large multi-purpose building. The pool was always clean and warm. Retirees possessed ample time to lodge complaints, so it was easier to do things right the first time.

Mariska stopped the cart in front of the community bulletin board to look for news. A notice hanging from a thumbtack, printed on neon pink paper, announced a new committee.

"Another club," said Darla. "This place has more clubs than a deck of cards."

Charlotte read the note, her eyes growing wider with every word.

"The *Corpse Committee*. Committee to get to the bottom of the mystery behind the body found in the backyard of Miss Charlotte Morgan."

Darla looked at Mariska.

"I guess we'll have to join that one."

"I did this morning. I saw it when I walked Miss Izzy. I wasn't sure how you'd feel about it, though, Charlotte."

"Well, I don't feel great being named as the benefactor of the *Corpse Committee*, but what can I do? I assume this is Penny's handiwork?"

Darla wrinkled her nose at the name of the community founder's wife.

"You know she has to get to the bottom of everything," said Mariska. "Gossip, trouble..."

"Glasses of scotch, her husband's bank account..." mumbled Darla.

Mariska giggled and slapped her friend's arm. "You're terrible."

The cart lurched forward and Charlotte clutched the sidebar.

Charlotte walked to the pool and threw her towel and bag on her usual chair. For the most part, she loved being semi-retired at twenty-six. When her grandmother died, Charlotte had inherited her prefab community home. Estelle had purchased the house for fifteen thousand dollars in full, so she had no mortgage.

Charlotte's father had died shortly after her birth, killed in a fall while working construction. Her mother died of cancer when she was eleven. Though her family wasn't rich, they had insurance, and with her modest needs, she knew she could live most of her life on her inheritance.

She had a small land lease fee to pay every month and easily made that amount doing work for an embroidery website owned by Mariska's son, Sebastian who lived in Maryland with his wife, Emily. The couple supplied Charlotte with an embroidery machine of her own, at which Charlotte spent two to ten hours a week stitching various critters on blankets and polos.

Charlotte spotted her handiwork on every towel and bag at the pool. The local ladies weren't shy about requesting items for themselves at the Pineapple Port discount of thirty percent off. At Christmas, Charlotte received so many orders from the locals that she barely had time to do her shopping. She'd added a t-shirt heat press to her collection of hardware and spent weeks afterward stamping pictures of grandkids.

Only recently, the urge to find a *calling* had begun creeping into her subconscious. She couldn't complain about her stitching work. With the industrial-sized embroidery machine tucked in her shed, there was no beating her commute to work. To ensure she never lost this gem of a job, she endeavored to find local sales as well. Being in Florida, she couldn't count how many anchors, shells, and boat names she'd stitched. In addition, everyone in Pineapple Port had a pet or knew someone with a pet, so she cranked out beach towels featuring West Highland terriers and cat-faced kitchen towels. She attended farmers' markets and community yard sales to supplement the website orders.

Still, she'd never actually dreamed of becoming an embroiderer. She felt like there had to be something better, something more *meaningful*. She wanted to feel passionate about her work. At twenty-six, she felt too old to live so aimlessly.

She'd hopped from teenager to retiree in the blink of an eye.

Charlotte stepped into the pool and waded to the center. Jackie Blankenship, the water aerobics leader, set down her boom box and popped in the instruction tape. The tape was superfluous; all the ladies, and a smattering of men, had the routine memorized. Jackie once tried to introduce a new tape, but the ensuing mutiny ended her dreams of novelty. She grumbled bitterly about it. It was no secret she regretted offering to run the program and the fact that no one would let her break the monotony of the routine added insult to injury.

"I was hoping it would rain," said Jackie to Charlotte as she walked by. "I don't know why I ever offered to run this stupid club."

"I know, Jackie," said Charlotte. "I know."

"The water is warmer again," said Mariska. "They turned off the heat last week and people nearly lost their minds. It dropped to 79."

"It might be more refreshing if it wasn't body temperature," said Charlotte.

"Oh, don't you even *try* and suggest that," said Darla. "Blasphemy."

Penny half-walked and half-swam to the group, her dark bob wet and slicked back across her scalp.

"I'd love for you to be a guest speaker at the new committee," Penny said to Charlotte as she arrived, her leathery skin crinkling as her mouth formed something like a smile. Charlotte wasn't sure if Penny was being friendly or had just successfully lured children into her gingerbread house.

"I saw the flyer. I'm guessing you'll have less to talk about if I don't show up."

Penny thrust out her chin with a level eight sniff *(How Dare You.)* "Is that a threat?"

"What? No. It's an observation. I'll come. I can't imagine the rumors if I don't."

"Yes, you have to come. This is very serious. We need to find out who this person is and what happened to them."

"I think I know who she is, but I would like to know what happened to her."

"You know who she is? It's a *she*?"

"It's that pawnshop fellow's mother," said Susan Hecht from the back of the pool. Half the ladies claimed to be deaf, but they always heard juicy gossip from several miles away.

"I thought it was his girlfriend," said another woman, new to the neighborhood. Charlotte had forgotten her name, but she knew she lived alone. She'd heard the woman kept twenty-five bowls of dog food scattered around her house, so if she dropped dead, her Pug wouldn't starve to death.

"He killed her for cheating," the woman added.

"I thought he was gay?" said Katherine O'Malley, tilting her head so the decorative flaps on her swimming cap flopped to one side like dominoes.

Charlotte rolled her eyes. "It might be Declan's *mother*, not his girlfriend."

"But he is gay, right?"

"*No.* I mean, I don't know. What does that matter? Either way, he didn't kill anyone."

"How do you know?" asked Susan.

"He's barely older than the bones. I doubt he killed his mother when he was eleven and buried her in my backyard."

"Declan is a funny name," said the new lady. "Maybe he killed her as a boy, like in that movie…"

"Oh…what was the name of that movie?" asked Penny. "I know what you mean. The little boy killed everyone."

"The Omen," said Charlotte, mentally thanking the neighborhood for her vast knowledge of old movies. "And no. Don't be ridiculous. Declan isn't Damien."

"Ah right—Damien," said Penny. "That's *like* Declan…"

"If he isn't gay, let me know?" asked Katherine. "My granddaughter is coming next week. I could set them up."

Katherine's granddaughter was an ex-beauty pageant winner. Charlotte felt an odd pang of anxiety and dread.

What was that?

She swallowed and vowed to drink less coffee in the mornings.

Katherine continued musing to herself, mumbling just loud enough for Charlotte to hear.

"Come to think of it... I think I set them up years ago and *she's* the one who told me he was gay... hm..."

"I'm sure I don't know," said Charlotte, her tone sharper than she intended it to be.

"Are you talking about the dead woman in your yard? The one Declan killed?" asked Andie Davis, wading into the pool in her bikini. Andie was only fifty, but her husband met the age requirement by a good ten years. The other ladies eyeballed her outfit and exchanged disapproving glances. Charlotte always wore a one-piece to avoid such scrutiny.

"Declan didn't kill her," said Charlotte, her voice growing shrill. "It's probably his *mother*, who went missing fifteen years ago."

"Sometimes kids kill their mothers," said Andie.

"Like Damien Omen Two," said Penny. "You can't close your mind to any possibility."

"Damien is a devil child from the movies. Declan is a *real person*," Charlotte said as steadily as possible to anyone who would listen.

"All the people on *Dateline* are real people, too," said Penny. "And now they're in jail."

Charlotte closed her eyes, took a deep breath, and counted to ten. It was a technique important to maintaining sanity in Pineapple Port.

"Please play the tape, Jackie," she said.

There was a commotion at the other end of the pool and Charlotte turned in time to see several ladies scolding a man who had swum into their lane. She looked at Mariska.

"I'm starting to think I need to hang out with people closer to my age more often. Y'all are driving me bonkers."

"I'm always telling you that," said Mariska as the water aerobics music blared, the recorded instructor's cheery voice offering words of encouragement.

Charlotte lifted her leg out to the side and then put it down again as the others fell silent. It was the most strenuous movement in the entire routine. She wasn't deluded enough to consider water aerobics real exercise, but it was easy on her creaky knees and it was nice to zone out and meditate when people weren't claiming the local pawn shop owner was a demon child.

In her mind's eye, she pictured sitting across from Declan in Mariska's house. She saw his green eyes, sparkling as he chuckled and the manliness of his chiseled cheekbones blending perfectly with the expressive wrinkles gathering on his forehead as he talked and worried. The top button of his blue polo was unbuttoned, revealing the v-notch of his throat and a smattering of dark chest hairs. On either side of the shirt's buttons, the thin fabric hung neatly from his well-developed pecs. She wanted to reach out and touch them. They looked firm. She inhaled, smelling his aftershave...

"What are you grinning about?' asked Darla.

Charlotte snapped from her thoughts. "Was I?"

Charlotte looked forward and raised her other leg.

"Nothing," she said.

CHAPTER SIX

Declan looked at the piece of paper in his hand then back at the ranch-style home in Pineapple Port. He'd received a call from Sheriff Marshall asking him to stop by and discuss the discovery of the bones, presumed to be his mother's. The address on the summons was 115 Flamingo Court, just a few houses down the street from Charlotte's. Declan knew the town of Charity was small, but he never imagined the police station would be a modular home in a retirement community. He checked the paper again, wondering if he'd misheard the address.

This made Andy Griffith look like the chief of the New York Police Department.

As he stared at the ceramic frog fishing in a tiny manmade pond in the front yard of the police precinct, a movement caught his eye. He glanced up in time to spot curtains drawing shut. Someone was watching him from the house.

Spurred into action, he climbed the three steps to the door and knocked. He still doubted the address but felt silly not trying if someone already had eyes on him.

A balding man answered the door wearing shorts and a white tank top. He was wiry, with deeply tanned skin and bowed legs. A riot of white hair raged from each armpit. Declan guessed him to be in his early seventies and didn't recognize him from the crime scene.

"Yes?" asked the man. His tone was brusque, bordering on annoyed.

"I was talking to your deputy out here," said Declan, nodding toward the fishing frog. "And he said this was the police station?"

The man looked at the frog and then squinted at Declan.

"I'm guessing I wrote down the wrong address?"

"No, you got the right place," said the man. "My office is being remodeled. I've been doing some things out of the house. I can't let the gears of justice grind to a halt just because the paint hasn't dried."

"No, of course not."

"And you keep your eyes off that frog, mister."

"Okay..."

"Come in," said the man, stepping back to make room. "I'm Sheriff Frank Marshall."

Declan chuckled and offered his hand to shake.

"You know, you should have become a marshal..."

The sheriff grunted as if in pain. He ignored Declan's hand and grabbed a t-shirt from a pile of folded clothes on his counter. He pulled it over his head.

Declan's gaze fell to the chest of the sheriff's tee and he bit his lower lip. The shirt was solid baby blue, but for two pink clamshells, one covering each breast.

Frank spotted Declan's growing smirk and glanced down at his chest.

"Dammit Darla," he said, ripping off the tee as if it was on fire. The shirt caught on his ear and he wrestled inside it before tossing it on the counter next to the folded pile and heading to the kitchen table.

"Follow me," he said, winded.

A scruffy tan dog came running to Declan, his whole body wriggling with excitement.

"Hey there, cutie," he said, squatting to pet the dog.

"He ain't cute, he's the ugliest damn dog in the world. Leave him be. He's old and he'll pee all over the place."

Declan sneaked a quick ear scratching and then stood.

Frank grabbed a pen and pad from his kitchen counter before sitting at the large wooden table. He motioned to the seat across from him.

"Have a seat right there, weirdo. I just have to ask you a couple of questions."

"What?" said Declan trying to stop in mid-sit, but he'd already dropped too far. He fell into the kitchen chair. "Did you just call me—"

"First question," said Frank cutting him short. "I'm not your psychiatrist, but I'd like to ask you about your childhood. Anything off? You don't have to get too graphic. Just the facts."

Declan closed his gaping mouth.

I must have heard that wrong.

He supposed it made sense that the police would question him about his mother while she was alive; the information could help to identify her killer.

"Well, my father was a drug addict," said Declan.

"I would have guessed booze, from your name."

Declan's jaw clenched. He swallowed hard and tried to relax. The last thing he needed was beef with the local sheriff, but the old man wasn't making things easy for him.

"Yes, Irish drunks are a delightful stereotype, but no, his poison was heroin."

"Delightful?"

"I was being sarcastic."

"Don't."

"Okaaay…"

"Booze, smack… shows a lack of restraint, either way. *You* a drunk?"

"No."

"Never?"

"I drink, socially; maybe a beer or two after work, but I wouldn't call myself a drunk, no."

"What about other people? Would *they* call you a drunk?"

"Not if they knew what was good for them."

Declan forced a chuckle.

Frank leaned forward on his elbows and stared into Declan's eyes.

"Was that sarcasm?"

"No. That was... uh... just a joke."

"Don't."

"Got it. Sorry."

"Now, again; would other people call you a drunk?"

"No."

"Drugs?"

"No."

"None? Smack? Horse? Nose candy?"

"Not unless you count heartburn pills and aspirin."

"Mixed? Is that something the kids are doing now?"

"No—I mean, I don't know. I meant *separately*. I don't take anything stronger than aspirin."

Frank jotted a note on his pad, using a pen marked with the logo of a cholesterol drug. The pen made Declan smile. Every time he dealt with the residents of Pineapple Port, they produced pens featuring drug advertisements, no doubt stolen from their doctors. He guessed no one in the community had purchased a pen in thirty years.

"It's funny," he said. "That pen you're using—"

"Tell me more about your dad," said Frank, cutting him short again.

"Uh... there isn't much to tell."

"Tell me anyway."

Declan leaned back in his chair and crossed his arms over his chest.

"Okay... well, he left when I was two or three. My mother raised me alone for a few years in New York, and then moved down here to be next to my grandmother."

"Mm-hm," said Frank, scribbling a few more notes. The pad of paper he used had *It's five o'clock somewhere!* stamped on it in hot pink. Declan scanned the house, spotting a frilly pillow and decorative plates on the wall.

"You and your wife live here long?" he asked.

Frank blessed him with his steely glare.

"Who said anything about my wife?"

"I was just making small talk."

"Don't. I hate that shit."

"Duly noted," said Declan, crossing his legs.

Frank looked at his crossed legs for a little too long, and he uncrossed them. This seemed to satisfy the sheriff and he returned to his notepad.

"Anything else I should know about your parents?"

"Well… when I was eleven, my mother left in the middle of the night and never came back. We never knew what happened to her. My grandmother reported her missing, but nothing ever came of it."

"Hm. I can see how that could mess you up."

"I guess. My grandmother was a big help, her and my uncle, Seamus. He lived here at the time but left to become an officer in Miami. He left his half of the Charity pawnshop to me for when I was old enough to take over."

"So he's police?"

"Was."

"Was?"

"He just retired. He's moving back here this week."

"Good for him."

"He was decorated," added Declan, feeling as though he had finally found some common ground with the sheriff.

"Oh, he must be so proud of you," mumbled Frank.

Declan scowled.

"Sheriff, have I done something to offend you?"

"Let's just say all your childhood hardships don't forgive your behavior now. I'm so sick of this new generation, always blaming their problems on their mommies and daddies."

"I haven't blamed anything on anyone."

"My mommy didn't buy me the right brand of organic waffles," said Frank in a whiney voice, ignoring Declan's protestations. "That's why I burned down the school."

"What the hell are you talking about?" said Declan, rising to his feet. "I didn't burn down a school."

"I'm talking about your sick little hobby, you wackjob."

The sheriff stood and pointed at Declan's chest with his crooked index finger. He stood a good six inches shorter but leaned forward like an aggressive bulldog. His posture gave

Declan pause, and he had to fight his rising anger. He hated the idea of flashing a temper and confirming the sheriff's impressive list of Irish stereotypes.

"What hobby?" he demanded to know.

"What hobby? *Building ships in a bottle.* You know what hobby, you pervert."

Frank stuck his stubby finger in Declan's face to punctuate the word *pervert*. It was all he could do not to slap it away and he clenched his fists at his sides to keep his hands still. He couldn't remember the last time he'd wanted to hit someone, let alone an elderly man recently spotted in a mermaid t-shirt.

Heh.

The image of the pink shell bikini top across Frank's chest brought a smirk to Declan's lips and he felt his anger subside. He released his fists and took a deep breath.

"Look, I came here to help you catch my mother's killer and all you've done is insult me."

Frank's head tilted to the side like a curious dog's.

"Catch your mother's—"

The fire in Frank's eyes died and his face fell slack. He grabbed a wad of papers from his breakfast bar and shuffled through them until he found the one he wanted.

"You're not Tommy Wickham?"

"I told you my name is *Declan Bingham.*"

The sheriff resumed shuffling through the paperwork and pulled another sheet.

"Christmas on a cracker. You think those bones they found at Charlotte's house are your mother's?"

"Yes. And I don't see how that makes me a weirdo *or* a pervert."

The sheriff waved a hand in front of him. "My mistake. I got you confused with this other kid, running around sticking his willy into koi ponds."

"His what?"

"You know…" Frank made a few quick pelvis thrusts to illustrate his point.

Declan recoiled.

"You thought I was violating koi ponds?" He laughed. "That's why you didn't like me talking about your frog pond."

The sheriff chuckled. "I didn't want you makin' eyes at Lil' Frankie."

"You named the ceramic frog Lil' Frankie? And *I'm* the weirdo?"

"Watch it. Darla named him. She calls him 'Lil' Frankie' because he catches about as many fish as I do."

"Darla's your wife? I met her. Her, Charlotte, and... Mariska? They were very kind to me after I realized the bones might be my mother's."

"Those three are never more than three feet apart. Anyway, I apologize. This office remodel has everything mixed up."

Declan nodded. "It's fine. I'm relieved. Let's start over."

"Okay. And if you want to pet Oscar, you go ahead."

Declan glanced at the dog who had flopped on the ground by his foot.

Frank looked over his notes. Declan watched him cross out the word *weirdo* in three separate places and *sick bastard* in one.

"So long and short of it, your mom disappeared and you had no idea why. No talk of a boyfriend or anything like that?"

"No. I mean, I was a kid so I wasn't thinking about things like that, but Mamó never said anything like that later in life either."

"Mamó?"

"My granny."

"Is your grandmother still alive? Can I talk to her?"

"No. She died two years ago. Emphysema."

"Those damn cigarettes, I bet. I lost a sister to them."

Declan nodded.

"Do you know where your mother worked?"

"Here, I think. She worked as a secretary at the building office, and then she also waitressed a bit, nights and weekends."

"You know where?"

"Orange Grill?" said Declan. "Something like that."

Frank grunted. "Nectarine's. Yeah, they went out of business close to ten years ago."

"That's pretty much all I know. I just recognized that

necklace. I'd given it to Mom for Christmas and she always wore it."

"I need to take a swab from your mouth so they can compare it to the DNA of the bones. Though they'll probably do the identifying by her teeth if they're in good shape."

"No problem."

"We'll have the tests back in a few days. Then we'll know for sure if it was your mom or not. I'm sorry, about the bones and my behavior today."

Declan shrugged. "No problem. I'm glad we got that cleared up."

The sheriff swabbed Declan's mouth, put the results in a clear jar, and sealed it. As he jotted his name on it, there was a knock on the door. He put down the jar and shook Declan's hand.

"That's it. You're free to go."

He opened his door, Declan following to leave.

A shifty-eyed young man in his late teens wearing jeans shorts and a torn t-shirt stood on the sheriff's steps. He was staring at the frog pond.

"Yeah, I got a call to show up here," he said, turning as Frank opened the door.

"What's your name?"

"Tommy. Tommy Wickham."

Declan swiveled to investigate the notorious pond lover. He glanced at the sheriff, who flashed him a quick smile and then turned his attention back to Tommy.

"Come on in, son," he said, putting his hand on Tommy's shoulder. "I just need to talk to you for a little bit."

CHAPTER SEVEN

Charlotte sat on her screened porch.

Her lanai.

She stared at the shallow gravesite behind her home. The police and forensic investigators had completed their tasks and removed the crime tape, but the yard would never feel the same. She shivered, thinking about all the years Declan's poor mother lay beneath her patio. She groaned, recalling last summer's luau-themed barbeque party.

People had danced the hula on Erin's grave.

My god. There might have been a conga line.

If there was a dead person in her backyard, where else might they be? She had seen enough horror movies to know that once someone disturbed a grave, all sorts of weird things started to happen. Now every time Abby stirred in her sleep, Charlotte sat straight up in bed, wondering if her dog's paranormal senses were tingling. Abby ran in her sleep a lot. She was exhausted.

As far as she knew, the investigators only found bones and the necklace. She hoped they'd also found something that would lead to Erin Bingham's killer. Everyone knew spirits grew less restless after avenging their deaths. That was Ghost 101. She hoped Erin was a nice lady, uninterested in haunting people. Declan seemed nice, so that boded well; his mother was probably nice, too. Charlotte couldn't imagine Declan haunting someone. Though, if she had to be haunted by someone, it wouldn't hurt to have a handsome ghost lurking about. It could be like The Ghost and Mrs. Muir.

Charlotte took a sip of her wine.

Great.

She was sitting around, drinking alone, fantasizing about being a young widow like Mrs. Muir, alone in a lighthouse with a ghost.

I'm even alone in my daydreams.

She needed to get out more. She needed to venture beyond Pineapple Port. Maybe go somewhere where people talked about movies more recent than 1947.

Charlotte stood and walked into the house. She wrote *get out more* on the chalkboard wall beneath solve mystery and bread, lettuce, and cookies. The chalkboard hadn't been painted for a week before it turned into a shopping list. She moved to put down the chalk and then changed her mind. She added The Ghost and Mrs. Muir on the board. She hadn't seen it in a while.

Charlotte saw something flash outside her kitchen window. It moved just above her fence line, round, head-shaped. She jumped and dropped the chalk.

Erin.

Already? She hadn't had the time to avenge a squirrel's death.

She froze, deciding whether to investigate or call for help.

Who could she call about a ghost?

A familiar tune began to play in her head.

Who ya gonna call? Ghostbusters!

Stop it. Damn it, Charlotte, concentrate.

She crept to the window and peeked outside.

She saw another flash of movement, this time heading toward her front yard.

She ran for the front door, alerting Abby, who tore around the corner, cutting her off and creating the first line of defense. It was everything she could do to avoid tripping over the dog.

She threw open the door and Abby burst outside.

"Whoa whoa whoa," yelled a man standing on the curb outside her home as Abby barreled toward him.

It was Harry Wagner. Harry had worked with Penny and

George to expand Pineapple Port, but at nearly eighty, he'd long since retired and now lived in one of the homes.

"Abby no," Charlotte called. "It's okay."

Abby did a tight loop around the man and then thumped her head into his knees, begging for pets.

Harry stared at Charlotte, his freckled head gleaming in the last of the afternoon sun.

"Were you just peeking over my fence?" asked Charlotte.

Harry grimaced.

"I hear you had some excitement."

"News travels fast. I'm afraid you missed all the excitement if that's what you were looking for. You scared me to death."

"I'm sorry. I was curious and I didn't want to bother you. How are you? I imagine it was a little upsetting."

"I'm fine. Although I won't be gardening any time soon."

"Hmm." Harry relented and offered Abby a quick pat on the butt. "Well, if you want someone to talk to, you know I'm no stranger to death."

Charlotte knew. Everyone knew. Harry was an ex-Chicago cop and loved sharing cold case stories. Investigating old, seemingly unsolvable crimes in the latter part of his police career had been the highlight of his life. He'd only solved four or five cases, but when played on repeat, they provided him with decades of stories for sharing. Charlotte braced herself, hoping she wasn't in for another encore performance of The Body in the Lake or her personal favorite, The Case of the They Thought He'd Killed Himself, But I Knew Better Because Everyone Else is an Idiot.

"I think I'm good, but thanks."

Harry nodded and looked at his shoes, but he didn't leave.

"Was there something else?" she asked, sure she knew the answer.

"I was wondering... maybe I could come to see the spot you found her?"

"You want to see the grave?"

"If I could..."

"Um..." she looked behind her as if the house might have an

opinion. "I guess..."

"Great."

Harry walked toward the door, pausing a moment to reach around the side of the house and produce a metal detector. He'd left it at the fence line. Charlotte recognized the contraption; she owned one herself. It sat, forgotten, in a closet somewhere. She hadn't been to the beach treasure hunting in a very long time. At fifteen, she'd waged a month-long Christmas season campaign for a metal detector, certain she could find riches on nearby beaches. Several quarters and hundreds of bottle caps later, the detector had found its way to a permanent home in her closet.

Charlotte scowled.

He'd been looking for a way to hop into the back yard and use it without telling her.

"I was thinking I might pass this over the crime scene a few times," he said.

"I can see that."

"Like I said, I didn't want to bother you, but the gate was locked..."

"Don't you think the crime guys did that already?"

"These guys," he said, shaking his head the way someone might after a child handed him a report card full of failing grades. "They aren't always as thorough as they should be. I just want to make sure they didn't miss anything. I have a lot of cold case experience, you know."

"I've heard that somewhere," she said, using her leg to push Abby back as the dog strained to get a good whiff of Harry's fascinating metal stick.

"It's really lucky I'm here. I'm sure we'll have this puzzle solved in no time."

Harry entered the house and made a beeline for the backyard. He was at the gravesite by the time Charlotte joined him.

"What made you pull up the concrete?" he asked.

"I wanted a garden. I don't know why so much of my backyard was paved. My neighbors have more grass."

"Your grandmother requested a larger patio during the

building," Harry mumbled, tucking his sifting scoop under his arm and switching on the metal detector. "Not sure why. Paid extra for it. Just made more work for my men."

"Probably just didn't want to mow the grass."

Harry shrugged.

"I can already see they made a mess of this," he said, pointing at the dirt around the gravesite. "I knew it."

As he bobbed his hand at the gravesite mess, his leather belt flopped in unison. Charlotte judged it a foot too long for his waist. The leather looked like hamsters had been chewing on it. She couldn't hold Harry's fashion sense against him; no one in the neighborhood would make the pages of Vogue anytime soon, but it looked like he'd punched the last three holes himself with a pair of scissors. It made her sad. She knew what it meant when the older residents started losing weight: a slow, but steady march to the end.

"I heard they identified the body as the mother of a shop owner around here?"

"Not officially, but there's a good chance it's Declan Bingham's mother. He owns the pawnshop in town."

"I should interview him. I know what questions to ask. I have a way of helping people remember important details."

"I'm sure," she said, yawning.

Harry placed his arm in the metal detector's cuff and passed the round white disc at the end over the shallow grave. Nothing pinged.

Harry walked away from the hole, sweeping back and forth. Finding nothing to the left of the grave, he moved toward a pile of dirt near the fence. Charlotte recognized it as the lump Katie made while digging for the skull. Harry passed the detector over it.

She heard a beep. It was a strong signal. Memories of treasure hunting burst vividly in her mind, and she suffered a shiver of excitement. She'd conditioned herself to react to metal detector pings like a Pavlovian dog drooling at the prospect of food.

"Part of the fence?" she asked. "A nail?"

Harry thrust out a raised palm to shush her.

She scowled but remained giddy as the detector sang its mechanized aria.

He passed the detector over the pile again and narrowed in on the hot spot. Grabbing his scoop, he dug and sifted until Charlotte heard the sound of metal on metal rattling in the can-like digging device. The object sounded small but solid.

Harry plucked out a small blob of metal. It looked like a tiny mushroom, with a cylindrical base and mushed top.

"That's a bullet," he said, his face glowing with pride. "I told you these yahoos down here don't know what they're doing. It's the damn heat. It makes them lazy."

"I guess you're right. Shouldn't you be wearing gloves?"

He looked at his fingers on the bullet.

"I'm holding it on the edges. There won't be any perp evidence on a spent bullet anyway."

"What about fingerprints from when they put the bullet in the gun?"

"Well, yeah, that. But it's old and, again, I'm holding it properly."

"You think that's what killed her?"

"Very probable, unless you've been out here shooting guns."

Charlotte chuckled, but she could tell by the way he was staring at her that he wasn't kidding.

"I don't have a gun," she said. "What are you going to do with it?"

He grimaced. "I'd like to send it to my guys back in Chicago..."

"I don't think you should do that. It should go with everything else they collected for the sake of continuity, don't you think?"

"They'll only mess it up." He slapped his thigh and smiled until it looked as though his face would break from the strain. "Boy, are they lucky I'm here."

"Why don't you take it to Frank? I'll go with you."

"Fine," he said switching off his detector. "I'd like that cocky little bastard to see how his people messed up, anyway."

Charlotte started back to her house and Harry followed,

staring at the bullet, grin still plastered to his face.

"Get me an evidence bag," he said as they walked in the back door.

Charlotte's lip twitched; annoyed by the way he'd barked his order.

"I'm fresh out of evidence bags."

"A plastic bag will do. I know you don't have any official evidence bags. I do, of course, but they're back at the house. I forgot to bring them. Dammit."

She opened a kitchen drawer and retrieved a sandwich bag.

"Easy there, Colombo," she mumbled, knowing he was a little deaf and probably wouldn't hear. "Here."

"You have a permanent marker?" he asked, dropping the bullet in the bag.

"I do," said Charlotte, opening another drawer.

She handed him a black Sharpie. He laid the bag on the counter and wrote on it as Charlotte read over his shoulder.

Bullet from—

"What's your address here?"

"118 Flamingo Court."

Bullet from 118 Flamingo Court – found by Harry Wagner.

Harry added his address and phone number on the opposite side. By the time he finished, his scrawl had nearly turned the entire bag black. Charlotte could barely see the bullet.

"Is that where they should mail the medal?" she asked.

"What's that?"

"Nothing. Don't you want to give them your email?"

"Oh, good idea," said Harry, scrawling it beneath his telephone number and plunging the bullet into total darkness.

Charlotte and Harry walked the few houses down to Sheriff Marshall's house.

"Did I ever tell you how I solved the Playground Killer case? The murder of Anthony Vera?"

"Once or twice," she said, quickening her pace.

Harry began an abbreviated version of the story, talking in a steady rhythm until Charlotte knocked on Frank's door and he answered.

"Hey, Char. How can I help you?"

"Harry found something." She pointed to him and he held up the sandwich bag. "It was near the grave. He found it with his metal detector."

"Seems your people missed it," said Harry.

Charlotte watched as a dark cloud passed over Frank's countenance.

"They weren't my people. They were from the big city."

Harry barked a scratchy, humorless laugh.

"Sorry. When you're from Chicago it's funny to hear people call Tampa the big city."

Sheriff Marshall ran his tongue over his teeth and reached to take the bag from Harry.

"What you paint the bag black for?" he asked, straining to see the bullet.

"I labeled it. Her pens were too fat."

"I beg your pardon," said Charlotte, pretending to be offended.

Frank looked at her and chuckled.

"Come on in," he said, grabbing a pair of reading glasses from the counter beside the door to study the object.

"It's a .380," said Harry.

"Might be a 9mm," said the Sheriff, squinting at it through his glasses. "Though I can barely make it out through the short story written on the bag. It could be a tiny cannon or a ham sandwich."

"It's a .380."

"Yeah, probably."

"Do you think it killed her?" asked Charlotte.

"Could be. Could be some weird coincidence."

Harry snorted. "I doubt it."

"You say this was in the grave?"

"It was in the pile of dirt Katie dug. A few feet away, up against the fence."

Frank nodded and put the bag on the end of his counter.

"I'll make sure this gets to the right people."

Harry's smile dropped and his gaze fell upon the bag. For a moment, Charlotte thought he might grab it and sprint out the door.

"I could take it somewhere if you tell me where," he said. "I don't mind."

"I got it," said Frank, sliding the bag farther from Harry's reach and ushering them both toward the door.

Outside, Charlotte waited for Harry to pick a direction and then with a quick goodbye, opted to walk the opposite way. All roads led to every other in the community; she could get home either way. She preferred to travel without another cold case story. She was living a cold case story, she didn't need more.

CHAPTER EIGHT

Charlotte didn't go directly to Declan's pawnshop. First, she borrowed Mariska's car and went food shopping. Then, she pretended to head for home, looped around driving aimlessly, and finally turned down the road that led to the pawnshop.

She wasn't sure who she was kidding. She didn't need to manufacture an excuse to see Declan. He needed to know about the bullet. The problem was she'd freshened her makeup before leaving her home; not something she normally did. It made her feel as if part of her mind had an ulterior motive for visiting the sexy salesman. A reason not related to the case. She pictured his chiseled jaw and the manly curve of his neck and felt a tingle.

Maybe it wasn't her *mind* with the ulterior motives.

Charlotte flew by the Hock o' Bell, taking it for an actual Taco Bell restaurant. The stucco walls and arches betrayed its former purpose. She'd thought Declan's restaurant repurposing idea was clever when she met him, but now she wondered if it wasn't a little confusing. How many people pulled into the parking lot searching for burritos, only to find creepy antique dolls and jewelry? Maybe he should sell food, too. He could have stuffed deer heads with hot dogs balanced on their antlers... serve everything on an endless supply of antique candy dishes...

She made an illegal U-turn and pulled into the shop's parking lot. An avalanche of nerves rumbled through her body. Declan was easy to talk to, she had nothing to fear, but she felt *weird* around him, as though he kept catching her *looking* at him.

When she talked to other people and they looked at her, it felt normal; after all, she was having a conversation with them. When she talked to Declan and he looked at her with those impossibly green eyes, she felt... *caught.*

"I'm being silly," she said aloud.

She'd so wanted to dismiss him as a money-hungry ambulance chaser, but he didn't seem like a ghoulish type. He seemed nice. Maybe even a little sad and vulnerable. In addition, didn't Darla and Mariska go to estate sales all the time to buy items from the dead? Wasn't that the same thing?

But wait... Half the residents of Pineapple Port thought Declan was gay, so the idea of hooking up with him might be more impossible than it already seemed. Granted, *she* didn't think he was gay, but then, she was less likely to jump to conclusions than the denizens of the Port. They thought any man who used hair gel was gay. They probably took one look at Declan's well-manicured nails and never looked back. Most of them had grown up in a time when a man who wore matching clothes was suspect.

Charlotte took a deep breath and opened her car door. She *needed* to talk to Declan. She had every right to be there. Nay, she was honor-bound to be there. First, she didn't feel right attending the *Corpse Committee* without his blessing. Of course, she also didn't feel great about telling him her neighborhood *had* a *Corpse Committee.*

Second, she needed to tell him about the bullet. He deserved to know about any evidence that could help solve his mother's murder.

Charlotte opened the shop door to the sound of a bell ringing. Not a gonging bell, like the shape of the building might imply; but an old-fashioned tinkling retail bell tied to the door hinge. The store appeared empty of people but stuffed with rows of furniture and trinkets. As she stepped inside, she stopped to admire a huge armoire that appeared large enough to lead to other lands. Her mind wandered. Did French children call C.S. Lewis' book *The Lion, the Witch and the Armoire*? What was the French word for *lion*? Was it Lyonnaise? No, that was a kind of

French fry. She didn't know the French word for witch... *Le witch?*

"Hello?"

Charlotte jumped and found Declan standing beside her.

"Why are you always sneaking up on me?" she asked, her hand pressed against her rapidly beating heart.

"I'm pretty sure you just came into my store. I didn't sneak my store *around you.*"

Charlotte let her gaze drop from his eyes to his toes and back again. He wore a red polo and khaki shorts; the polo once again hanging neatly from the slope of his perky pecs.

So the blue polo wasn't responsible for making you look well built.

It had to be what was *underneath* the polo.

Dammit.

Charlotte cleared her throat and looked away.

"That would be quite a trick," she said.

"What?"

"Sneaking your store around me."

"Oh. Right. That's my point."

Declan looked away and then came back to her.

Why do you *look flustered? We can't* both *be flustered.*

"Sorry, you're right. My fault. My mind was a million miles away," she said, largely to keep herself from saying something even more awkward.

"That happens with you I've noticed."

Charlotte nodded.

"Old habit," she muttered, looking around the store to avoid his eyes.

"Why's that?"

Charlotte ignored his question.

"Hey, you don't happen to know..." she trailed off, realizing how weird she was about to sound.

"What?"

"You don't know the French word for lion, do you?"

"Did you come here to ask me that?"

"No..." She took a few steps away, dragging her finger along a low walnut bureau as she moved as if testing it for dust. She didn't know why she did it. But now, the urge to check her finger for dust was overwhelming.

"Nice shop," she said, rubbing her fingers together.

I don't feel dust... don't look. He'll know. Don't look...

"Thank you."

"It isn't nearly as smarmy as I thought it would be," she added, taking a quick look at her fingers.

No dust.

"Uh... thanks, I guess. I should use that in my ads: *Hock o'Bell: Not nearly as smarmy as you think.*"

"I didn't mean—"

"No. No problem. I had a big blowout last month and sold most of my smarm. Can I help you with something? How are you?"

"I'm good. I suppose I should be the one asking you, though."

Declan shrugged. "It's upsetting, of course, but in my heart, I knew my mother didn't leave me. Part of me knew she was gone."

"Did they confirm it was her? Did you hear?"

"No, but the timing and the necklace... I don't see how it couldn't be."

Charlotte nodded.

"Now I just need to find out why and how it happened," he said, running his fingers through his dark hair. One wavy curl fell on his forehead as he dropped his hand, making him look like Superman. Superman in a polo and khakis; which she reasoned was more Clark Kent's style, but he didn't have those glasses on that tricked people into thinking he was an entirely different, incredibly built, handsome guy.

"Do you ever wear glasses?" she asked.

"What?" He raised one eyebrow. "Why would I wear glasses? You mean sunglasses?"

"No, I mean *glasses* glasses. Like, with thick black frames."

"Uh... no. Should I ask you why you ask? Or will I regret that?"

Charlotte shrugged. "No, don't ask. I think *I'll* regret it if you do."

"Fair enough. Can I ask why you stopped by one more time with the *tiniest* bit of hope that you might answer?"

"Oh. Sorry. I have two things to tell you. First, Harry Wagner came by my house. He's an ex-cop who used to work cold cases. He's a little obsessed with them. Anyway, he showed up with a metal detector and found a bullet in my backyard."

"A bullet? Where they found the body?"

"Yes. We gave it to Frank—er, Sheriff Marshall, so he can pass it on to the forensic people."

"Who would shoot my mother?" Declan wondered aloud. "Not only shoot her but take the time to bury her. It's not like she was shot walking into a convenience store robbery or something."

"It might not be related. It could be some crazy coincidence."

"I guess… Thank you." He thrust his hands in his pockets and then seemed to catch himself as his thoughts began to drift. He focused on her and she felt the urge to duck behind the nearest sofa.

"You said there were two things?"

"Oh right." Charlotte looked at the ground and traced a circle on the floor with her foot. "Um… the lady who owns Pineapple Port, Penny, started a committee to address your mother's discovery."

"A committee?"

"There's a committee for everything. Someone sneezes funny and they start the Funny Sneezes Committee."

"Really. What are they calling this one? The Skeleton in Charlotte's Yard Committee?"

Charlotte felt her face growing hot with embarrassment. "Uh… *worse.*"

Declan stared at her, awaiting her answer. She considered lying, but as she looked down and into her purse, she spotted the folded committee flyer. She had to tell him the truth; he would find out, anyway.

"*The Corpse Committee.*"

Declan bit his lip. "Oh boy. That's catchier than my

suggestion."

"They like alliteration. Sorry."

"*Crime Committee* might have been good."

"I think they hoped the sensational name would attract more attendees. They once had a committee to discuss hiring a new organic lawn service and called it the *Deadly Poison Club*."

"Well, at least they didn't call Mom's committee the *Corpse Club*. That sounds like a teenage paranormal series."

Charlotte laughed.

"Well, whatever they call it, it isn't necessarily a bad idea. A lot of the older residents have been here since before your mother's murder, and someone might remember something. You never know."

"That would be great. They'll probably find very little evidence with the bones. I don't have high hopes."

"I brought you a flyer," said Charlotte. She handed him the pink sheet of paper with *Corpse Committee* across the top in bold letters. Beneath the title was a picture of a chalk outline.

Declan looked at the flyer and then back at her.

"Wow."

"Sorry. But the date and time are on there if you want to attend."

"I will," he said, folding the sheet. "My uncle will, too."

"Your uncle lives nearby?"

"He's moving back from Miami. He's retiring here."

"Oh, well I bet it will be nice to have him near."

"We'll see about that," he said, nodding his head from side to side. "He's a character."

Charlotte looked around the store, unsure what to say next.

"Okay, well, I thought you'd like to know about the group and the bullet. Maybe you could bring some photos of your mother? They might jog someone's memory?"

"Good idea. I will."

Charlotte took a few steps toward the door.

"And you could bring your, uh… significant other if you like," she said, turning.

He smiled. "My dog?"

"Do you have a dog?"

"No."

"Oh, well, I wouldn't anyway. Some of the ladies carry their little rat dogs around with them and they don't get along with other dogs. By *other*, I meant if you had, you know... someone special in your life."

"Someone special in my life," echoed Declan. "You sound like a greeting card."

Charlotte opened her mouth, frantic to better phrase her thought. He held up a palm to stop her from speaking.

"Got it. I was just messing with you. I know half of Pineapple Port thinks I'm gay."

Charlotte took a deep breath and puffed her cheeks, exhaling with a pop of her lips.

"I'd say it's closer to sixty percent... but I'm guessing you're *not* by the way you phrased that?"

"*Just* by the way I phrased that?"

"Well, you have to admit you hit a lot of the stereotypes. You've got a nice haircut, your nails are buffed, you're well dressed, you look like you work out, you're handso—"

Charlotte stopped and glanced at Declan to see if he'd registered where her last word was heading.

He laughed. "Okay, you've convinced me. I've had it wrong all these years..."

She closed her eyes and pinched the bridge of her nose with her hand. "Sorry," she said, shaking her head.

"Don't worry about it. I get it. You like your men a little more rough around the edges. A little more lumberjacky."

"No. I mean, that's not what I meant..." she paused. "Lumberjacky?"

He shrugged. "If it isn't a word, it should be."

"Well, I'll alert the *Declan's Sexual Preference Committee* that they have it all wrong."

"No. Don't tell them. I don't discourage the rumor. I may *en*courage it from time to time. For one, it makes them think I have better taste than I do. They also used to try to set me up with their granddaughters..."

"Oh…" Charlotte recalled Katherine planning to do just that. "Well, what's wrong with a little match-making? Maybe the woman of your dreams is one of their granddaughters."

"Maybe, but I was running out of polite ways to decline. I didn't want every failed setup to lose me a potential customer, and I imagine the granddaughters don't appreciate being thrown at every man within a five-mile radius of Pineapple Port, either."

She chuckled. "I've been thrown at more than a few grandsons, so I feel your pain. They mean well, but it's pretty awful."

He nodded and an awkward silence fell for a minute or two.

"Anyway… I'm good on that front," he said.

"Okay," she said, taking his comment to mean he already had a girlfriend. "I guess I'll see you at the meeting."

The bell chimed above her head as she opened the door to leave.

"See you there," he called as she left. "Thanks for stopping by."

She waved without turning, replaying the conversation in her head. Declan *had* to have a girlfriend. He was capable of getting a girlfriend without any help from the Pineapple Port matchmakers.

More than capable.

A strange feeling of relief washed over her. Maybe now that strange tension she felt whenever he was near would dissipate. The relief mingled with another emotion.

What is that?

Ah.

Disappointment.

She started her car and pulled out of the parking spot. Declan stood in the window of the shop and waved as she pulled away.

She sighed.

Why did he have to be so darn hot?

CHAPTER NINE

Charlotte, Darla, and Mariska walked into the meeting room of the Pineapple Port clubhouse. Someone had set out the usual array of cookies and punch, though Charlotte thought the arrangement felt a tad festive for a *Corpse Committee*. At least they hadn't made cookies in the shape of chalk outlines. Some of the ladies had a real flair for theme baking.

Andie paused beside her and surveyed the cookie situation. She leaned toward Charlotte.

"Store-bought. Cheap, too," she mumbled before taking three and moving to her seat.

A pile of yoga mats and a smattering of inflatable exercise balls sat in the corner of the large room, which doubled as the floor exercise studio on Tuesday and Thursday mornings. Charlotte avoided the yoga classes. Most of the residents expelled gas frequently when walking, talking, or playing cards. She'd accepted long ago that strange bodily noises were a common occurrence for older people, but she also knew she'd never be able to keep a straight face in a yoga class. She was only human. Throw on some woodwind massage music, a group of ladies attempting downward dog, and a symphony of body noises, and a Buddhist monk would burst into giggles.

Folding chairs arranged in a semicircle awaited members of the newly formed group. Charlotte took her usual seat between Darla and Mariska. Darla was a little deaf in her left ear and Mariska a little deaf in her right, so sitting between them in the correct configuration solved most communication problems.

Penny sat in the only padded chair in the room. She kept it locked in the clubhouse closet for occasions like this. After a few more people arrived, she distributed an agenda printed on neon yellow paper. At the top, it said *Corpse Club* in large letters.

"I thought it was the *Corpse Committee*?" said Darla.

"Oh no," said Charlotte, dropping her chin to her chest.

She raised her hand. Penny pointed to her.

"Yes, Charlotte?"

"I'd like to suggest we change the name to *Crime Club*. That way, once this mystery is solved, the club could be more all-purpose. I doubt we'll find more bodies, but maybe we could address missing lawn statues or the occasional car break-in."

"Or people who don't return juicers they borrowed," said Althea Moore, her eyes shifting toward Jackie Blankenship.

"Oh Althea, I'll bring it back tomorrow," hissed Jackie.

"I second that. I like *Crime Club* much better," said Mariska. "*Corpse Club* sounds gruesome. It's like the Mickey Mouse Club, but horrible."

A few others mumbled and nodded their heads.

"Fine," said Penny. "Should we vote on that now? All in favor of changing the name to *Crime Club* raise your hands."

All but a woman in black and Penny raised their hands. Everyone stared at the dissenter until she, too, raised her hand.

"I just thought *corpse* sounded more dramatic," she said. "I don't care. Nothing matters."

"Fine," said Penny. "Passed. From now on this group will be known as the *Crime Club*."

"How often will we meet?" asked Harry. "Weekly? Monthly doesn't seem like enough during the heat of the investigation. When I worked cold cases we used to—"

"Weekly seems like a lot," said Penny, cutting him short.

"I think once a month would be fine," said Darla. "We could always have an emergency meeting if some new facts came to light."

The group nodded in unison. Everyone loved the thrill of an emergency meeting.

"Fine. Well, to get things started, I think everyone should know that they bungled the investigation already," said Harry.

Frank groaned. Jaws fell and a smattering of gasps rippled through the group.

Oh boy. Here we go.

"I went to Charlotte's house with my metal detector, my everyday metal detector—"

"As opposed to his *formal* metal detector," whispered Darla.

"The one with the bow tie," added Mariska.

Charlotte snorted a laugh and the three of them burst into giggles. Harry shot them a nasty look and continued.

"I found a bullet. A .380."

Gasps rang out a second time.

"Sheriff Marshall said it might be a 9mm," said Charlotte.

"So he says. I know what I found."

Frank shrugged and rolled his eyes.

"They missed a bullet?" asked Jackie, the reluctant water aerobics queen, still dodging dirty looks from Althea, Rightful Owner of the Juicer.

"They did," said Harry. "We need to do something about the shoddy detective work around here. What if it had been you or me? I don't want these slackadoodles working on my case."

"Slackadoodles?" echoed Charlotte. "Is that like a lazy Labradoodle?"

Darla shrugged.

"I don't think this is something that happens here all the time, Harry," said Mariska.

"You never know. You never know."

"I think before we get into any of the details of the case, we should identify the victim formally," said Charlotte. "Do any of you even know her name?"

Most of the group shook their heads. Charlotte knew fifty percent of the attendees were the same people who attended every meeting and had no interest in the topic. They came for the cookies and punch, hoping beyond hope each time that someone would bring homemade.

"She's the pawnshop owner's sister," said Penny.

"*Mother*," corrected Charlotte. "Her name was Erin Bingham. Does that name ring a bell for anyone?"

There was a low murmur accompanied by synchronized head shaking. Al Taliaferro, who'd been staring at his shoes or possibly napping, threw back his head and turned his attention to Harry.

"You think she was shot?" he asked.

"We don't know yet. That remains to be determined."

"Erin Bingham," said Penny, scratching her chin. "I think she used to work at George's office."

"Declan said she did," said Charlotte.

"I said what?"

Heads swiveled toward the voice. Declan and an older man walked toward the group, grabbing seats as they passed the collection of folding chairs in the corner. The second man stood three inches shorter than Declan and had a much thicker build. He shared Declan's sharp nose and dark hair, but his temples were speckled with gray. Declan held a manila envelope in his hand.

"That must be his boyfriend," whispered Katherine O'Malley.

Declan's explanation for not dispelling rumors to avoid matchmaking made even more sense if Katherine's self-centered grandchild was one of the girls thrown his way. Charlotte had met her and not been a fan. Rather than admit her grandchild needed a lesson in manners and humility, Katherine clung to the idea that Declan simply wasn't interested in women at all.

Charlotte stood. "Everyone, this is Declan. We don't have definitive proof yet, but we suspect the woman found was his mother."

A low chant of apologies and tsk noises filled the room. One tiny voice asked, "what woman?" and someone hushed her.

Declan held up a hand in an abbreviated wave.

"Sorry, I'm late. This is my uncle, Seamus. I just picked him up at the airport."

"Hello, all. Hello ladies," he added with a naughty wink.

One of the ladies giggled.

Declan set his empty chair across from Charlotte and sat down. His uncle opened his chair and sat behind Declan because the gentleman beside Declan pretended not to see Seamus and refused to make room for him in the circle.

"Would you like some punch? Some cookies?" Celia Jackson asked Seamus.

"No, thank you. Unless you made them, then I might have to try them."

Celia smiled and shook her head, a bright blush rising to her cheeks.

"Declan, I was just saying I think your mother worked for my husband," said Penny.

"She did. She had two jobs. She worked in the office here and on weekend nights she worked at a restaurant called Nectarine's."

"Oh, I miss that place," said Agnes Salzmann.

Several women agreed. "They had the best French toast..." said one.

"I'll talk to George about it," said Penny. "Maybe he'll remember something that will help."

"Where is George?" asked Frank. "Shouldn't he be here?"

"He had to talk to the sprinkler man. The timers are all screwy."

Charlotte nodded. George was an avid gardener and if one sprinkler didn't sprinkle, she could imagine he was losing his mind.

"I knew it. I was soaked the other day while walking by your place at two o'clock in the afternoon," said Andie.

Penny dismissed her by throwing her nose in the air and looking away. The comment hadn't even registered a sniff. Charlotte wondered if the silent sniff might be the worst sniff of all.

"You should know the investigators already messed up your case," said Harry to Declan, preparing to retell his tale.

"I already told him all that, Harry," said Charlotte.

"Did you tell him I found the bullet with my metal detector?"

"I did."

Harry grimaced and sat back, arms crossed over his chest.

"I gave the bullet to the appropriate authorities," said Frank.

Harry grunted.

The sheriff scanned the group.

"Does anyone here own a gun?"

Several of the ladies seemed alarmed.

"My husband has several guns," said Penny.

"I have a handgun," said Al.

"I think my husband has a handgun in the safe," said Ginny Aleshire. "I think he might have a rifle, too, and some sticky things."

"Sticky things?" asked Frank.

"You know, *sticky* things. Sticks you use to beat people. Everybody has them."

Charlotte slid her gaze toward Darla.

"What the hell is Ginny's husband up to?"

"I don't know, but I'm going to make a mental note not to piss him off."

Frank held up a hand to stop the rising tide of chatter. "Well, anyone with a gun, I'd like to collect them for ballistics testing."

"I was going to suggest that," said Harry.

"You don't think one of us could have killed her, do you Frank?" asked Jackie.

"I'm not saying that, but getting your weapon cleared is the easiest way to remove yourself from suspicion. If they decide to do a house-by-house search for weapons, you don't want to be the one hiding your gun. Bring them to me now and we'll get them tested against the bullet."

"That I found," mumbled Harry.

"Of course none of us did it," said Penny. "But I'll tell George to bring by his guns, Sheriff. We want to help in every way possible. Things like this don't happen in Pineapple Port."

"I brought some pictures," said Declan. He stood and slipped a pile of papers from his manila envelope. He handed a sheet to each person in the circle.

"Charlotte thought seeing my mother might help people remember her, maybe help with the investigation."

Everyone took a photo and stared at it. A few offered nods of appreciation.

"Such a beautiful girl," said Mariska, shaking her head.

Charlotte looked at the photo of the dark-haired woman. She was very pretty, with a pert nose, full lips, and startling green eyes. She could see Declan's face in hers.

"You favored her," said Darla, noticing the same thing.

Declan nodded.

A silence fell over the group.

"Can anyone think of anything else?" asked Charlotte. "Penny, now that you've seen her, does she look familiar?"

Penny offered a level seven sniff. Seven meant *True Agitation.*

"I'm not sure. She looks like anyone. I didn't get to the office much. I was raising my babies. But I did some of the bookwork and I remember seeing her name on the payroll."

Al stared at the photo, his usually tan face paler than usual.

"Al?" asked Charlotte. "Do you recognize her?"

"I... I do," he said. "I worked for George and I remember seeing her at the office. But I never saw her outside the office. I don't know anything about her. You said she was shot, right?"

"We don't know for sure," said Frank.

"Probably, though," said Harry. "I found a bullet, after all."

"I set up a Facebook group for the *Corpse Club*," said Penny.

Declan looked at Charlotte, his eyes wide. Charlotte shook her head and looked down, trying not to laugh.

"*Crime* Club," said Charlotte, after taking a second to compose herself. "Remember, Penny? We voted to change the name."

"Right, yes," said Penny. "I'll have to change the name of the group. Anyway, I'll send you all a link. Go and join and I'll post any updates there."

"I don't trust the Face Place," said Agnes. "I won't do it. You can't make me."

Penny huffed.

As the meeting adjourned, attendees gravitated toward

Declan and Charlotte walked outside. Jackie asked her about getting some dishtowels embroidered with Scottish terriers on them for her daughter's birthday and they talked until she saw Declan exit the building. She assured Jackie she'd stitch whatever she needed and excused herself. Seamus approached and started a conversation with Jackie.

"Thanks for coming," said Charlotte to Declan when he stepped outside. "Sorry if you were swarmed in there. You're like a celebrity around here now."

"Oh, thanks for the invite. Seamus, this is Charlotte. They found the bones in her backyard."

Seamus paused his conversation with Jackie and thrust forward his large paw to shake.

"Nice to meet you. My nephew's told me all about you."

"About how you found the body," said Declan.

"Right," agreed Seamus. "About the bones."

Seamus turned back to Jackie and Charlotte watched as the pool aerobics queen offered him a demure smile. For no-nonsense Jackie, it was category four hurricane flirting. She could pull a face muscle fluttering her eyelids like that without stretching first.

"That seemed like a successful meeting," said Declan. "Who knows, maybe something will come of it."

"I never dreamed so many people here had guns," said Charlotte.

"Well, a lot of our founding fathers did and I'm sure there are a few of them living here."

Charlotte laughed.

"Well…" he said, swinging his arms. "Back to the shop."

Charlotte nodded and said goodbye to both of the Irishmen. She watched them walk toward the parking lot as Mariska appeared in the doorway, cookie crumbs nestled on the shelf created by her bust line.

"Was that Declan?" she asked.

"Yep."

"Why don't you ask him over for a drink?"

"Really? I thought you thought he was gay?"

"I saw the way he looked at you. That man is not gay."

Charlotte looked back at Declan's retreating form.

"I think he has a girlfriend."

Mariska shrugged. "Maybe she's not all that."

Charlotte laughed.

"What? You don't think I know the hip lingo?"

She shook her head, still snickering. "You're crazy anyway, Mar. Anytime someone looks in my direction you think they're five minutes away from proposing marriage."

"They probably are. You're gorgeous."

"Gorgeous to you, maybe, but you have low standards."

"Gorgeous to everyone," said Mariska, grabbing her and sneaking in a second hug for the day.

Charlotte grimaced and pretended to hate it.

"We never should have let you live in that house by yourself for so long. You've gotten too used to it."

The two of them began strolling back to the golf cart.

"You and Bob and Frank and Darla were always right across the street. And whenever I wanted I could sleep over."

"Like after you watched a scary movie," said Mariska, chuckling at the memory.

"Exactly. It was a dream being the queen of my castle."

"Yes, but both your mother and grandmother weren't huggy things. As much as I loved Estelle, she wasn't the warmest person. And now you jump at the slightest touch. I've been trying to hug it out of you for years, but I worry you'll never let anyone get close to you."

"Wait," said Charlotte, stopping. "You're telling me this hug routine of yours is some sort of physical therapy?"

"Well..." said Mariska, her eyes growing moist. "That and I love you."

Mariska clamped her arms around her once more and she submitted to the third hug of the day. When it became apparent Mariska was in for the long haul, Charlotte struggled to pull her arms free and hugged her back. They stood that way, rocking back and forth until Darla approached.

"Oh no," said Darla. "Who died now?"

CHAPTER TEN

Charlotte walked home, poured herself a glass of wine, and sat on her back porch, book on her lap, once again staring at Erin Bingham's shallow grave.

"Hey Erin, I met your son," she said aloud.

No answer. Good.

"He's very cute."

Nothing.

A part of her wished she'd never met Declan. If she hadn't, the bones would have remained bones and not become a *person*. The more time she spent thinking about Erin, wondering what happened to her, the more she felt like she knew her.

A tiny part of her thought that maybe Erin *would* answer. She just hoped it would be when she *expected* it and she wasn't going to just open her bathroom door sometime to find Erin standing in the hallway. When she was young, Mariska used to enter the house with no announcement. Charlotte would turn a corner to find a shape standing in her hall or kitchen. Half the time they'd both yelp and then stand there panting, hands on their hearts.

"What happened Erin? Just talk enough to tell me what happened."

She couldn't help but wonder about Erin's last hours.

"Were you afraid? Did you know you were going to die? Did—"

Charlotte fell silent. It made her upset to think of Erin in fear for her life.

Abby groaned and rolled onto her back, her legs in the air like a dying cockroach. She didn't look like a dog with extra-sensory perception alarms blaring.

"Whenever you're ready, Erin," she mumbled.

Charlotte wanted to fill the grave and make it go away, but she worried disturbing it might ruin some chance of finding Erin's killer. The crime tape came down before Harry arrived and found the bullet, so she didn't trust the police to tell her when it was safe to touch the area. What if she'd covered the grave before Harry came round? What if, while digging, she'd knocked the bullet through the fence and into the yard next door? Harry might never have found the most important piece of evidence.

She wished she could fast-forward and discover the results of the forensic testing. Or, as long as she was giving herself superpowers, she wished she could see into the past, and identify Erin's killer. She could give both Declan and his mother peace.

Charlotte closed her eyes and rested her head on the back of her chair. Sans superpowers, she'd have to use her mind to find Erin's killer. *Think.* There had to be an angle; some breadcrumb that would lead to better clues. She felt responsible somehow, for owning the property beneath which Erin had rested for so many years. She was obsessed.

She was passionate.

Hm.

Isn't this what she'd wanted? A passionate interest in something? She couldn't make a career of finding bones in her yard, but...

The sound of Abby's deep bark made Charlotte jump and slosh wine onto her shorts. She heard a knock and set down her glass to walk to the front door.

"Al," said Charlotte, finding Al Taliaferro on her doorstep.

"How you doin' Charlotte?"

Al ran a hand over his head. Towering over the five-foot-nothing man, she could see every sun-damaged inch of his scalp through the strips of his thinning black hair. It was unusual to have yet another member of the community at her door, but at least he'd had the decency to knock instead of peeping over her fence.

"What's up?"

Al wrung his hands, eyes darting left and right.

"Uh… Mind if I talk to you for a bit?"

"No, of course not."

She waited for Al to begin, but he stood, silent, shifting his weight from one foot to another. She realized Al's conversation required more than a chat on the stoop.

"Want to come in?"

Al nodded and stepped into the house, careful to avoid the bounding terrier determined to steal his attention.

"Can I get you something to drink? Wine? Beer?"

"You got scotch?"

"Do I live in Pineapple Port?" She flashed him a smile. Scotch was a popular drink in the neighborhood. She thought it tasted like earwax, but she always kept some on hand.

Charlotte put ice in a glass and poured. She handed it to Al.

"Let's sit on the lanai," she said, leading the way to where her wine awaited her return. She decided right then to say *lanai* a million times a day until she became desensitized to it.

Al followed her. He froze at the threshold, staring at the gravesite through the screen.

"That where they found her?"

"Yes. That's where Katie found her. Just to the right of the lanai."

Al swallowed and walked into the porch. He sat across from Charlotte, who retrieved her glass and took a sip.

"So how can I help you, here in my lanai?" she asked.

Al didn't flinch. She could probably answer all his questions with *lanai* in it and he wouldn't bat an eye.

"I have information about the girl. About those bones."

Charlotte forgot about the *lanai* game.

"What? You do?"

"I didn't kill her," said Al. He gulped his scotch.

"I didn't think you did."

"I just have some information that probably don't mean nothin'."

"Okay..."

She considered suggesting to Al that he tell his story to Frank, but she didn't want to scare him away. What could it hurt if she heard it first...

"Go ahead," she said, using her most reassuring tone.

Al took a deep breath.

"I was coming back from Sandy's... That was a bar that used to be three towns over. It's gone now. Anyway, I was coming back and I'd been drinking. I'm not going to pretend I wasn't. I was drunk. I was driving with one eye closed."

She winced and he saw it.

"Hey, keep in mind this was fifteen years ago. Back then, nobody thought twice about driving drunk."

"Fifteen years ago wasn't the fifties, Al."

"I just mean it's worse now. I mean better. You know what I mean."

"Understood."

"Anyway, something happened... I forget what. I had to change the radio or I dropped my cigarette... I don't remember. I just know I looked down for a second, and when I looked up, I saw this woman walkin' down the road. No, more like *jogging* down the road."

He took another drink from his glass until only the clinking ice remained. She stood and retrieved the bottle of scotch. She refilled his glass and sat back down.

"Thanks," he said, grabbing the glass the moment it left her fingers. "Anyway, I remember she was wearin' a white blouse with a big red belt. She looked like a ghost. I was headed right for her. She was moving funny, y'know? Weavin' back and forth. I remember because it confused me. I didn't know which way to swerve."

"Like *she* was drunk?"

"Yeah, I guess. I dunno. It all happened in a split second. She was stumblin' back and forth. It seemed like she was everywhere. I swerved and I missed her."

Al paused and stared at her. She tried not to react; worried any judgment on her part would silence him. Maybe serving as his confessor had been a poor idea. There'd been murmurs in the neighborhood that Al was once connected to the New Jersey Mafia, but, that rumor followed almost everyone from New York or New Jersey whose name ended with a vowel. It wasn't unusual for the victims of the stereotyping to not only embrace the rumor but encourage it, much like Declan had done with his tall tales. Pineapple Port was crawling with ex-Tony Soprano wannabes.

"Charlotte?"

Charlotte's attention snapped back. "I'm sorry. My mind wandered."

Al grimaced. "That's okay. I'm probably scarin' you. You think I killed that poor girl."

"But you didn't?"

"No. No..."

"You didn't hit her with your car?"

"No, I... I mean I don't think so." He paused to take another sip. "I didn't hear a scream, didn't see her on the road in the rearview, didn't feel a thump. I told myself I'd imagined it. Like I said, she looked like a ghost, but—"

Al finished his glass and put it on the table. He put his face in his hands and breathed deeply.

"But what?"

"But it was right *here*," said Al, sitting up and pointing at the ground with his stubby index finger. "Right where your house is; where they were building the new part of the Port. I never would have thought about it again, but it was right freakin' *here*."

Charlotte looked out at the grave.

"Did you bury her?"

"No, that's the thing. I didn't bury her. I never got out of the damn car. I slowed down... but I never got out. I told myself I'd imagined her and I went home. I was pretty shaken up to tell you the truth. Laughin' with nerves."

"You said everything was a little fuzzy. Are you *sure* you didn't bury her?"

"How could I forget buryin' someone? I'm not that old. And I'm not that stupid to tell you I was in the same *state* the day she disappeared if I did bury her. Hell, I couldn't live with myself all these years knowing I'd killed a girl and buried her. I know people got a thing about certain Italians buryin' people under cement, but to be honest, the sight of blood makes me sick. I wouldn't have been able to touch her."

Al leaned forward in his chair, his voice dropping to a conspiratorial whisper.

"Char, I was a *plumber*. I knew maybe one connected guy and he was a nobody. I might let people around here think what they want about my past. Maybe I don't correct them when they start dreamin' up stories if you know what I mean. But I ain't never killed nobody."

Charlotte sat back in her chair, deep in thought.

"She couldn't have been knocked into a hole somehow," she mumbled. "They couldn't have built over her; someone would have noticed."

"Unless they were afraid it would stop construction? I can't stop thinking about it... thinking someone might have found her by the side of the road and thrown her in a hole just to avoid delays."

"Oh gosh... you think? I mean, even the greediest bastard wouldn't pave over a dead girl to avoid stalling construction, would he?"

Al shrugged. "Probably not, but I dunno. Stranger things have happened. Just because I wasn't connected, doesn't mean I didn't hear stories, if you know what I mean."

"Are you sure it was Erin Bingham?"

"No. Like I said, I'm not sure about nothin' except I didn't bury no one. That picture her kid brought, though, it sort of looked like her, but I dunno. Gave me the sweats."

"Did you see her again? Did you see Erin at the office here again?"

Al shrugged. "I only went in the office once in a while. I

wouldn't have noticed when she was there or when she was gone."

"Why are you telling *me* this?"

"Aw Char, I'm scared," said Al, rattling his ice. "I'm scared to tell the sheriff. I thought I'd bounce it off you, see what you thought."

"But why me?"

"Because you found her. Maybe you know stuff I don't. And 'cuz you're smart. Everybody knows it. You make a killing on trivia night. You and your nose always in those books," he thrust a thumb toward the living room where Charlotte's book Stonehenge stood. "And you're close to Frank. I thought maybe you could help me out there, make sure he doesn't arrest me? I know I didn't do anything to her, but I'd feel better if I told him about it. Maybe it could help in some little way."

Charlotte bit her lip, considering the possibilities and the best way to handle this new information.

"Do you mind if I make a phone call?"

"You callin' the cops?" asked Al, beginning to stand.

"No, I'm going to call Declan. I want to see if he knows what his mother was wearing when she went missing."

"Oh, like if it wasn't white then it wasn't her? That's smart. See? I never thought about that. That's good. That's good. Be careful how you tell him, though. He might not be so happy with me, y'know... that maybe I almost hit his mom with my car and all."

"I'm just going to ask him about the clothes right now."

Al settled back into his chair.

"Okay. You call him."

Charlotte found her phone and dialed the number on the card Declan had given her the day they met.

"Hello?"

"Declan? It's Charlotte. Quick question. What was your mother wearing when she disappeared?"

"What was she wearing? Why?"

"I just need to know. It's probably nothing."

"I don't know," he said after a pause. "I was asleep when she left. She was wearing her pajamas the last time I saw her. If she went out, she probably got redressed."

"Were they white?"

"What?"

"Her pajamas."

"Oh, no, they were navy, I do remember that. Like a cotton shorts outfit with little dots all over them. The dots were green, I think."

"Was her car missing? Did she take it?"

"No. Wherever she went, she walked, or was picked up."

"Where did you live then? Was it within walking distance of my house?"

"Of your house? I... I guess it was. Your part of the community wasn't there then, but yes, we were just outside of Pineapple Port on your side of the development."

"Hm..." said Charlotte, looking at Al. Declan's information didn't rule out the possibility that he *had* seen Erin on the road that night.

"What's this about? Did you hear something?" asked Declan.

"No, I'll tell you later. It's probably nothing. I have to go, okay?"

He sighed. "Not really. I don't see why—"

"I just can't this second. I'll talk to you soon, bye."

She hung up and rubbed her lips with the knuckle of her left index finger, staring at Al, who had moved into the kitchen to hover near the scotch.

"What he say?" he asked.

"The last time Declan saw his mother she was wearing navy pajamas."

"So it wasn't her," said Al, his face awash with relief.

"Not necessarily. He said she disappeared after he went to bed. If she decided to leave the house she would have changed."

"Aah," he grunted, face collapsing into a frown. "You got me all excited there for a second. I better have a drink."

He poured himself another, an act that barely registered for Charlotte as she imagined a girl in white, captured in headlights, running down the street. It was a haunting image.

"Even if it wasn't Erin, I wonder what happened to the girl you did see," she mumbled.

"Maybe it was a ghost. Maybe I was seein' things. It all happened so fast. Nobody ever said anythin' about finding nobody on the side of the road. Honestly, I might have imagined the whole thing."

"So you didn't see reports about Erin missing? On the news?"

"Nah. It wasn't like today with the news everywhere, twenty-four hours a day. I never heard about her missing. I don't even know if it was around the same time, to be honest. It's just eatin' at me."

"Al," said Charlotte, adopting her most serious face. "Please promise me you'll tell Frank this story."

He scowled. "I dunno… I *want* to…"

"It's the right thing to do. I'm sure it's nothing. It's just the right thing to do."

Al nodded and thrust his hands into the pockets of his khaki shorts. He started pulling out keys, a Leatherman knife, loose aspirin, gum, and bits of paper, piling it all on her counter. His pockets were like a magical clown car, contents never-ending.

"What are you doing?"

"I thought I'd leave my stuff here, in case he takes me to jail. I don't trust those guys, I'll never get it back."

"You don't have to do that. You're not going to jail."

Al stopped and stared at her.

"I promise. And if you do, I'll take all your stuff to your wife for safekeeping, okay?"

He started stuffing things back into his pockets.

"Okay, Char," he said, clapping her shoulder when he'd finished. "I'll go over there right now. I'll do it."

She clapped him back. "Good man."

"Thanks," he said, pausing at the door. "It felt good to get that off my chest."

"Well, it will feel even better to tell the sheriff."

"I dunno. He's a hardass."

Charlotte snickered. She loved how honest everyone became after the age of seventy.

"You can trust him. What if I went with you?"

"Would you?" Al beamed. "I was just about to ask. That would be nice of you. I'd feel better."

"No problem. Let me grab my flip-flops."

Charlotte and Al walked down the street and knocked on Frank's door. Darla answered, wearing a flowing caftan in turquoise and brown.

"Charlotte—what brings you here?" her face clouded with confusion. "With Al?"

"She's here in case I need someone to hold my stuff," said Al.

Darla's face twisted with confusion. "*What?*"

"Al has something to tell Frank," said Charlotte. "I'm here for moral support."

"Tell him to come back tomorrow," said a gruff voice from inside the house.

"Oh nonsense, come on in," said Darla.

Charlotte stepped inside in time to catch Frank rolling his eyes and pantomiming shooting himself in the head with his finger.

"Dammit, Frank, don't do that. It's gruesome," snapped Darla.

"Do what?" he asked, winking at Charlotte.

Frank stood and shook Al's hand.

"Whatcha got for me?"

Al told half his story before Frank asked him to stop.

"Two things. One, do you want a lawyer?"

"Nah, I'm sure it was just a dream. I just thought I should tell someone."

"Okay, second thing…"

Frank looked at Darla. "Darling, love of my life, you have to leave. I can't have you gasping and saying *oh my word* after every sentence."

Darla scowled.

"Fine. Can I get anyone a cup of coffee?"

"No, thank you," said Charlotte. "But I'll take a glass of wine."

"That's my girl," said Darla, heading into the kitchen.

Frank took notes as Al finished his story.

"Okay, you're free to go, Al. Got it all on paper. If we need to contact you again I'm assuming you'll be around?"

Al nodded. "Where would I go?"

Frank and Al said their goodbyes as Charlotte sipped her wine. When Al left, Darla turned to her husband.

"You're not going to arrest him?"

"For what?"

"He admitted to driving drunk."

"I can't arrest a man for driving drunk fifteen years ago. If I could, I'd have to arrest everyone in the damn neighborhood. This isn't exactly a taxi crowd around here."

"But he killed that girl."

"He's not sure he hit anyone, or even if what he saw was true. And if he'd killed her, they would have found her on the side of the road, not in a grave."

Darla grunted and pushed her nose to the side to make it appear broken. "Unless he buried her. I heard he's got *connections*, you know."

Frank waved her away. "The only thing that man's got connections to is his television's remote control. Oh, and hey, Charlotte, you might like to know I got the autopsy report back right before you stopped by."

"Really? Already? Is it her? Did they find anything?"

"It *is* Erin Bingham," said Frank, flopping back into his comfy chair.

"Oh no." Charlotte suffered a wave of sadness. She knew the victim *had* to be Declan's mother, but she'd hoped it wasn't.

"Did you tell Declan?"

"I'm going to give him a call in the morning. They also found a chip in one of her ribs that looked like it could have been caused by a bullet."

"Then the bullet Harry found killed her?"

"Probably. There was also scratching around that chip. They don't know what caused it. Did the dog get ahold of any rib bones?"

"No. Just the skull and jaw. I never saw Katie grab anything else."

"What about Abby?"

"She wasn't out there. She prefers the air conditioning."

"Oh, you spoil that dog," said Darla.

"And you didn't touch anything?" asked Frank.

Charlotte shook her head.

"Hm."

"Is that your official sheriff's evaluation of the situation?" asked Darla. "Hm?"

Frank nodded. "Mm-hm."

CHAPTER ELEVEN

Charlotte left Darla's house and returned to her own. She hopped in the shower and stood under the water, staring at her loofah mitt, replaying Al's story over again in her head.

Could Al have killed Erin Bingham?

She couldn't picture Al getting out of his car, dragging Erin's body away from the road, digging a hole, and burying her. He was a hundred and thirty pounds and five feet tall on his best day, holding a sack of flour and wearing his highest-heeled loafers. If Declan's height came from his mother, Al would have struggled to drag her dead weight, even as a younger man. The chance that he also had a shovel in his car and dug a grave, all the while so drunk that he had to drive with one eye closed, didn't seem likely.

In addition, her home was under construction when Erin went missing. It seemed odd that Al would have hidden a body in a work zone, where the daily activity of building made her discovery more probable. A person didn't have to be in the mafia to see the stupidity of such a move.

No version of Al burying Erin made sense, but the coincidence of Erin's disappearance matching Al's memories of a young woman alone on the stretch of road between Pineapple Port and Declan's old home was interesting.

She wanted to call Declan, but she also dreaded the idea.

Charlotte reached for the soap and grimaced at her loofah mitt. She hated loofah mitts. Every year, Mariska found a reason to give her a gift basket with a scrubby item in it and she felt guilty throwing them out. She forced herself to use the evil loofahs for a month or two until it felt less ungrateful to toss them.

She liked the idea of exfoliation. Nobody wanted to walk around covered in dead skin. And to their credit, loofah mitts were better than those scrubby balls of crinoline that looked like headband decorations for seven-year-old pageant girls. Their sole purpose was to decorate bath-themed gift baskets that people bought for quasi-friends. Bath baskets required little thought, but had an air of thoughtfulness, like roses from a gas station.

But loofah mitts were too wide and slipped off her hand. A person with a paw large enough to fit into one could play tennis without a racket.

She preferred scrubby gloves. Tight-fitting gloves allowed her to employ all the nimbleness her fingers could afford. The loofah mitt was like beating herself clean with a club. Loofah was also too scratchy; she wanted to slough dead skin cells, not scale a fish. The mitt looked soft and inviting in the gift basket, but once wet, it curled up like a dead insect and dried with an impenetrable exoskeleton. She could wear it like a cuff and block bullets like Wonder Woman. What good was a mitt that turned into an unchewable hamster tunnel after one use?

She considered soaking the loofah to keep it from hardening overnight, but she worried that fully hydrated, it might spring to life. She didn't want to wake up one morning to find it clamped on her face. A day later her chest would explode like *Alien*, unleashing an army of loofah mitt larva upon the world.

She needed to throw out the mitt and end her misery, but she hated wasting something Mariska bought.

Maybe I could toss the loofah as part of my new self-improvement policy...

Charlotte glanced toward the kitchen, where her chalkboard awaited. As she did, she realized the hot water had dropped a few degrees.

How long have I been standing here pondering loofahs?

Charlotte bathed using the bath gloves she'd purchased for herself, stepped out of the shower, and wrapped a towel around her body. She leaned back into the shower, pinched the loofah with two fingers, and dropped it into the trash.

As she combed her hair, her eyes darted back and forth from her foggy mirror to the loofah in the trash. She didn't trust it there. She felt like it was angry with her. She plucked the loofah out of the trash and walked it to the kitchen trash, where it would remain hidden under her sink, *secured behind cabinet doors.*

She returned to her room and slipped into sweat shorts and a cotton tank top, trying to remember what she'd been thinking about before the loofah stole her attention.

Oh, right. Al's involvement in Erin's death.

She might have solved the whole mystery by now if she spent as much time thinking about Al and Erin as she did about killer loofahs.

Charlotte stared at the clock on her kitchen wall and wondered if it was too late to call Declan. It was only seven, but seven was like midnight in Pineapple Port.

I shouldn't get involved... still... Declan deserves to know...

She knew she should let Frank call Declan in the morning, but it was *killing her.*

She wandered to her chalk wall and wrote *stop LM situation.* It was code for addressing Mariska's loofah mitt tendencies. She had to nip future loofah purchases in the bud. It was the adult thing to do. Mariska wouldn't be insulted. She'd probably be happy to avoid the expenditure of keeping her swimming in loofahs.

She picked up a book and tried to read it but couldn't concentrate. She put down the aged paperback and found her cell phone.

She knew her mind wandered whenever faced with a dilemma. The official term was *avoidance.* For months after her mother's death, she'd stopped speaking and begun reading two or three books a day. If she couldn't physically remove herself from an unpleasant situation, her mind packed up and left of its own volition. Years later, she couldn't shake the habit, but normally, it wasn't a problem. Usually, she didn't have a dead woman in her yard.

The loofahs had kept her from thinking about telling Declan that his mother was officially dead.

Before her mind could hide, she maneuvered to her recent calls and dialed.

Ha. I moved too fast for you, brain.

"Hello?"

The moment Charlotte heard Declan's voice she realized she couldn't tell him her news over the phone. It wouldn't allow him to see her face; to see that she felt confident Al wasn't his mother's killer. On the phone, he might get angry and hang up on her. He could call Frank and demand to know why no one had told him about Al's reckless driving or the autopsy reports and then Frank would be furious with her.

"Hello?" repeated Declan.

Charlotte remained silent. She'd spent twenty minutes thinking about a loofah and two seconds planning a very serious call about a potential murder.

I didn't think this out at all.

"Charlotte, I have caller ID. I know it's you."

She looked at the phone, horrified.

Damn modern-day technology.

Charlotte chewed at her lip, trying to invent a reason why she might have called. She didn't want to tell him the real reason for her call, but they weren't in a hey-I-just-called-to-say-hi sort of relationship.

Should I invite myself to his house? I wonder what his house looks like. I bet it's modern and neat. For some reason, I picture hardwood floors and a leather sofa, but not a cheesy faux leather one, a nice one. I wonder—

"Charlotte?"

Declan? Oh right... how the hell have I survived for twenty-six years? I have the attention span of a—

A squirrel hopped by her window and she followed its

progress, wondering what skinny little Florida squirrels ate.

We don't have acorns around here. Do we? Wait—

She realized she was holding a phone to her ear.

"Hello?" she said.

"There you are. I couldn't hear you."

"Uh..."

Charlotte imitated a poor connection.

"Wait... I... erp... I... eh... moving... bet... Here. Is this better?"

"There you go. Much better. We must have had a bad connection."

"Yep. Sorry. Hey, are you at home?"

"I'm at home."

"I have some information about the case. About your mom. Would you mind if I came over to tell you?"

Good. Breathe. Focus...

"Just a second."

Charlotte heard a muffled yell as if Declan had covered the phone to scream at someone.

"Sorry. My uncle is here and he was being... uh... loud. What is it? What did you find out?"

"I'd rather tell you in person. It's sensitive."

Charlotte cringed. She didn't even know what *it's sensitive* meant, but she'd heard people say it in movies. It sounded ridiculous. She might as well have told him it was 'top secret' or 'black ops.'

"Okay, sure, I guess," said Declan, his voice sounding deflated. "Do you want me to come to you?"

Charlotte's eyes darted around her home. She'd never been embarrassed about it before, but Declan had called it a *dorm room*. She was mortified for him to see it again.

"No. I'll come to you."

Declan gave her his address and she wrote it on her wall in chalk.

"I'll be there in a few minutes."

She stared at Declan's address on her wall. Her stomach felt funny again. She circled the address to emphasize the seriousness of her visit. The circle started at the top, looped around, and then dipped down to complete the ring.

It reminded her of something.

It looks like a heart.

She released a frustrated grunt, put down the chalk, and jogged to her bedroom to remove her lay-around clothes. She pulled thong underwear from her bureau drawer and slipped into them. She loved thongs. Growing up in a retirement community meant coming face-to-butt with an endless array of panty lines. Every tush had some configuration of granny panty lines; even some of the men. Not only were panty lines unattractive on a young person, but they involved the word *panty*, possibly the worst word in the English language. Charlotte couldn't even say *panties* without cringing and giggling. Even 1959's *Anatomy of a Murder* with Jimmy Stewart had a ten-minute shtick about how they couldn't say panties in the courtroom without the gallery cracking up.

Thongs made her feel *young*. Not many other things did in the Port.

She planned to wear thongs until her butt grazed the backs of her knees. She didn't know how old was too old for a thong. Maybe never. Maybe her generation would fill retirement homes with thong-wearing octogenarians, everyone wearing thongs the way their grandmothers wore scarves and housedresses.

She noticed the elastic unraveling on the thong she'd chosen and threw it back into her drawer. She pulled out a sexy, lacy pair and stepped into them. She hadn't worn that pair in some time, so it was a good opportunity to slip it into rotation. She didn't want to wear her underwear unevenly.

That was why she chose that pair.

She looked at herself in the mirror and assured herself of that fact.

That is why I chose this pair. Not because it is my sexiest pair. Because it was feeling unloved.

Charlotte grabbed shorts, paused, and then opened her closet. She plucked a sky blue summer dress from the rack and slipped into it. It, perhaps, showed a little too much leg, but it was easier to step into a dress. No buttons or zippers. Shorts were high maintenance.

Yes, shorts are a lot of work. The dress is much easier. Saving time is efficient.

She put on her usual makeup; mascara, lipstick, and a dusting of blush, and then opened the cabinet under the sink. She collected five crinoline wash balls and a forgotten loofah lurking in the back of the cabinet. She marched them all to the kitchen trash and then took the trash to the outside bin.

She didn't want to come home at night to that many angry, abandoned bath products.

Loofahs safely in the trash, she ran back inside and grabbed a cold bottle of white wine from her refrigerator. It was only polite to bring a gift when visiting a person's home for the first time. She patted Abby on the head and left. Declan's home was less than a mile away, so she put the bottle of wine in the basket of her bike and wheeled out of Pineapple Port.

She felt as though her body was about to crawl out of her skin. Nerves jangling, she stared at the bottle of wine, wondering if it would be rude to arrive with it half empty.

CHAPTER TWELVE

Declan and Seamus walked into Declan's stucco home in Charity, Florida, just on the outskirts of the Pineapple Port community. The house stood barely half a mile from the modest modular home in which he'd lived as a child. Declan could still see the two-bedroom home he'd shared with his mother in his mind's eye. He could walk through it and see the red, crushed velvet sofa and the checkered white and yellow linoleum kitchen floor. Crushed velvet seemed like an odd fabric choice for sticky Florida, but his mother had loved that sofa. It made Declan smile to think about her telling him not to put his feet on the cushions.

Sometimes he jogged past his old home, but it made him sad to see the unruly grass and the screen door hanging at an awkward angle from its hinges. Declan's grandmother had moved him to her home in Tampa after his mother's disappearance, and whoever purchased his home after he left wasn't endeavoring to win any curb appeal competitions. Declan could only imagine the rundown interior. When planned neighborhoods like Pineapple Port appeared in Charity, no one wanted to buy stand-alone modular homes without access to pools and community centers. If it wasn't for the rusty Chevy truck parked outside, Declan would have thought his childhood home abandoned.

As Seamus walked into Declan's new home, he whistled with appreciation.

"Nice place. How many bedrooms?"

"Thanks. Just two. You'll be staying in the office slash guest room."

"What? Where's the kids' room?"

Declan chuckled. "Riiight."

"You got a girl?"

"Not at the moment. Can I get you a beer?"

"Yes, sir," said Seamus, flopping into Declan's large brown sofa. "Damn. Is this real leather?"

"Yes. That was an estate sale item I decided to keep. The guy was a furniture importer."

"Nice."

He popped a beer and brought it to his uncle. Seamus took a long swig and then lazily surveyed the room. He glanced out the slider door and then craned his neck to gain a better view of the backyard.

"Is that a pool?" he asked.

"Just a little one. A lap pool. We don't get the ocean breezes you have in Miami."

"Any idea what a place like this would have cost me in Miami?"

"Charity is a long way from Miami... and this is hardly a mansion."

"It's nice though," said Seamus, taking another long draught of his beer. "You have it made here. That place we went is *full* of ladies on the prowl."

Declan scowled, confused. "Are you talking about Pineapple Port?"

"Yeah. Pineapple Port. Wall-to-wall ladies. I bet most of their husbands are dead, too."

Declan froze, the bottle inches from his lips. He lowered the beer to his lap.

"Like the older ladies, do you?"

"Oh yeah," said Seamus, dragging out the word 'yeah' until it sounded as if he was talking about the juiciest burger he'd ever eaten. He leaned forward to rest his forearms on his knees.

"Young guys have it all wrong," he said, in a conspiratorial whisper. "They're all hot for the pretty young things, but those girls won't do anything but break your heart. The real love is with the older ladies."

"Really..."

Seamus took a swig of his beer and then nodded, staring into middle distance.

"Oh yeah. It's all about the older ladies."

"How old are you again?"

"Fifty-five."

"And these ladies... just how old are we talking?"

He shrugged. "The girl who taught me everything I know was seventy-two," he said. "But I think the sweet spot is mid to late sixties."

Declan nodded in slow motion. This was a side of his uncle he'd never seen. Talking about Seamus' love life was uncomfortable enough, but this chat had taken a hard right into Weird Town.

"Right. So how many older girlfriends have you had?"

"Four," Seamus counted on one hand and then waggled his pinky. "Four and a half."

Declan laughed. "How do you have half a girlfriend? Was she super short?"

"She died. We'd only been dating two months, but she was something special."

"Oh."

He squinted at his uncle, waiting for him to laugh and tell him he was kidding. Instead, Seamus stared at the floor, silent, and then stood to fetch another beer.

"She might have been the one," he said as he opened the refrigerator. "But fate is a cruel mistress. Cancer, cancer, emphysema, heart attack, and unexplained."

"What's that?"

"That's how I lost my last five loves. Cancer, cancer, emphysema, heart attack, and unexplained. It's the only downside to dating older ladies. I keep outliving them."

"Who was unexplained?"

"Violet. Probably a heart thing. I think she was still pining for her ex-husband. She never seemed totally with *me*, y'know? Especially in bed."

"Oh wow. You've got to warn me before you say things like that."

Seamus took a sip of his new beer and sighed. "I thought I could make her forget him. The bastard ran away with his home care nurse, but he never left Violet's heart."

Declan laughed beer into his nose and covered his face with his hand to keep it from pouring into his lap.

"Come on, Seamus," he sputtered between coughs. "You're pulling my leg."

Seamus walked over and sat back on the sofa.

"You think it's funny, but these older ladies are real, y'know? I know you don't get it. You've got the hots for the young one."

"What young one?"

"You know, *the* young one. The only chick in a room full of hens. I could see you have it for her from a mile away."

"Charlotte? I just met her. I don't know what you're talking about."

"Oh, you've got it bad. Don't deny it. I might like them older, but even I could appreciate the stems on that flower."

"Are you suddenly channeling Humphrey Bogart or something? I feel like I just walked into a film noir."

"A film war?"

"Film *noir*. You know, an old forties drama where people said things like 'hey, check out the stems on that gal.'"

"What? She had long legs. You had to have noticed them."

"She does have ni—*long* legs, it was just the way you said it. I get what you meant."

"I bet you do," said Seamus, winking.

"Whatever. Anyway, you're wrong about Charlotte. Her whole neighborhood thinks I'm gay, anyway."

"I don't doubt it. You're just so damn pretty."

"Very funny."

Seamus threw a pillow at him, his booming laugh echoing from the cathedral ceiling.

Declan snatched the pillow from the air just as his phone

rang. He winged it back at his uncle and stood to retrieve his phone.

"Speak of the devil. It's Charlotte," he said, looking at the caller ID.

"Ooooh," said Seamus, following with a string of kissing noises.

Declan waved at him to be quiet.

"Hello?"

He repeated his greeting until Charlotte began to talk. It seemed they had a bad connection.

"Are you at home?' she asked.

"I'm home."

"I'm home," said Seamus in a breathy voice. "I'm naked and waiting for you."

"Just a second," he said, covering the phone. "Cut it out. Charlotte has information about mom."

"Yeah? What?"

"I don't know yet. Shut up for a second and maybe I can find out."

He uncovered the phone. "Sorry. My uncle is here and he was being... uh... loud. What is it?"

He begged Charlotte to reveal her information, but she insisted on delivering the news in person. It worried him. People never traveled to deliver good news.

"I'm in Charity. You know the Hibiscus Community? I'm 398 Sandtrap Drive."

"Guess they were running out of *nice* golfing street names," said Charlotte.

"Well, at least I'm not on Dog Leg Lane."

"Or Ball Washer Way. I'll be there in a few minutes."

Declan hung up and found his uncle staring at him.

"What?"

"Oh, you are so done. Look at that smile."

"What?" he repeated, frowning. "She made a golf joke. I can't smile?"

"Is she coming over here? Tell you what, you guys chat and I'll just sit here and scream *get in the hole!* every once in a while. I can be punny, too."

"You're disgusting. She's a nice girl."

"And pretty."

"And pretty."

"And smart."

"And smart."

"And nice rack."

"Alright already. You're an idiot. Whatever you do, don't tell Charlotte she has ga-ga gams or something when she gets here, copper."

Seamus laughed. "She does," he said, putting his empty bottle on the counter and opening the refrigerator to retrieve another.

Declan threw him a dirty look, snatched the empty bottle, and put it in the trash.

CHAPTER THIRTEEN

Ten minutes later the doorbell rang and Declan answered to find Charlotte on his stoop. She wore a simple summer dress that framed her elegant collarbones and, he had to admit, the aforementioned nice rack. Declan's eyes darted back to her face, worried that his eyes would telegraph his thoughts directly into her brain. His more off-color thoughts were echoes of Seamus' comments, but there was no way to explain that to her through telepathy.

"Hi," she said, holding up a bottle. "I brought wine."

"Oh. Well, thank you."

Charlotte's face twitched.

"Was bringing wine weird? It felt strange to dump all this information on you and leave. I thought the wine would be a nice way to pretend it was just a normal visit. Plus, I've never been to your house before so it's like a housewarming gift, right?"

"Sure, no, I appreciate it. It's a nice change from my uncle, who brought nothing but two weeks of dirty laundry and plans to drink every beer in the house. What's weird is that I haven't asked you in yet. Come in."

Charlotte entered and he took the wine from her. He moved to the kitchen to uncork it.

"Hi Seamus," said Charlotte, wandering into the living room. She offered a wave at hip level.

"Hello, lass." He stood from his place on the sofa and strode over to her, opening his arms and wrapping her in a bear hug.

Seamus looked at Declan as he hugged her and waggled his eyebrows. Declan gritted his teeth and waved at him to leave her alone.

"She's too young for you. Let her go."

Seamus flashed one last grin and then stepped back.

"So I hear you have some information for us?"

Charlotte's hands fluttered to smooth her dress, knocked akimbo by Seamus' energetic embrace.

"Yes, I do."

"Here you go," said Declan, handing her a glass of wine. "Sorry about that. Have a seat."

Seamus flopped down on the sofa and patted the cushion next to him.

Charlotte looked at the spot and paused.

"Sit right there," said Declan, motioning for her to sit in a matching standalone chair. "Ignore him. He's just goofing with you. You aren't even his type."

"Oh," said Charlotte, sitting.

She balanced the wine on her thigh and offered a tight smile.

Declan saw her frozen features and realized what he'd said.

"I mean, not that you're not gorgeous or anything. I just meant he likes old ladies. I mean *older* ladies."

Seamus nodded. "Nice recovery, slick."

Charlotte laughed and Declan thought he saw her shoulders relax.

"I wasn't offended. Anyway, yes, I have news for you both."

Declan held out a glass of wine for Seamus and he raised his upper lip in disgust.

"I'll take a beer," he said, handing him his latest empty.

Declan grimaced and set the glass of wine in front of his seat. He walked briskly to the kitchen, opened a beer, and returned to thrust it at his uncle.

"When exactly are you moving out?" he muttered.

Seamus took the beer and smiled.

"Okay," said Declan, sitting and facing Charlotte. "Ready now. What's up?"

"Two things. Al Taliaferro stopped at my house after the meeting."

"He was the squirrelly little guy at the meeting, right?" asked Seamus. "The guy who kept asking if Erin was shot?"

"Yes, exactly. How did you know?"

Seamus shrugged. "It's a cop thing."

"Well, your instincts were right. Now I know why that detail was so important to him. About the time your mother went missing, he saw a woman in a white shirt and red belt stumbling down the road. He swerved to avoid her and doesn't think he hit her."

"Doesn't *think*? Did he go back?" asked Declan, horrified. "Was it her?"

"No. I mean, he didn't go back, so he doesn't know if it was her. He'd been drinking and thinks he might have imagined the whole thing, but felt obligated to report the incident because it happened in front of my lot."

"Wow," said Declan, putting his hand over his mouth while he absorbed the story.

"It doesn't work," said Seamus. "You found her in a grave. She didn't get hit by a car and go spinning into an open grave."

"And we found a bullet. That doesn't mesh either," said Charlotte. "I wonder if maybe Al saw her running from someone, but he didn't see anyone else. He thinks he imagined the whole thing."

"He sounds like Towline to me," muttered Seamus.

Declan looked at him. "What?"

"Towline. He was one of our CIs."

"Confidential informant," said Charlotte, jumping in her seat. Her wine sloshed and she scrambled to keep it from spilling on her lap.

The two men stared at her and Declan thought he saw her blush. The corner of his mouth curled into a smile. It was cute how enthusiastic she seemed, though he had no idea what had inspired her outburst.

"Confidential informant," she said. "Sorry. I watch too many crime dramas. I got a little excited there."

Seamus shot Declan a sidelong glance and he realized his uncle had caught him grinning again. He cleared his throat to squelch his smile.

"Right. CI means confidential informant. Anyway, Towline lied like he breathed if it kept him out of trouble."

"Why did they call him Towline?" asked Declan.

"Well, Smiley, glad you asked."

He glowered at Seamus, who ignored him. He imagined it would take more than a glare to frighten his beefy uncle into behaving.

"The guys on the boat that he worked called him Towline because he was so full of bullshit he had to tow it behind him."

Charlotte laughed and looked at Declan.

"Is that *your* nickname?" she asked. "Smiley?"

Seamus opened his mouth to answer but Declan cut him off. "No."

Charlotte took a sip of her wine. "So, you think Al is lying about something?"

Seamus shrugged. "I've found people will sometimes tell little lies to make themselves feel better about the *big* lie they're hiding. The whole 'I imagined a girl on the road' story sounds fishy. Towline used to do that. Tell us about a crime, leaving out the parts that incriminated him."

"Do you think Al hit her and buried her? Or you think he knows more than he's saying?"

"Either, neither, both. Can't say."

Seamus rubbed the tip of his beer bottle with his thumb and stared at it, as if deep in thought. After a moment, his head snapped up and he looked at Charlotte.

"Wait; what did you say Al said this girl was wearing?"

"A white shirt and a red belt."

"That's right, but not the belt... Why would he notice a belt, in the dark, drunk?"

"What do you mean that's right?" asked Declan. "How would you know what she was wearing?"

Seamus took a drink from his beer, eyes staring at the floor.

"Seamus, how would you know what she was wearing?"

"Because I saw her that night."

"What? You never said that before."

Seamus stared at his bottle, silent. Declan put down his wine glass to keep from throwing it at his uncle. He took a deep breath, composed himself, and refocused.

"Tell me now," he said, his voice steady and flat. "All of it."

Seamus sighed.

"After my brother ran off, your mother and I had a thing. She was pretty messed up and I felt bad for her. I guess I was trying to comfort her and things went too far. I fought it for almost a year, but... she meant something to me. She did."

"And you saw her the night she disappeared?"

"Things were getting serious. She'd been dating another guy and she told me she was breaking it off with him. We were going to make a go of it. I was going to adopt you, the whole thing."

Declan swallowed. Having Seamus in his life after his dad disappeared might have changed his life. At the same time, he was infuriated at the idea Seamus had taken advantage of his mother during a difficult period. Even more, so that he'd never mentioned it.

"Go on."

"Erin stopped by; it was pretty late, maybe nine or ten. She told me she was going to see this other guy and end things with him. She was wearing a white blouse and a skirt. A jeans skirt. No belt that I remember and I've got an eye for details like that."

"So, she left and that was the last you saw of her?"

"Yes. I should have gone with her. I..."

Seamus trailed off and looked away.

"You, *what*?" asked Declan.

"I loved her. What do you want me to say?"

"I want you to tell me what happened to her."

"I don't know." Seamus jabbed at the air with the hand that held his beer. "She left and I never saw her again. I didn't know the other guy. I didn't know anything that would help the police. I got scared my brother's criminal history would keep everyone, especially the police, from believing me. You have to understand—the Bingham name was mud around here after all the shit your dad pulled trying to feed his drug habit. I did what I could and then I moved to Miami to be away from it all."

"You never told the police she was seeing someone?" asked Charlotte.

"I told the police she'd been dating someone, I just never told them that she and I were involved. I didn't want them pegging me for the jealous boyfriend. I didn't want them wasting time investigating *me*. She hid the other guy's identity from me, afraid I'd be jealous, I guess. I had nothing. After she disappeared I asked around. No one knew she was dating someone, me, *or* the other guy. Erin wasn't a big talker."

Declan rubbed his face with both hands and swept back his hair. He wanted to scream. The answer to all his questions seemed so close, yet this new chance had already come and gone over a decade earlier.

"Could she have been seeing Al?" he asked Charlotte. "What else did Al say?"

"Nothing, really, and I doubt they were dating. You know how you said you got your height from your mother's side? I don't know how tall she was, but Al is barely over five feet."

"Erin was tall. Five-nine, five-ten. Your height," said Seamus.

"He's also wildly devoted to his wife," added Charlotte. "I once heard him refer to them as two chunks of ricotta in the same cannoli."

Declan's lip twitched. "Ew."

"Yeah. Even two meatballs on the same spaghetti seem more romantic. He was a plumber, not a poet."

"Or two pepperoni on the same pizza."

"Two spoons in the same gelato."

"You two have issues," muttered Seamus.

Charlotte glanced at Declan and then looked away.

"Anyway, my point is, Al and your mother would be an odd couple. It isn't impossible, but when Al told me the story I didn't get the impression he knew your mother. He was connecting his shaky memory with the disappearance of a woman he didn't know."

"He should tell the police his story," said Seamus.

"I took Al right across the street to Sheriff Marshall and he told him everything he told me, so it's on the record now."

"That's good," said Declan. "That's something."

He looked at Seamus. His wordplay with Charlotte had been a welcome distraction, but frustration and anger began to ooze through his veins like slow, black blood.

Seamus met his gaze and then turned to Charlotte.

"You said you had two things?"

Charlotte nodded. "Frank let me know he got the autopsy report."

Declan's eyes grew wide. "What did it say?"

"Frank?" asked Seamus.

"Sheriff Marshall," said Charlotte. "He's like my unofficial uncle."

"Good thing he's an unofficial uncle," muttered Declan. "Less chance he slept with your mom."

Seamus' eyes flashed with anger.

"Let's not do the passive-aggressive thing, huh, boyo?" he barked, sitting forward. "You want to hit me, *hit me*. I told you I'm sorry. Sorry I didn't tell you about your mom and me, and sorry I couldn't protect her."

Declan stood. Seamus stood with him. The mix of rage and sorrow roiling in Declan's chest made it hard for him to focus as he stared at his uncle, unsure of what to do. He felt like a teenager again. He'd been an angry kid after the death of his mother. He'd gotten into fights and hung out with the wrong crowds. He'd spent the last seven years reinventing himself only to have his hard-earned poise dissipate as quickly as a Florida afternoon rainstorm. He was an angry teenager again. Staring at his uncle, he longed to focus his pain into one punch... *he longed for the release.*

"I'm sorry," said Seamus, his voice low and soft. "You have no idea how sorry I am."

Declan looked away, focusing on the steady ticking of his kitchen wall clock.

Breathe.

After a moment, he released his fists and sat down. Seamus sat as well.

"I want to see the autopsy report," said Declan.

"Frank plans on sharing the full report with you tomorrow," said Charlotte. Her voice sounded timid. Declan realized his behavior must have taken her by surprise.

"I'm sorry," he said, holding a lifted palm toward her. "I'm sorry if I upset you. It's been a weird couple of days and I nearly took it out on the wrong person. I'm sorry to you, too, Seamus."

"No worries," said Seamus, patting Declan's knee. "I understand more than you know."

"Touching the knee is pushing it."

Seamus withdrew his hand. "Sorry."

"I can't imagine what you're going through," said Charlotte. "For what it is worth, you'll know everything in the report tomorrow."

"It doesn't matter. I didn't need a report to tell me she was dead. I knew it."

He stared at the floor for a moment and then looked up at her.

"Sorry. Go on. Anything else?"

"They found a chip in her rib that could have been caused by the bullet."

"So that rules out Al, too," said Seamus.

"Probably. But there was one odd thing. They said there was a bunch of scratching around the chip."

Seamus scowled. "What does that mean? What kind of scratching?"

"Frank didn't know. He said there was a sizeable chip missing and scratching that didn't look like it was related to the bullet striking the rib."

"Something that happened over the years?" asked Declan. "What about that dog?"

"Katie mouthed her jaw and skull, but they didn't uncover the rest of the body until long after she was locked up next door."

"I wish they'd offered some ideas about what caused it. I

can't help but think that's an important detail."

"They didn't know and Frank didn't speculate."

Declan sighed.

"So, do you want me out?" asked Seamus. "I understand if you do. I can get a room somewhere until I find a place."

"No," said Declan, deflated, his anger gone. "It's a lot to take in. Maybe you and Mom would have been great together. I don't know. I was a kid. This whole situation is just bringing old frustrations to the surface. I'm sure you did what you could."

"I did. It's what drove me to work with the police in Miami. I never stopped asking questions, but I never found anything that led me to your mother. Part of me thought maybe she just…"

As Seamus trailed off Declan saw his uncle's eyes shining wet with tears.

"You thought she might have left you?"

Seamus nodded and wiped his eyes on the back of his arm.

"Yeah. I thought maybe the other guy had talked her into running away with him."

Declan nodded. "Sometimes I thought she left without me, too."

Seamus sniffed. "Are we supposed to hug now?"

"We can skip it."

"I'm sorry I don't have more information for you," said Charlotte.

"Oh, I appreciate everything you've done, you've been great," said Declan. "Sorry about our behavior."

"Especially the sappy stuff," added Seamus.

"Maybe once you read the whole report you'll see something that rings a bell."

"Yep," said Seamus, standing and slapping his belly. "If there are two things I learned in this life, it's that they never make it easy for you."

"What's the second thing?" asked Charlotte.

"Never try to bathe a cat."

CHAPTER FOURTEEN

"Well," said Seamus, looking at his watch. "I have a date. Gotta go."

"You have a date?" asked Declan. "You've barely been here for twenty-four hours. How can you have a date?"

"It's with someone from your neck of the swamp," he said, looking at Charlotte.

"From Pineapple Port? It's got to be nearly nine. No one there is awake at this hour."

"Oh, you'd be surprised."

"Would it *kill* you to put that in the trash?" asked Declan looking at the bottle his uncle had left on the table.

"Who is it?' asked Charlotte. "You *have* to tell me who it is."

Seamus opened the front door, caressing it with his fingers.

"I don't kiss and tell," he said in a low, sexy tone. Seamus winked and closed the door behind him.

Charlotte looked at Declan.

"Did he just feel up your door?"

"That *was* unsettling."

She mulled Seamus' oddness a moment longer.

"Do you know who it is?"

"Who?"

"His date."

"No. He said he had a thing for older ladies, but that was about it."

"I bet it was Jackie. They were canoodling outside the

meeting. Damn. If I brought this gossip to Mariska and Darla they'd bake me muffins for a month."

Declan laughed. "I promise to tell you as soon as he tells me, but I demand twenty percent of the muffin haul."

"Ten."

"Fine."

"Yea, thank you."

Charlotte clapped her hands with glee but stopped when she detected Declan's smirk.

She nodded toward the front door. "Are you two close?"

"Seamus and me?" Declan's crooked the corner of his mouth, causing a dimple to flash to life. "Funny you should ask after how we acted tonight."

"It was a *little* tense there for a second. I was afraid I'd have to dive out of the way to avoid becoming collateral damage."

"We wouldn't have swung at each other." He swirled his wine and watched it kiss the lip of his glass. "Probably."

Charlotte pictured the men squaring off in her mind. Part of her found it thrilling. The way Declan's arms flexed as he clenched his fists, the little bulge along his jawline as he grit his teeth... *When had this primal urge to watch men fight developed?* The emotion in the room had erupted so suddenly. It was as if Declan had morphed from a smooth, cool vampire into a snarling werewolf at the first sign of trouble.

The muscle in Declan's biceps twitched as he swirled his wine.

Charlotte wanted to touch it.

She felt her face grow warm and she looked away, certain that he could read her mind and worried her thoughts were moving from PG-13 to R.

Am I under obligation to give him a parental warning?

Every time she saw Declan he seemed more attractive. Maybe she was just thrilled to find someone who wasn't thrown at her by one of the Pineapple matchmakers. While she'd often daydreamed about bumping into a handsome stranger at the food store, she'd never imagined she'd meet someone over a grave. Especially one in her back yard.

Declan moved to sit down and she snapped back to the issue at hand. Namely, Declan's *hands*. She was staring at them. They were so perfect; long and tipped with buffed, manicured nails that said, "Hi there, I take pride in my appearance." They combined nicely with his old khaki shorts, which added, *not that I'm vain or anything* to the conversation. What if he had swung that beautiful hand at Seamus? *He might have broken a knuckle.* What if they'd started grappling and he got all rumpled and sweaty. What if he'd had to take off his shirt...

"Are you counting something?" said Declan.

Charlotte realized she'd started ticking on her fingers how many months it had been since her last date. She'd hit seven by the time Declan interrupted.

"Uh..." Charlotte grabbed her glass from the table to keep her hands still.

"No," she said, the number nine screaming in her head.

Nine? Really?

"I —"

And how long since...

Declan's green-speckled eyes locked on her as he waited for an explanation. She liked the little divot above his lip. *What was that called?* She'd have to look it up. She liked the way that divot created the inverted arch in the center of his lip and the way the curve echoed the curve on either side of his mouth. Why hadn't she ever noticed that little divot on anyone's face before? *He wasn't the only one who had one, was he?*

She casually touched her finger to her upper lip to be sure she had that arch as well.

She did.

That's good.

It would be difficult to find a self-help group for people without lip arches.

"Sorry," she said. "My mind wandered."

"That happens a lot with you."

Charlotte took a sip of her wine to drown the strange googly feeling in her stomach and chest.

"About you and Seamus," she said, straining to return to

their conversation. "I meant, did you keep in touch?"

"On and off. Not long after Mom disappeared he offered to take me to Miami, but he couldn't afford a kid. I think he was counting on Mom's insurance to help, but the insurance company delayed it for years. No body."

"So your grandmother raised you."

"Yep."

"Sounds like we have that in common. Well, first my real grandmother and then grandmothers by proxy."

"That's right, you never explained to me how you ended up the youngest girl in Pineapple Port. But first, can I get you some more wine?"

Charlotte looked at her glass, surprised to find it empty.

"Sure. Thank you. I'm not keeping you up am I?"

Declan laughed. "It isn't even nine yet."

"Sometimes I forget not everyone goes to bed at sundown."

Declan filled her glass and splashed a bit in his own.

"Okay. Tell me your tale."

"Well, there isn't much to tell…" She stared at the freshened wine. She wanted to pick it up. *Is it too soon? How long should I let it sit before I can start drinking again without appearing desperate for it?* She wanted something to do with her hands…

Uh oh.

Declan was looking at her again with that expectant and oddly penetrating glance.

"Um… well, my father died when I was a baby. My mother died when I was eleven. Cancer. I ended up with my grandmother in Pineapple Port. Then she died not long after that."

"But who took care of you?"

"Pineapple Port. Mostly Mariska and Darla. Mariska was my grandmother's best friend."

"One of them adopted you?"

"Not officially. I think Frank handled the details and shuffled some paperwork. I'm not sure. They arranged it so I could continue living in my grandmother's house, but when I was younger I slept over at Mariska's quite a bit. It was like having a mom who lived next door."

"Huh. On your own that young. I bet a lot of kids dream about that."

"Probably. Too bad I was a pretty good kid. I didn't take advantage of the situation the way I should have. I decorated the house to my fourteen-year-old tastes, of course."

"Ah, right, I remember," said Declan, grinning.

"I know, I know... you said it looked like a dorm."

"It just lacked a certain... sophistication?"

Charlotte laughed.

"You're right. And to think you didn't even go down the hallway to experience it in all its glory. You should see my bedroom."

Did I just say that?

Charlotte grabbed her wine glass and took a sip. Her eyes darted around Declan's home, focusing anywhere but on him.

It was a nice house, with a high ceiling in the main living area and an open concept. It looked too new for it to be his childhood home.

"Did you live here with your grandmother?"

"No. She lived in Tampa. After she died I came back here and bought this place."

"Why would you come back to Charity? I mean, I know we have a nice new food store now, but... it isn't exactly a hotbed of culture and entertainment."

"Seamus' ex-business partner at the pawnshop died and I took over. Plus, it's cheaper here."

"That's true."

"And something was drawing me back anyway. Roots. Maybe nostalgia."

"Maybe you wanted to be here in case your mom ever returned."

Charlotte froze. She'd expressed her opinion before thinking it through; Declan hadn't asked her to psychoanalyze him, especially with the blow of his mother's confirmed death still so raw.

"I'm sorry. I didn't mean to—"

"No, it's okay," said Declan. "You're probably right."

He leaned forward to retrieve the television remote.

"You want to watch a movie or something?"

She heard the chatter of commercials blaring through the surround sound speakers as he adjusted the volume. She sighed. She'd upset him and now he needed distraction from her.

"There might be something on the movie channels," he said, flipping to the guide. "I can't do anything streaming right now. For some reason, my so-called smart TV doesn't have any sound when I try and use the smart features. Not through the surround sound, anyway."

"I should probably go," she said.

"Not a movie buff?"

"No, it isn't that... Wait; did you say you can't get sound when you use the smart TV features?"

"Yeah. It's new and I haven't figured it all out yet."

"Do you have an optical cable?"

Declan knit his brow. "I think so..."

She put down her glass and walked to the cabinet next to the television where the electronics sat. One side of the cabinet was open to allow Declan to use his remote, and the other closed. She opened the closed side and knelt in front of it.

"Do you mind if I look?"

"I guess not..."

Charlotte turned the cable box sideways and studied the back of it. She followed a cord with her fingers and saw that it led to the stereo system that ran the surround sound.

"See this?"

Declan knelt beside her and peered into the cabinet, their faces close. His otherwise subtle shaving scent filled the small cabinet area. She wished she'd remembered to wear perfume. She never remembered to do that.

"That's the optical cable, right?" he asked.

"Right. That's the problem."

"But it worked before."

Their lips were so close Charlotte could lick his nose. As soon as that thought popped into her mind, it became almost impossible *not* to lick his nose.

"It worked with the old TV, I mean," he added, his voice suddenly much softer.

Charlotte swallowed.

"Thing is," she said, also speaking softly in the tight space. "You've got it leading directly from the sound system to the cable box, so it isn't working with the television directly. The smart TV needs that."

"Really?"

Declan leaned farther in to see.

Both of them were on their hands and knees, side by side. His hip grazed hers and then bounced away. A second later, it returned, lightly pressing against her hip. There it remained.

The phrase *joined at the hip* ping-ponged through her mind. She'd never enjoyed that phrase so much.

"You need the cable to go from the sound system directly to the television. Watch."

Charlotte reached in to pluck the optical cable from the back of the cable box, but lost her balance and fell against Declan. He lifted a hand to steady her, his palm resting against her hipbone, his fingers brushing her waist.

"Easy there," he said.

"Sorry," she said, flashing a quick smile. She watched as a tiny bead of sweat appeared at Declan's hairline and began its travels down his brow.

"The equipment gives off a lot of heat," she said.

He leaned back and wiped his brow.

"Yes. I wonder if that's normal."

Charlotte pulled the optical cable toward the television connection.

"Good thing you have an extra-long cable. I think we're going to make it."

"Uh... good."

He cleared his throat.

Declan pulled the television away from the wall to grant her access to the ports on the opposite side. She strained to reach them while he stood beside her and held the stand to keep the television from toppling. She felt a warm breeze on her chest. The television sat on a mantle above a fireplace, and she stood on the low hearth to reach the back cable ports. This put her breasts at eye level with Declan as he steadied the television and she leaned toward him. She could feel his breath between her breasts.

Declan's eyes glanced up to catch her looking and he turned his face to the side.

"Almost there?" he asked.

Charlotte spotted the port.

"Almost."

She slipped the optical wire into its square hole and stepped down.

"There. Try it now."

Declan set the television back on the mantle and grabbed the remote. He loaded a movie streaming service and picked a random selection from his purchased queue. The sound of voices filled the room.

"You did it," he said. "Who knew you were such a nerd?"

Charlotte laughed. "Everyone, except you, apparently."

"Where did you learn to do that?"

"I just happened to set up a similar thing at my house. You managed to get me during the month that information was still in my head."

"I don't know about that. I think maybe you're just a genius."

"I wish."

"So do you want to watch something?"

Charlotte looked at the screen. Two people were kissing, grappling with each other, and about to fall into bed.

"Not this," he said, quickly hitting pause. "It's a murder mystery, not... uh..."

"Porn?"

"Right."

Declan had paused the film seconds before a man's tongue grazed a woman's breast, her nipple visible through the thin fabric of her chemise.

"Oh," she said, an involuntary noise that escaped her lips as she looked away. "I... uh..."

"I could make popcorn..."

He looked at the screen, spotted the paused scene, and quickly hit play.

Groans of pleasure filled the room, amplified by surround sound.

Every nerve in Charlotte's body hummed with energy.

The wine, she thought, glancing at the second empty glass sitting on the table. White wine always made her giddy. She looked at Declan and knew she couldn't be trusted with him. The countdown until she made a fool of herself began in *10... 9...*

"No, I should go," she said. "I'll come to hook up your washer and dryer tomorrow."

Declan laughed as he fumbled to turn off the television.

"I can't tell you how wonderful it is to have a tech geek living just a few blocks away."

Charlotte walked to the door and he jogged to beat her there. He opened the door.

"Thanks for coming over. Now I'll have some idea of what to expect when I read the autopsy tomorrow."

"No problem."

Declan held out his hand and Charlotte shook it. The exchange felt strangely formal.

"Okay... see ya," she said, walking out the door.

She was near her bike when Declan called her.

"Oh, and it's *lion*," he said.

"What's that?"

"The French word for *lion* is *lion*."

Charlotte grinned. "Thank you. Good to know."

She paused.

"What's the little divot above a person's upper lip called?"

Declan's brow knitted.

"What am I? Your own personal Google?"

She laughed and waved as she straddled her bike to head for home.

She replayed their interaction in her head as she pedaled

until she reached the part where she'd fixed his television. Her eyes grew wide at the memory.

Oh no. Please tell me I didn't say that.

She slapped a hand across her mouth.

"Good thing you have an extra-long cable?"

CHAPTER FIFTEEN

Seamus knocked on Jackie's door and she answered a moment later.

"Aren't you a vision in blue," he said, admiring her aquamarine tunic with matching turquoise jewelry.

"Why thank you. Ready?"

"First, a gift."

Seamus pulled his hands from behind his back to reveal what he had been hiding.

"Thank you. It's—it's a package of bacon?"

"You said you loved bacon. And flowers are so overdone."

Jackie turned the flat package of meat over to inspect the other side. "And maple, too, wonderful."

"It was between that and the pepper-edged. It was a tough call, but I made it."

"Well, you've chosen wisely. And, it's nice to know you listen. I'll put this in the fridge."

Seamus nodded. "Yeah, it occurred to me it wouldn't be such a great idea to give it to you in the car."

Jackie trotted to her kitchen and returned a moment later to walk with Seamus to his Toyota Highlander.

"So where is it you want me to take you?" he asked. "You made it sound like a big secret."

"Oh, it is. It is exactly a secret. A secret club. You even need to know the password to get in."

"Really? Gorgeous *and* mysterious. You're a keeper."

He chuckled as Jackie smiled and batted her eyelashes.

"You can only get the password if you're on their list or recommended by a member," she said.

"So you're officially recommending me? I'm honored."

"No, you're my *guest*. That's different. We'll see if I recommend you."

"Still not sure after I brought salty pork products? Oh boy. Tough nut. Guess I better be on my best behavior."

"Don't be too good," drawled Jackie.

Seamus winked. "Not a problem."

They pulled beside a large warehouse located fifteen minutes inland. There were twenty cars already there, and they took their place beside them in the huge lot.

A large, ponytailed man in his mid-thirties greeted them at the entrance. He had a dagger tattooed on the side of his neck. Seamus eyeballed him, calculating his chances against him in a tussle. He gave himself a fifty-fifty shot.

"Hey Miss Jackie," said Ponytail.

"O'Toole, Newman and Pickford."

The man opened the door and held it for them as they entered. "You know you don't have to—"

Jackie nodded and walked inside, holding aloft a hand to quiet the bouncer as she moved.

"He seems very familiar with you," said Seamus, giving the giant one last glance.

Jackie shrugged. "I like it here. I come a lot."

"And what kind of password was that? I'll never be able to come here if I have to remember all that nonsense."

"It's easy to remember," said Jackie above the rising music as they passed through a narrow hallway with tin walls. "O'Toole, Newman and Pickford... Peter, Paul, and Mary."

Seamus stepped into the main room and his jaw fell slack. A sea of smartly dressed retirees filled the giant warehouse space. A DJ stood on a large stage spinning tunes. Though the current song was from before his time, he recognized it as *Yakity Yak* by the Coasters.

"It's an old people dance club."

"Fifties, sixties, and a smattering of seventies music. It cycles so when the seventy-year-olds get tired, the sixties music starts, and the sixty-year-olds dance until it is time for the fifty-year-olds to step in."

"So no one has a heart attack."

"Most of the time. Want a drink? It's a little easier to talk by the bar."

They meandered to a large and well-stocked bar located against the east wall.

"I'll take a tequila sunrise, Joe," said Jackie to the young man pouring.

"Whiskey for me," said Seamus.

"Ice?"

He raised an eyebrow. Joe nodded and poured it straight.

"What do I owe you?" asked Seamus.

Joe's eyes darted toward Jackie and he shook his head. "On the house."

Seamus looked at Jackie.

"You own this place, don't you?"

"What? What makes you say that?"

"The way everyone treats you. Defers to you. It's pretty obvious."

"Well... not a lot of people know, so keep it to yourself."

"You have partners?"

"Just me."

"What about your neighbors in Pineapple Port? Do they know?"

Jackie shook her head. "They think I'm just another happy patron."

"You *are* a woman of mystery," said Seamus, finishing his glass and motioning for another.

"You still won't be able to get in here without me until someone recommends you and you're approved," said Jackie, a saucy smile creeping to her lips. "And after tonight you'll have to start paying for the whiskey."

"Then make it a double," Seamus called over his shoulder.

Jackie laughed.

"I think I'll be able to get in," said Seamus. "I have friends in management."

Jackie stared at him, a smile lingering. Seamus had seen that look before.

Oh, she's done. She's in love with me.

He leaned in and kissed her. He wanted to think about how lovely she looked, but he couldn't stop thinking about the fact that she owned the club. As their lips separated, his gaze wandered to the huge, industrial-style bar and the endless racks of booze.

Best. Girlfriend. Ever.

"So you were a cop, right?" asked Jackie.

"Afraid I'll bust you for your underground club?"

"It's not as illegal as people might think. Making people *think* it's illegal is part of my marketing plan. It makes it more exciting for everyone."

"Ha! One last caper, huh? Like getting to sneak out on their parents again."

"Something like that. There is a poker room in the back. That isn't entirely legal."

Jackie pointed to a door and he looked at it.

"Reeeally..."

"Tonight isn't poker night; don't get any ideas."

"When is it?"

"I'll tell you if and when the time is right."

Seamus grinned. "Tough broad."

He was about to lean in to steal another kiss when his attention drew to the far corner of the dance floor. In a large booth, six people were making out like overheated teenagers. Every one of them had to be in their late sixties, if not older. There were bald heads, cheap shoes, and bright plastic jewelry flashing everywhere. One couple tumbled out of their seat on the floor and began giggling.

"That group needs to get a room," he said.

Jackie groaned. "It's the X."

"X? Ecstasy?"

Jackie nodded. "They love it. There are strict rules about selling or consuming drugs on the premises, but they take it before they come, and then..." she raised the corner of her upper lip and threw a finger in the direction of a man and woman clutching each other in a desperate attempt to meld bodies together. "...*that.*"

"Where do they get it?"

"I don't know. I haven't decided what to do about it yet. Once they're here they aren't technically doing anything wrong, but I get tired of turning the firehose on them to get them to leave at the end of the night. Plus, sometimes they start feeling up people not involved in their little—"

Jackie cut short.

"Al!" she called across the room. "Al!"

A short man standing near the X group turned his head toward Jackie. He pointed to his chest and Jackie nodded, pointing to her feet. Al shuffled over.

Can't Help Falling in Love by Elvis swelled. Some of the fast dancers downshifted, some left the floor, and a new crowd of slow-dancing couples moved in to take their place. Blue spotlights swirled slowly around the dance floor.

"Al, what are you doing over there?" Jackie asked as he drew near.

"What?"

"*You know what.* Why are you skulking about with that crowd?"

"Aw... I wanted to try it. Don't you want to try it?"

"No, I do not. Do you know where they buy it?"

"No. Thing is I *had* two. A friend of mine had a couple and gave them to me."

"Who?"

Al scowled.

"I'm no snitch."

She rolled her eyes.

"Anyway, I was going to take them before I came today, but I lost them. The worst part is I think I left them on Charlotte's counter."

Seamus' ears perked at the sound of Charlotte's name.

"Charlotte, the young one?"

Al looked at him. "Yeah, Charlotte Morgan."

"You and Charlotte were going to do X together? Is she the friend who gave them to you?"

"What? No. I emptied my pockets on her counter when I got all scared—"

Al stopped and looked at Seamus.

"Anyway," he said. "She has nothing to do with it. I'm just too embarrassed to ask her if I left them there."

"Well, stay away from those people," said Jackie. "That stuff could be dangerous and I'm sure Tina doesn't want you rubbing all over her. She comes here to dance. Go dance with your wife."

"Yeah yeah," said Al, turning.

"Drive safe," called Seamus.

Al turned and looked at him, his eyebrows tilted with concern. Seamus waved and Al offered a curt nod before heading back to his wife.

Seamus chuckled. "This place is crazy. How did you come up with the idea?"

Jackie sighed.

"My husband was a slum lord. We made a lot of money on the suffering of others. When he died... I wanted to give back. I spent most of our money fixing up the places he'd let run down for years, building neighborhood parks, and doing what I could. When I started to run out of money, I spent the last of it on this building and started the club. Everyone who works here grew up in my husband's substandard housing. I give them jobs and help any way I can."

Seamus looked over at Joe. Though not as large as the doorman, he had tattoo sleeves on both arms and looked as though he had been around the block, as did the DJ.

"Wow. That's something, Jackie. You must be so proud."

She shrugged.

Seamus looked at his feet. "You've been so honest with me... I feel like I should be honest with you."

"I would hope so."

He took a deep breath. "I wasn't a cop in Miami."

"You weren't? What were you?"

Seamus smiled. "If I told you, I'd have to kill you."

Jackie put her hand against his cheek, drawing him in for a kiss.

"I'm harder to kill than you think," she whispered.

"I bet," he said. "That's okay. I like a challenge."

He grabbed her hand and led her to the dance floor.

CHAPTER SIXTEEN

"I hope you don't mind," said Mariska as she and Charlotte walked to her car. "I told Dottie I would give her a ride to her daughter's on the way."

It wasn't unusual for Pineapple Portians to request rides from Mariska on nail day. Her trips to the salon were predictable and a staple of her relationship with Charlotte. Mariska had her nails intricately painted once a month, and in the time it took to finish, Charlotte had her eyebrows waxed and her nails done more simply, usually just a buff.

"No problem," said Charlotte. "I'd rather take Dottie than have her try and drive herself. Then we'd all be in trouble."

Dottie was eighty-five. She'd had her license taken away years ago, but that didn't stop her from making an occasional trip to the store. The last time she'd returned dragging a political poster under her car, the potential senator's frozen grin slowly wearing away beneath her undercarriage.

Mariska opened her sunroof and they rolled the few blocks to Dottie's house, careful to avoid the Sandhill cranes congregating in the road. Dottie's neighbor fed the redheaded cranes, defying the neighborhood ordinance against it. He threw them bread and hot dogs under the cover of predawn darkness, but the birds stayed at his house until nearly noon, defeating the whole purpose of his skullduggery. When he left town to visit his children, the angry Sandhills pecked away half his siding and all the screening of his neighbor's porch, searching for their regular meal. His illegal bird soup kitchen had to be the worst-kept secret in town.

The door to Dottie's home flew open before Mariska had a chance to put her car in park. The short, white-haired woman puttered out, encaged by a walker with tennis balls plugged to both front feet. She turned slower than a clock's second hand, grabbed the handle of her front door, and slammed it shut as if it had just insulted her. The shockwave unhinged the plastic numeral two in her mounted home address and it swiveled upside down, rocking back and forth like a pendulum.

After her ferocious burst of energy, Dottie locked the door and shuffled to Mariska's car with all the speed of a buffering video. Charlotte hopped out and offered help, but the woman waved her away with an angry grunt. Dottie collapsed into the front seat of Mariska's VW Jetta and then slammed its door into her walker, repeatedly, until it gave up and toppled out of the way.

Mariska covered her ears as Dottie yanked the passenger door shut with a thunderous clap. Charlotte, who knew better than to sit in the car when Dottie closed her door, collapsed the walker and put it in Mariska's trunk.

Dottie had the legs of an eighty-five-year-old woman and the arms of a steelworker with a secret passion for mixed martial arts. She sat her purse on her lap. Without a word or nod to Mariska, she looked forward and twiddled her thumbs, ready to go.

Charlotte slid into the backseat.

"It's on Citrus, right Dottie?" asked Mariska as she pulled away from the curb.

"What's that?"

"Your daughter; she lives on Citrus, right?"

"No. She lives on Citrus."

"Right, okay, dear."

They pulled onto the highway and Dottie's head began to bob as if she was listening to heavy metal music. Charlotte shimmied to sit behind Mariska to gain a better view of Dottie's face, curious as to what expression might accompany her rhythmic head-banging. The new angle revealed that Dottie wasn't bobbing her head; her wig was flipping back and forth on her scalp. The breeze caused by the open sunroof made it look as though her white curls cordially tipped hello to every passerby, except that Dottie had never been that friendly in her life.

Charlotte covered her mouth, trying not to laugh. She caught Mariska's eye in her rearview mirror and pointed to her head and then Dottie. Mariska glanced over and saw the wig flapping in the breeze.

"Oh."

Mariska tried to stifle a laugh, but only delayed it long enough to build pressure for a lip explosion.

"Dottie, your wig..."

Dottie didn't register the comment and Mariska started laughing too hard to try again. A strong gust flipped the wig back until it stood straight above Dottie's head like an open teapot, supported by the headrest that towered over the tiny woman. Her wispy white hair danced in the breeze like cilia beneath her raised cap of curls. She didn't notice. As the curls flung back, Charlotte squealed with giggles and clamped a second hand over her mouth. A tear of laughter rolled down Mariska's cheek.

Dottie's daughter lived nearby, and Mariska pulled in front of her home a minute later. As Mariska braked, Dottie's hair flopped back onto her head, settling in place as if it had never moved. She shot a look at Charlotte and touched her hand to her head.

"Did you touch my head?" she barked.

"No. Absolutely not."

Charlotte hopped out of the car, wiping tears of laughter from her eyes. She retrieved the walker and set it up, nearly losing a hip to the car door as Dottie flung it open and stepped out onto the curb. She tried to help Dottie to her walker, but the woman ripped her arm from her grasp.

"I can walk," she said.

"Sorry."

Charlotte weaved around Dottie and sat back in the

passenger seat. She refused to look at Mariska until they were moving. Ten feet down the road, the two women looked at each other and cackled once more.

"Oh, by the way," said Charlotte as they laughed together. "I decided I hate loofah mitts."

Mariska's laughing slowed.

"Hate them?"

"Hate them."

"Okay."

"And those rainbow-colored crinoline balls."

"But they're so pretty."

"Horrible. Impossible to use. They look like My Pretty Pony poops."

Mariska huffed.

"Fine," she said after a moment. "But your baths must be awfully boring."

Only one other woman sat in Another Nail salon. The owners were Vietnamese and most people assumed they'd misunderstood the English idiom *Another nail in the coffin*, but with the salon located in the middle of retirement country, Charlotte felt confident they hadn't misunderstood anything.

The woman enjoying her nail buff was Susan Strazza, a familiar Pineapple Port resident. Mariska and Charlotte waved and said hello before taking their places in their favorite pedicure chairs. Charlotte knew she spent too much of her meager income on pedicures, but she liked them and she lived in Florida. She imagined the money that people in Maine saved on pedicures they turned around and spent on socks.

As warm water filled the foot bowl, Charlotte ran through the various settings of her massage chair. She liked the shiatsu setting that poked her hard beneath the shoulder blades, but it took some skill to force the mechanical thumb to stick in just the right position.

"So anything new?" asked Mariska.

"A lot. I went to see Declan last night."

"Did you?"

"I was there when that Declan fellow was picking through poor dead Laurie's things," said Susan without turning. "He said her miniature tea set was *darling*. Straight men don't say *darling* so I wouldn't get your hopes up."

"I'm sure he was surrounded by old ladies and trying to be polite," said Mariska.

Susan scoffed.

"And that has nothing to do with anything anyway," said Charlotte. "I went to talk to him, not to marry him."

Susan chose not to respond.

"Did he kiss you?" asked Mariska in her version of a conspiratorial whisper. Mariska's whisper voice was so loud that the nail tech's family back in Vietnam could probably hear her.

"No. We... we might have had a moment though."

"Oh," said Mariska, her face blooming with surprised delight as if someone had goosed her.

"But, *again*, that isn't why I went there. Al Taliaferro came to my house after the meeting yesterday. He told me—"

Charlotte spotted Susan tilting toward her like a tree in a strong breeze. She leaned closer to Mariska to whisper.

"He told me he thought he nearly hit a girl on the side of the road with his car about the time that Erin went missing."

"What?"

Susan's head swiveled. "What?"

"I said Al told me his secret pizzelle recipe."

"Oh," said Susan. "I already have that."

Mariska lightly slapped Charlotte's arm to regain her attention.

"Did he—?"

"I don't think he did," she said, cutting Mariska's incompetent whispering short.

"Oh good. That would be terrible."

"I'll give you more details later, but I don't think the two things are related. I had him tell his story to Frank just in case. He wanted to."

"Oh double good. Frank should know."

"Frank doesn't even eat pizzelles," said Susan, craning her neck to look at them. "I tried to give him one once and he turned it down."

"That's funny," said Charlotte. "He ate a whole plate of mine and then asked for more."

Susan caught eyes with Charlotte in the mirrored wall behind her nail tech, scowled, and looked away.

"You're terrible," said Mariska. "So, you told Declan about Al?"

"Yes. That, and—"

Charlotte trailed off and glanced at Susan. She covered her mouth and leaned toward Mariska.

"Frank got the autopsy back, and it *is* Declan's mom."

"Oh, that's a shame."

"You want eyebrow today?" asked the girl working on Charlotte's toes.

"Yes, thank you."

"You want mustache?" the girl asked, rubbing her finger under her nose.

Charlotte groaned. Every time she came to the salon one of the girls scolded her for the gunslinger's mustache they insisted she had. Charlotte didn't see any mustache, but they managed to shame her into agreeing to have the invisible hairs removed fifty percent of the time.

"Sure."

Susan's phone rang and the nail tech held it to her ear to avoid ruining her manicure.

"Hello?' said Susan, much too loudly. The nail tech winced and leaned away from her.

"What? Oh. I'll be right there."

She nodded to the tech to hang up the phone and pulled her nails out of the tiny nail driers. The tech dropped the phone into her handbag on the floor.

"Is everything okay, Susan?" asked Mariska.

With her foot, Susan pushed her purse toward the woman at the checkout counter and pointed at it with a bright pink nail. Familiar with the drill, the cashier picked up the purse, retrieved

Susan's wallet, and extracted the appropriate amount of cash.

"There are police cars all around George and Penny's house."

"What?" said Charlotte. "Are they okay?"

Susan shrugged. "I said *police*, not *ambulance*."

Mariska's phone rang and she scrambled to pull it from her pocketbook.

"Hello?"

Mariska put her hand over the phone. "It's Darla."

"Susan just went running out of here," said Mariska, watching Susan do just that. "Something about police cars at George and Penny's? Are they okay? Is there an ambulance?"

There was a pause before Mariska added, "We'll be there as soon as we're done. Call me if you hear anything else."

"What is it?"

"Oh, you'll never believe it."

"What?"

"They think George killed Declan's mother."

CHAPTER SEVENTEEN

By the time Charlotte and Mariska took their beautiful toes back to Pineapple Port, a crowd had gathered around George and Penny Sambrooke's home. Mariska pulled over and parked not far from the scene and the two of them walked straight to Darla, who stood with the others behind the crime tape at the edge of George's beloved lawn.

"Crime tape in Pineapple Port twice in one week," said Mariska, ending her thought with a series of disapproving tongue-clucking noises.

"What's going on?" asked Charlotte.

Darla turned, revealing her t-shirt, blue, with the words, *I'm not old, I'm vintage* stamped across the chest. Charlotte had given it to her for Christmas the year before, and she smiled to see her wearing it.

"Oh, girls, I'm so glad you're here."

"Did Frank tell you what's going on?"

"He got a phone call this morning," she said, walking away from the crowd and motioning them to follow.

Charlotte glanced at the crowd and saw several sets of eyes follow their progress. They strolled until they were out of earshot.

"Go on," said Mariska. "We're far enough away."

"Have you *heard* you whisper? No? You know who has? *Everyone.*"

"Oh, just talk," said Mariska, scowling.

"Fine."

Darla stopped and crouched toward the other two, speaking low.

"So, Frank got a call; an anonymous call. Frank said it sounded like a man but the voice was funny like he was talking through one of those voice changer thingies, so he couldn't be sure. The man said George killed Erin Bingham and he could prove it."

"That's crazy," said Charlotte. "George has barely said four words since I met him and now he's a killer?"

"It's always the quiet ones," said Mariska, shaking her head.

"I think he just can't get a word in when Penny is around," said Darla.

"Did he say anything else?" asked Charlotte. "How could he prove it?"

"He said the proof was buried underneath the orange tree in George's backyard."

Mariska gasped and covered her mouth.

"He buried her under the orange tree."

Darla and Charlotte looked at her, brows furrowed.

"He buried her in my backyard. Remember?"

"Oh, right," said Mariska, her hand slowly dropping from her face. Her palm had barely passed her chin before it shot back up and she gasped again.

"He buried the *weapon* under the orange tree."

"Or his other victims," said Darla. "He could be a serial killer."

Mariska gasped again.

"You're going to hyperventilate," said Charlotte.

Mariska moved her hand to the side of her face and shook her head, seemingly dumbfounded by all the possibilities.

"How would this other person know George was the killer or about what's under his orange tree?" asked Charlotte. "Unless they killed her together..."

"Oh no," said Darla. "I didn't even think of that. Poor girl; killed by two people."

"I don't think the number of murderers makes you *more*

dead," said Charlotte.

"It just seems scarier."

"Where's Frank now?"

"Standing by the orange tree while the crime guys dig up the evidence."

"Can you call him and ask him what's going on?"

Darla twisted her lips into a tiny knot. "I'm not supposed to call him when he's working."

Charlotte considered this, trying to picture the layout of George's yard in her mind.

"Isn't there a hedge between George's yard and Jenny Teacup's?"

Jenny Teacup's last name was Teehan, but she collected antique tea sets. Someone called her Jenny Teacup once, and the nickname stuck. This supported Charlotte's supposition that retirement communities were a lot like high school. She'd attended both high school and Pineapple Port simultaneously, so she knew better than anyone.

Darla nodded slowly. "There's that gorgeous bougainvillea hedge between his house and Jenny's; George's pride and joy. Why?"

"We could stand behind the hedge and whisper to Frank."

Darla's and Mariska's eyes both flashed wide and white.

"Brilliant, girl," said Darla. "Let's go."

With furtive glances toward the crowd, the three women walked the long way around the block until they reached Jenny Teacup's home. They had seen Jenny in the crowd with the others, so they walked brazenly past her house and into her backyard. Standing as close to the orange tree as they could get, Darla peeked between the hedge branches until she spotted her husband.

"I have to get his attention," whispered Darla. "There are state cops nearby."

"Text him," said Charlotte.

"I guess one little text can't hurt, but I don't have my phone."

"I have my phone," said Mariska, pulling it from her pocketbook and handing it to Darla. Darla looked at it as if it were a Chinese puzzle box and then finally flipped it open.

"Sweetie, you need to upgrade this phone. You need to get yourself a smartphone."

"Phones aren't supposed to be smart."

"Will you two hens hush?" said Charlotte.

"Hush, hush, sweet Charlotte," mumbled Darla, putting the phone against her ear as Mariska giggled.

Charlotte rolled her eyes. She didn't dare say another word or Darla and Mariska would start cackling. It took very little for them to catch the giggles.

They heard Frank's phone ping on the opposite side of the hedge and he excused himself to look at the text. He read it, looked at the hedge, and then moved toward them.

"Frank," hissed Darla through the leaves.

"Darla, I'm in the middle of official business. I can't talk to you right now."

"I need you to tell us what's going on."

"I don't know yet. They've been digging a while, but they haven't found anything. I can't be here talking to you."

"You tell me everything you know or I'll reach through this damn bush and pat your bald head."

She reached through the bush and touched Frank's face.

"Darla. For the love of…"

"We'll be here; you just tell us what you see as you see it."

"Got something," said another voice.

"Who is *us*?" asked Frank, peeking through the leaves.

"Mariska and Char—"

"Never mind. I know who," he said. "Am I supposed to sit here and look like a crazy person talking to myself?"

"You don't have to talk all the time. Just the important stuff. Cover your mouth with your hand. Come on, you're a sheriff."

Charlotte heard Frank sigh. The four of them stood in silence for several minutes.

"This is so exciting," said Mariska in her stage whisper.

Charlotte put her finger against her lip to shush her.

Mariska pulled an imaginary zipper across her lips.

"It looks like a box," whispered Frank from the opposite side of the hedge.

"A box?" said Darla. "Like a treasure chest or like a cardboard box?"

"Like a shoebox, but metal."

"They gonna open it?"

"I don't know… I guess they are… hold on, they're looking at it."

They all held as still as possible.

"They opened it. It wasn't locked. It's full of papers."

"Papers? Not a gun?"

"Or a knife?" said Mariska, poking Darla in the ribs.

"Or a knife?" echoed Darla into the hedge.

"No, it's all papers. He's trying to open one to read it. He's got those gloves on so it's hard."

"Oh, I would imagine that's hard," said Mariska. "I can't grab anything small when I wear my dishwashing gloves."

"Whatcha got there, Billy?" asked Frank in a much louder tone. The three women jumped at the sound of his voice and Darla fell sideways and then into the bush. Mariska and Charlotte rushed to extract her before her thrashing made too much noise.

"Looks like love letters," said another man. "Between George and Erin."

Mariska and Darla gasped, even as Darla tried to remove a flower plastered to her cheek.

"You're going to inhale that flower and choke to death," said Charlotte.

"George was having an affair," said Darla.

"It looks like he killed Declan's mom and it's the *affair* that worries you?"

"Oh, that too," said Mariska. "Terrible."

Darla nodded in agreement.

"But I can't believe George cheated on Penny. He's always so quiet."

"It's always the quiet ones," said Mariska again.

"Erin must have been fifteen years younger than him, too."

"It's always the young ones," said Mariska.

"Frank!" whispered Darla as loudly as she could.

Frank walked back toward the hedge.

"Darla, not now."

"Get me copies."

"What?"

"Get me copies of the love letters."

"I can't do that."

"Tell them you want to review them for clues or something."

Frank grunted.

"I'll see what I can do. But I don't want to hear a peep out of you the next time I come home from the Bourbon Club a little snockered."

"Fine. You get a one-time pass."

"Fine," said Frank, walking away.

"What are you smiling about?" asked Mariska.

Charlotte looked up.

"What? Was I? Nothing. Just thinking I should probably tell Declan about this new development."

"Aaah…"

Mariska tried to wink, but it looked more like a small stroke. She was a terrible winker.

CHAPTER EIGHTEEN

Entering Charlotte's neighborhood, Declan spotted an elderly man on the side of the road gripping a radar gun. His black t-shirt, tan shorts, knee-high tube socks, and tennis shoes didn't appear to be standard-issue but he pointed the gun as if Declan was barreling down on him, intent to kill.

He slowed to two miles less than the speed limit of fifteen miles per hour. As he passed, the man lowered his gun and wagged a bony finger at him.

Declan rolled over two speed bumps and waved to six people walking their dogs before he reached Charlotte's house. Even the people behind the wheels of golf carts had dogs nestled on the seats beside them or, in one case, jogging alongside. Did Pineapple Port force residents to own dogs by neighborhood bylaw? Did a cat count? What about a beefy hamster with a junk food addiction?

Though all the modular homes in Pineapple Port were similar, Charlotte's was one of the few sans lawn art, standing unique in its blandness. Declan passed plastic flamingos, gazing balls, birdbaths, flags both American and football, smiling frogs, and fake alligators lurking on lawns. Charlotte displayed only a smattering of reedy plants and a colorful ceramic pot where he presumed a plant had once lived and died.

Declan parked and walked halfway up the driveway before Charlotte burst through the front door to meet him on the walkway.

"Hello," she said.

"Hi."

Charlotte looked lovely in another simple summer slip-on dress, this one red with hibiscus scattered across it. Her breast-length auburn hair hung loose and framed her face. Much like her sparsely garnished home, she wore little makeup, but her fine features and hazel eyes needed little decoration. As a bonus, her height forced her summer dress to stop at mid-thigh, whereas on a smaller girl the frock would have brushed the tops of her knees. Declan found himself staring at her shapely, tan legs and averted his gaze.

"So... does everyone in your neighborhood have a dog?" he asked. "I must have seen half a dozen driving in."

"Everyone except the cat ladies, but we dog-people don't talk to them much," she said, chuckling to show she was kidding. "A local puppy mill was shut down a few years ago and nearly everyone ended up adopting one."

"Ah. That makes sense."

As they fell silent, he found his gaze beginning to trace the line of her body again.

"You said you had something to tell me?" he asked, finding her eyes.

"I do."

"Should we go in?"

Charlotte glanced back at her home and squinted her right eye, plumping the apple of her cheek. She appeared in pain.

"I was thinking maybe we could grab some sushi at Katana Kuts?" she said. "Are you hungry?"

Declan looked at Charlotte's modular home and wondered if his comment about her decorating skills had him banned from the premises.

"Sure. I could eat."

"You do like sushi?"

"Yes."

"Great. We'll go Dutch. I'm not asking you to pay for me."

"Well, I expect you to pay for *me*. After all, you asked *me* out."

Charlotte's mouth opened.

"I'm not asking you out. I just thought... I mean, I'm fine with treating you since it was my idea but—"

"I'm kidding," he said, grinning as he watched her scramble. He glanced at the only vehicle in her driveway, a red golf cart. "I'll drive, hop in."

Declan opened his passenger-side door. Charlotte flashed him an odd look and stepped inside.

By the time he reached his seat, he knew he had to ask.

"What was that look for?"

"What look?"

"When I opened the door for you, you looked at me like I was nuts."

"Oh, I was just surprised you opened the door for me. It's unusual nowadays."

"Years of opening doors for my grandmother, I guess."

"It's nice," she mumbled.

"Speaking of unusual," he said, turning his head to pull out of the driveway. "There was a guy just inside the entrance to Pineapple Port with a speed gun, but he wasn't wearing a uniform. Any idea what that was about?"

Charlotte laughed. "Oh, you mean Tony. That wasn't a speed gun. Did you see the wire hanging from it?"

"Yes."

"It's a painted hairdryer. He pretends it's a speed gun to slow people down when they enter the neighborhood. It's his unofficial job."

Declan chuckled. "Well, it worked. I slowed down."

"Oh, he's very convincing. He freaked out one of my neighbors' tweaker grandson. The kid thought he was about to be pulled over and made his getaway. She didn't see him for two days."

Katana Kuts was empty but for one other couple. All the early birds had come and gone. Two half-filled cups of coffee sat on the sushi bar with an empty sugar packet dispenser between them. As they sat, a man stepped forward and grabbed the two mugs. He scowled at the empty sugar container and replaced it with a full one.

"They took the sugar again," he said, shaking his head.

"You have to start using poured sugar, in bowls," said Charlotte. "They can't slip those in their purses."

"I did put some in bowls," said the man, nodding toward a sugar bowl sitting a few feet down the bar. "Then they take all the Sweet n' Low."

"Most people worry about young punks coming into their businesses…" said Declan.

"Yeah, for me it's retirees. You said it. Sugar packets, creamers, soy sauce… even chopsticks. I have to ration everything."

Charlotte leaned toward Declan and whispered. "We have a lady in the neighborhood who paints chopsticks with lacquer and sells them at craft fairs as decorative hair sticks, so I could maybe solve that little mystery for him…"

"Seriously?"

She nodded. "I have a pair. Sometimes she even hot-glues little flowers to them. People with free time can be *very* enterprising."

"And sticky-fingered."

"Sticky fingers are never a problem. They steal the handi-wipe packets from barbeque places, too."

A tiny dark-haired waitress scampered from the back of the building to Declan's side as he looked over the menu. She stood close, her face nearly rested on his elbow. He could feel the hairs on his arm move when she breathed. He fought the urge to pet her.

"What can I get you?" she asked, peering up at him like Oliver Twist in search of a handout.

"Um…" Declan tried to speak, but the girl's face was so close it was as if she'd stolen all the available oxygen. In addition to feeling claustrophobic, he was terrified that the moment he opened his mouth she'd smell everything he'd eaten the previous week.

She tugged on his sleeve.

"Maybe you want something to drink?"

"Um, Charlotte? Do you know what you want to drink?" he asked, tilting back his head and speaking directly to the ceiling.

The waitress dashed to Charlotte's side. Charlotte's arm touched Declan's as she leaned to avoid inhaling the server's hair. She murmured her order, lips grazing the girl's forehead.

Unsure of an item, the waitress stood on the bottom bar of a nearby barstool and crawled across Charlotte's lap to peer at the menu. She read the name of the drink Charlotte pointed to phonetically until she had it memorized. Then she hopped off the stool like a Pomeranian and scurried away.

Charlotte and Declan looked at each other and then looked away to avoid giggling.

A moment later, the waitress' face arose like whack-a-mole beside Declan's elbow again. He yelped and jumped, knocking his chopsticks to the ground.

"Jeez, sorry," he said as she handed him a new pair of chopsticks in a paper sheath. "I didn't see you coming."

Declan asked for a martini and inquired about one of the more obscure appetizers. The waitress again hopped onto the bottom rung of a stool and crawled across his lap. She explained several appetizers by reading what the menu said verbatim, which was unhelpful since most of the descriptions read like a random game of Scrabble in the first place.

"I feel violated," whispered Declan when she left to fetch their drinks.

"You might be pregnant," said Charlotte. "I haven't felt so loved since Abby fell asleep on my face."

"What did you get that was so complicated?"

"A saki cosmopolitan. What did you get?"

"A martini. But I made the mistake of asking about the Happy Maki. Why are things always *happy* in Japanese restaurants? Just once, maybe I'd like to try the *Sashimi of Discontent* or the *Heartbroken Hand Roll*.

Charlotte laughed and Declan made a mental note to make her laugh more often. It felt even better than inspiring a new widow to chuckle as he sifted through her beloved's belongings. He couldn't remember the last time he'd had so much fun and he was only eating sushi.

I need to hang out with younger people more often.

They received their drinks and the waitress disappeared. Declan planned to finish his martini while he and Charlotte talked about her news and then order food.

That's when he heard the noise.

click click

Declan turned to find their tiny friend positioned a foot behind his seat. She stood smiling and clicking her pen as she awaited their food order.

click click

Declan felt the hair on the back of his neck rising.

click click

I can hear her breathing.

"Um..." Declan's fingers crawled back to the menu and the waitress stepped forward to rest her head on his elbow, awaiting his order.

"We're going to hold off ordering for just a bit," he said.

The waitress grinned. "Okay, that's good. Okay."

She scuttled back to the kitchen.

Declan released a sigh of relief. Another second and she would have been perched in his lap like a ventriloquist's doll.

"Did you ever see that movie *The Ring*?" he asked Charlotte.

Charlotte covered her face as she snorted saki cosmo into her nose.

Score.

Charlotte finished her cocktail and asked for a small bottle of cold sake, which arrived in a metal tree full of saki cups. When Declan ordered a glass of wine, the bartender misunderstood and brought two glasses.

Charlotte stared at her empty cocktail glass, saki tree, a glass of wine, and soy sauce bowl.

"I'm one fetal pig away from looking like I brought a seventh-grade chemistry kit to dinner."

"So, you should probably tell me your news before the waitress returns or before all those liquids converge in your stomach to create a homemade bomb."

"Good point."

She turned to Declan and stared into his eyes for a moment.

"What's wrong?" he asked.

"I'm not sure how to tell you this... But they're questioning someone about your mother's murder."

Declan leaned forward, his hand slipping from the edge of the bar. He nearly fell from his stool.

"Careful," said Charlotte, pressing against his shoulder to keep him steady. "This is the one time the waitress isn't here to break your fall."

"Really? Who?" he asked, doing his best to right himself gracefully.

"Well, that's just it. It's George, and I'm finding it hard to believe it."

"Who the hell is George?"

"One of my neighbors. He owns Pineapple Port. Frank got an anonymous tip that there was something buried beneath George's orange tree, and they found a box of love letters between him and your mother."

"Love letters?"

"That's the word. We're pumping Frank for more information."

"Why hasn't anyone contacted me?"

"I guess they don't have any official news yet. Love letters don't make a person a murderer. You can't tell Frank I told you."

Declan realized his jaw was hanging slack and shut his mouth. He turned back to the counter and took a sip of wine.

"So you're saying it's possible my mother was dating George and he killed her, buried her on his land, and built a house on top of her?"

Charlotte shrugged. "I doubt it. He's never hit me as the murdering type. Of course, he's never hit me as the cheating type either..."

"He's married?"

"To Penny. She was at that meeting of the *Crime Committee*. The one in charge."

"And they were married when…"

Charlotte nodded. "If it even happened. Like I said, I don't know all the facts yet. I just wanted to keep you in the loop."

Declan's shoulders slumped. "I don't think I'm in the mood for the Happy Maki now."

"I'm sorry," said Charlotte. "I thought you'd like to know."

"Oh and I do. I appreciate it. But I can't talk to Frank?"

"Not yet. If he finds out I'm telling you things he'll cut me off and then you won't have a man on the inside."

"So you're my man on the inside? My confidential informant?"

Charlotte smiled. "I'm your CI."

"And my private eye."

"Who doesn't lie."

"Because you're sweet as pie."

"And you're my gu—" Charlotte stopped short. "I mean, *the* guy."

"Okay, you're too good at this. You're starting to scare me now. Buh-bye."

"Why?"

"Let's call it a tie."

"Fine."

"Good."

Charlotte looked at him, a tiny smile growing on her face.

"Don't say it," he said.

She pressed her lips together as if it took all her strength not to speak.

"Don't you do it…"

She shook her head and picked up her saki.

"I'll *try*," she mumbled into the cup.

He pretended not to hear and turned his head so she couldn't see him smile.

I think I like this girl.

This girl, who found my mother in her back yard.

CHAPTER NINETEEN

The next evening was the official meeting of the Bourbon Club, when Mariska's husband Bob, Frank, and a revolving handful of other local men collected in Mariska's lanai to drink. They thought they were being clever calling it a "club," forgetting that women invented book clubs that had more to do with wine and a night away from the kids than great literature.

Charlotte, Mariska, and Darla gathered in Mariska's living room behind the glass sliding door that led to the Bourbon Club. The club had a running gag that women weren't allowed in the lanai unless they brought snacks. The only female allowed full access was Miss Izzy. The slider door remained cracked wide enough for Miss Izzy to waddle back and forth between the men and women, exploring which group was most likely to feed her. The ladies began the evening as the easier marks, but two or three drinks later, Izzy wrapped the men around her little paw and the Cheez-Its fell like rain from a bourbon-infused cloud.

"Frank cough up any more news about George?" Charlotte asked Darla as she sank lower into Bob's man-eating La-Z-Boy.

"They took his guns," said Darla. "They're going to match them against that bullet Harry found."

"Is he in jail?"

"They're holding him as long as they can, but I don't know if a box of love letters is enough to make a case against him."

"This is so horrible," said Mariska. "Penny has to be a mess."

"We should go talk to her," said Darla.

"We should."

"Maybe she knows something," suggested Charlotte.

"Exactly," said Darla. "Maybe she knew about the affair."

"Maybe she knew about the murder."

Mariska gasped. "You don't think…"

Charlotte shrugged. "I don't know what I think anymore. I know I didn't think I'd ever find a body in my backyard."

"I don't know how much help Penny will be," said Darla.

"If you discovered your husband was having an affair, and then the girl in that affair went missing, you might not be inclined to start *looking* for her. Penny might have seen more than she knows. At the time, she might have considered Erin's disappearance luck, no matter what evidence she found lying around."

"Like a gun," whispered Mariska. "Or bloody gloves. Or clothes covered in mud…"

"If I found out Frank was having an affair, it's not the *girl* who would go missing," muttered Darla.

Miss Izzy wandered in from the porch and set up camp at Charlotte's feet, her ridiculous ears swirling in search of crinkling paper and crunching cracker noises. Charlotte took a pretzel from the snack bowl on the lamp table beside her and tossed it to the dog, who snapped it out of the air.

"She loves her baldies," said Mariska.

"Baldies?"

"The pretzels. No salt."

"Ugh." Charlotte scowled. "No wonder they were the worst pretzels I've ever eaten."

Charlotte rocked several times to extract herself from her chair and walked to the lanai. She moved the sliding door wider than the exact width of Miss Izzy's body and stuck her head in the room.

"Did you ask for a guest pass?" asked Dave, a heavyset blond who lived on the other side of the neighborhood.

Dave was a woodworker who came in handy whenever someone needed crown molding or a door shimmed. Most of the men in Pineapple Port were once blue-collar workers, but even the ex-business men had practical living skills and hidden talents. Charlotte found it comforting to know there was always an ex-plumber or amateur electrician nearby in case of emergency. She worried the only talent her generation of retirees would possess was the ability to clear a video game level in record time, or text someone a message without looking at the phone.

"She didn't ask *Lance* for permission," said Bob, a goofy grin on his face.

Charlotte smirked. Bob had been a Lance Corporal in the marines. Somewhere around his third bourbon he, and everyone else began to refer to him as *Lance*. While *Bob* was so quiet he made monks look like chatterboxes, *Lance* could be a handful.

"Frank, did they get the ballistics test back on George's guns?" asked Charlotte.

Frank tilted to look past Charlotte into the living room, glowering at Darla. Charlotte turned in time to see Darla return his hard stare with a grin and a happy little wave.

"No. We'll probably know tomorrow," he said. "And inform my wife I'm not telling her another damn thing."

"What if it is a match? Is that it? One hundred percent proof he did it?"

Frank raised his glass to his lips and paused to consider.

"It wouldn't look good."

"But *Lance* is looking good," said Bob.

"Here here. To Lance," the men all held their glasses in salute.

Charlotte groaned and turned to rejoin the ladies.

"What's going on out there?" asked Darla.

"Lance has arrived."

Mariska dropped her face into her hands. "Oh no."

"It's bad enough dealing with one man," said Darla, patting Mariska on the shoulder. "You have to deal with *two*, you poor, poor woman."

"Oh," said Mariska, sitting up. "That reminds me. Charlotte, you have a date tomorrow."

Charlotte fell into her chair. "What?"

"Gladys's grandson, Brad, is going to be visiting and I volunteered you to keep him company for a few hours tomorrow."

"Are you out of your mind? We had a deal you weren't going to set me up with anyone anymore."

"This guy is rich," said Darla. "We thought we'd make an exception. He's good-lookin', too."

Charlotte scowled. "Isn't it a teeny bit of a warning sign that he needs his grandmother to set him up on dates?"

Mariska and Darla looked at each other.

"I don't know that he *needs* to be set up…" said Mariska.

"I think maybe he just broke up with someone," said Darla.

"Great. I get to be his rebound date while he's away from home. How can I say no?"

"It's just been so long," said Mariska, tilting her head to the side and staring as if Charlotte were dying of an incurable disease. "We were worried you've forgotten how much fun it can be to take your nose out of your books and talk to someone your own age."

"Not that we aren't fascinating," said Darla. "But chatting with someone *your* age and of the opposite sex might be good for you."

Staring into middle distance and feeling sorry for herself, Charlotte took a baldy pretzel and put it in her mouth. She immediately regretted it.

"These things taste like cardboard."

"Don't change the subject," said Mariska. "Will you take him around tomorrow? Maybe get some lunch? I'll pay."

"You don't have to *pay*," said Charlotte. "First of all, *he* should pay. I'm the one providing a tour service. Fine. Whatever. This neighborhood's going down the tubes anyway. It's all murder, sex, and lust."

"Did someone call Lance?" said Bob, entering the room. He smiled, his half-staff eyes sweeping over the group. "Hello, ladies…"

"You are going to regret this tomorrow, mister," said

Mariska, waggling a crooked finger at him.

"If I had a penny for every time I heard that," said Bob. "I'd be a pennynair."

He attempted a wink before sauntering down the hall to the bathroom. Charlotte could hear him ping-ponging off the walls as he walked.

"That man," muttered Mariska.

Charlotte chuckled. She loved Lance.

"So... I was thinking..." said Charlotte, grabbing another pretzel. She nearly had it to her lips when she realized what it was, wrinkled her nose, and tossed it to the dog. "Let's approach this like a *Dateline* episode. What if it isn't George who killed Declan's mom?"

"I hope it isn't," said Mariska.

"Me too, but I mean, if it isn't George, who is it? Who are our suspects?"

"It's always the husband," said Darla.

"It's always the husband," echoed Mariska.

"Her husband was already dead," said Charlotte.

"Then the boyfriend," said Darla. "*Dateline* is pretty one-note that way. Husbands or boyfriends, they are your choices."

"But the boyfriend *is* George," said Mariska.

"Oh, right. Well, the motives are always sex or money. Did she have life insurance?"

Charlotte opened her eyes wide. "Yes," she said, sitting up as far as the chair would allow. "And she had two boyfriends."

The other women's mouths formed two perfect Os of surprise. They looked like the Christmas caroler statues that Mariska pulled out for display every holiday.

"Two?" they said in unison.

"When I was at Declan's, Seamus admitted that *he* was dating Erin at the time of her death."

"Who's Seamus?" asked Darla.

"Declan's uncle. Remember? He came to the *Crime Committee* meeting with him."

Mariska's eyes popped wide. "His uncle? He was dating his own *sister*?"

Charlotte pursed her lips and tilted her head to stare at Mariska from beneath her lowered brow. "His uncle from the *other* side of the family. He might be a murderer, but he isn't a total sicko."

"Oh. Whew. That's good."

"But I thought she was having an affair with George?" asked Darla.

"Maybe she was. Seamus said that the night she went missing she told him she was breaking up with her boyfriend. She was going to try and make it work with Seamus and he was going to adopt Declan—the whole thing. She left to break up with the boyfriend and he never saw her again."

"So George *did* kill her," said Mariska.

"Seamus said he didn't know who the other boyfriend was. She didn't say. So it wasn't necessarily George."

"Did Declan go to live with Seamus?" asked Darla.

"That's just it," said Charlotte. "It sounded as if Seamus freaked out after Erin died. He said he tried to look into her disappearance, but came up empty. He was worried the cops would try to pin a murder on him, because his brother, Erin's dead husband and Declan's dad, had been a terrible drug addict and gotten in a lot of trouble with the local law. He thought maybe he could support Declan on Erin's insurance money, but the money was delayed."

"No body," said Darla. "They always hold the insurance check waiting for proof of death on *Dateline*. Makes the murderers furious."

"Exactly. Seamus moved to Miami and Declan went to live with his grandmother."

"Poor boy," said Mariska. "That must have been terrible for him."

Charlotte's face pinched as she realized the weight of what she was implying. "When it comes to possible suspects, Seamus looks pretty good. He was the boyfriend *and* someone who could have collected on her insurance by adopting Declan."

"That would be *awful* if Declan's uncle killed his mother," said Darla.

Charlotte nodded. "He seemed like a pretty nice guy. Odd, but nice."

"Is there anyone else? What if the other boyfriend wasn't George?" asked Mariska.

"You don't think she had three boyfriends, do you?" said Darla. "That seems like a lot."

"I don't know. Maybe her friends kept pushing guys on her, trying to get her to date more..." said Charlotte looking away to appear as innocent as possible.

Darla nodded in agreement until a look of realization washed across her face and her gaze locked back on Charlotte.

"Oh I get it," she said. "Like we're pushing guys on you."

Charlotte offered a mirthless smile.

"Speaking of which, before you human traffic me to this guy, are we going to see Penny tomorrow morning? Maybe she'll know something."

"Yes, let's do that," said Mariska. "She could use some support. Maybe we can catch her at poolside breakfast, but if not we'll go knock on her door."

"We'll go pump her for information," said Darla.

"Is she cute? Are you taking volunteers?" asked Bob, appearing once again in the living room. "Lance is here. He'll volunteer. But first, a beer."

"Your zipper is down, idiot," said Mariska.

Bob looked down and worked the zipper of his khaki shorts back up.

"It's not my fault. The women back there are aggressive..." he mumbled, throwing a finger in the direction of the bathroom.

Charlotte laughed.

Mariska rolled her eyes and scowled.

CHAPTER TWENTY

Charlotte spotted Darla scampering toward the table where she and Mariska sat, her caftan flapping in the breeze behind her. The third Wednesday of every month was Poolside Breakfast, where a good portion of the Port gathered to share eggs in the community center overlooking the pool. Charlotte and Mariska sat at their usual table, but Frank and Bob were absent.

"Where's Frank?" asked Mariska as Darla slipped into her seat. "I can tell you Bob didn't feel up to breakfast this morning. Lance did quite a number on him last night."

"Frank was a little slow but he had to go to work. Charlotte, you need to make him and Bob those hangover concoctions of yours."

"The Red-eye Jedi," said Charlotte. "Mind tricks you into thinking you don't have a hangover."

"How does it do that?" asked Mariska.

"It's full of vodka."

"Oh. Hm."

"Oh," yelped Darla. "I almost forgot. Frank got a call. The ballistics came back and the bullet didn't match any of George's guns."

"Oh, that's wonderful," said Mariska.

Charlotte looked up in time to see Penny in the doorway.

"And as if on cue, there's Penny."

All heads swiveled to watch as Penny entered the room. She wore her best pearls, a silk tank, and tan skort. As gazes fell upon her she lifted her chin and weaved her way between the oglers to Mariska's table.

"Hi, Penny," said Mariska. "We were going to come to see you today if you didn't come to breakfast. How are you doing?"

"I'm just fine. I assume you've heard the news?"

"The bullet didn't match," said Darla. "Frank called you?"

"Frank called me. And yes, the bullet didn't match any of George's guns. Of course, it didn't match."

"What's that?" asked Harry from two tables to the left. "My bullet?"

"*The* bullet," said Penny.

"But they still have those letters. Maybe he ditched the gun."

Penny glared at him.

"Don't be ridiculous. Those letters are fakes or taken out of proportion. My George never had an affair with his secretary. That would be so... so..."

Penny curled her hands into fists as she tried to find her word.

"Cliché?" offered Charlotte.

"Yes," said Penny, pointing at her. "Cliché. A man and his secretary. It's ridiculous. They told me they can't even be sure the letters they found are between George and that girl. They're misleading. They might be anyone's letters. She isn't the only person in the world named Erin."

"George said they aren't his?" asked Darla.

"Of course he did."

"Can't they do handwriting analysis on them?" asked Harry.

Penny whirled on him and released the fabled Level Ten Sniff. Before Harry could say another word she stormed off, calling "*You people*" over her shoulder as she left.

"Huh," grunted Harry, moving from his table to Mariska's. "I thought for sure it was George."

"Maybe the letters aren't as damning as we thought," said Charlotte.

"Maybe not," said Harry. "Or maybe they just need to find more evidence. Hair or blood or the gun. He buried the letters, maybe he buried other things."

"Or maybe it wasn't George," said Darla. Charlotte could see she was getting annoyed with Harry for joining the group without asking.

"Did you know Declan's uncle was dating her?" asked Mariska.

"Seamus?" said Harry, his ears perking. "He was dating his... uh..."

"Sister-in-law," said Darla. "That confused us for a second, too."

"Mariska," whispered Charlotte, touching her hand. "You can't gossip about something this serious."

Darla overheard and scowled. "Harry, we know you want to solve the mystery and relive your glory days but we can't help you."

"But what's this about the uncle? You think he did it? It still has to be George, don't you think?"

Charlotte shook her head. "We don't know. We were just playing *Dateline*. On that show, it's always the husband or the boyfriend, and Seamus was dating her, that's all. It's hardly evidence."

"That and the insurance money," said Mariska.

Charlotte kicked her under the table.

"Ow. What?"

"What insurance money?" asked Harry.

Mariska rubbed her leg. Her face fell as Harry asked his question.

"Oh," she said.

"Nothing," said Charlotte. "Leave it to the real police."

Harry turned on her, his mouth set in a short, tight line.

"I *am* real police."

"Not anymore," said Charlotte. "Not officially. You found the bullet and that was great, but don't start any rumors about Seamus. You know how this neighborhood can get. We were just playing, coming up with alternative theories."

"Playing *Dateline*."

"Exactly."

"You know none of those people are detectives. They're

talking heads and half-assed reporters."

"Don't get wound up about it, Harry. We just don't want the neighborhood buzzing with rumors."

Harry stood.

"I don't gossip." He held their gazes a moment longer and then returned to his table, sitting with his back to the group.

"Poor Harry," said Mariska. "He just wants to be useful."

"You can't start rumors," said Charlotte. "No more talking about our theories unless we're alone in your house."

Mariska nodded. Then her eyes lit up.

"What is it?" asked Charlotte. "Did you think of something?"

"No," said Mariska, pointing. "Here come the eggs. I'm starving."

Charlotte spotted the waiter approaching with their covered tray of breakfast foods. She was about to turn and pull her napkin to her lap when she noticed a familiar figure sitting at a table on the other side of the room.

"Seamus," she said.

"You said we can't talk about it here," mumbled Mariska, watching the waiter reveal their menagerie of delight the way a raccoon might eyeball a lidless trashcan.

"No, *Seamus*," repeated Charlotte in a hissed whisper. "He's over there in the corner."

Mariska's and Darla's gazes tore away from the food.

"He's with Jackie," said Darla. "He's over there canoodling with Jackie."

"Well that's nice," said Mariska, pulling a sausage link from the tray to her plate. "She's been alone for a while now. They make a nice couple."

"A nice couple," screeched Darla. She glanced around to see if her yelp had garnered any attention and then leaned in to continue at a lower volume. "He might be the murderer, remember?"

"Oh. That wouldn't be good." Mariska looked at Jackie as she slipped a chunk of sausage into her mouth.

"No, that would be bad."

"I have better sausage than this," said Mariska, chewing. "I bought sausage the other day you can only get in Michigan. It is the most wonderful thing you've ever eaten."

"Did you order it online?" asked Darla.

"No, I got it at the store."

"You said you can only get it in Michigan."

"You can only get it in Michigan. I don't know how I got it here."

Darla opened her mouth to continue and then shut it. She looked at Charlotte, who could only shake her head. She constantly marveled at how easily her two friends were distracted. She must have absorbed that behavior herself through osmosis.

"So do we tell Jackie? Do we warn her that her new beau might be a gun-totin' maniac?"

Charlotte sighed and shrugged.

Darla scooped scrambled eggs in slow motion, her mind clearly elsewhere as she left a trail of fluffy yellow crumbles on her plate.

"I don't want to start trouble but I also don't want to find Jackie skinned alive."

"Skinned alive?" said Mariska, stabbing another sausage. "You think he'd do that?"

"It's a figure of speech," said Darla.

"Where? Where is suggesting a man might skin your friend alive a figure of speech?"

"Kentucky. And I thought you didn't like those sausages..."

"You two," said Charlotte, finally reaching the end of her rope. "We have a problem here. Jackie could be in danger. Maybe... I don't know. Maybe I should talk to Declan first?"

"But that's his uncle," said Darla. "I don't see that conversation going well."

"No," agreed Charlotte. "Me neither. It's bad enough that he just found out his mother is dead. Maybe we can just plant the seed in Jackie's head."

"Plant the seed that her boyfriend wants to kill her?" asked Mariska.

"That's a hell of a seed. Maybe we should just slap warning

lights on the man and hit the sirens," said Darla.

"What does that even mean?" asked Charlotte.

Darla shrugged. "You know. I dunno. Whatever."

Charlotte took a piece of bacon from the communal platter. "I just want this mystery solved so everything can go back to normal. Get Frank to hurry up, will you?"

Darla chuckled. "I don't think he's moving that fast today, darlin'."

Charlotte's eyes darted back to Jackie and Seamus between each bite of what little breakfast she ate. The two appeared friendly. Jackie couldn't stop laughing and made a point to lightly slap Seamus' arm after every other thing he said. She assumed it was Jackie he'd left to see the night she visited Declan, as she'd suspected. The man moved fast. He hadn't been in town for more than a day and he already had a girlfriend.

He had good taste. Jackie was barely sixty and appeared in her early fifties. She was smart and funny and widowed over six years. Matchmaking efforts had failed in the past; Jackie never clicked with any of the neighborhood widowers. It made Charlotte happy to see her with someone.

On the other hand, she'd always hoped Jackie would find someone a little less murdery.

CHAPTER TWENTY-ONE

"That was a lovely breakfast," said Seamus as he and Jackie strolled away from the Pineapple Port community center. "Thank you."

"Do you think anyone saw you?"

"I know Declan's lady did. Her eyes followed me like she was a trailer hitched to my truck."

"Declan's lady? In *there*?"

"The young one. Tall, pretty..."

"Oh, Charlotte."

Jackie stopped, her eyes wide with surprise, and placed her hand on his chest. Seamus flexed his pecs, first the left and then the right. Jackie snatched her hand back, blushing.

Still got it.

"You didn't tell me they were a thing," she said.

"I don't know that they are... yet. I might be tellin' tales out of school, but I'd bet dollars to cents that they *will* be."

"That's wonderful. She's a nice girl. And she's been alone almost as long as—" Jackie cut short and began to walk again.

"As long as what? As long as a summer's day?"

"Yes. As long as a summer's day."

Jackie slipped her tiny hand in his and he watched her as they walked. The side of her mouth curled in a smile. With her face tilted down, and that grin growing, she looked like Erin might, had she lived to grow old with him. The second he'd met Jackie, he'd known his return to Charity had been the right move.

"A penny for your thoughts," he said, leaning toward her and whispering in her ear.

She giggled.

"Do you ever say a single sentence that isn't some colorful turn of phrase?"

"I'm Irish, dear, we're a colorful people."

"You only have a hint of an accent left, but it's beautiful. You must have charmed the ladies in Miami."

"Oh, they were dying to meet me. Linin' up around the block, they were."

"How is it you're still single?"

"I'm one of those *unlucky* leprechauns, I guess."

Jackie giggled again. She put her free hand over her mouth to stifle her laugh and stopped walking. Still holding Seamus' hand with her left, she stared into his eyes.

"I should go," she said. "I have things I need to do today. Water aerobics is at ten-thirty."

She said the phrase *water aerobics* as if it were as joyful a task as mucking a horse stall.

"Well, thank you again for the invite, my love," said Seamus, raising her hand to kiss it.

Jackie blushed and looked away from him as his lips touched the back of her hand. She smelled like lilacs.

"I'll see you soon?" she asked.

"Very soon. The story of life is quicker than the blink of an eye, the story of love is hello, goodbye."

"That's lovely. Is that from one of your Irish poets?"

"Jimi Hendrix."

Jackie grinned and twirled on her heel to leave. He remained in place as she walked toward her home. She looked over her shoulder and offered a wave as she left. He waved then, and twice more when she glanced to see if he was still watching. She turned the corner and disappeared behind a little white home with a giant metal crane in the front yard.

Lord, they love their lawn ornaments in this place.

"You're a fast mover," said a voice.

Seamus turned to find a man striding toward him. He recognized him as the fellow from the meeting Declan had taken him to about Erin's discovery.

The man with the bullet.

Harry.

"What's that now?" he asked, forcing a smile on his face. He didn't like the man's tone but he'd always found you can catch more flies with honey, a saying he knew was also *not* Irish. It didn't make any sense. *Who wanted to catch flies? And more importantly, if you had some nice honey, why would you want it full of flies?*

"I mean with Jackie there," said Harry, stopping. He sounded out of breath as if he'd been trying hard to catch them. "You two seem to have hit it off very quickly."

Seamus thrust his hands in his pockets and grinned. "A woman as charming as she, is like a four-leaf clover."

"Lucky? Lucky to have found you? Something to be plucked?"

Seamus laughed. "I meant *hard to find.* Though I like your first interpretation better I think."

Harry mimicked Seamus by slipping his own hands in his pockets, trying very hard to appear non-threatening and casual. Seamus decided he trusted the man even less.

"You used to live around here?" asked Harry.

"I did."

"I don't remember you, but I didn't know that many people in the area back then. What made you come back?"

"I was retired. Miami held no charms for me anymore and I missed my nephew."

"Right... Declan. Horrible about his mother, isn't it? She would have been your sister-in-law, right? It must have been awful when she went missing. Were you here when it happened?"

"I was."

"Were you close? I mean, your brother was dead by then, right? It was probably nice to have you nearby to do man-chores, paint and change oil, that sort of thing. Maybe help with

Declan? Boy needs a man in his life…"

"She was a lovely girl."

"Right. Of course, she was. Terrible. Is that what made you move to Miami after that? The whole *terrible* situation?"

Seamus studied the man. He seemed very familiar with the timeline of his living situations. He also seemed pale, even to an Irishman. A fine sheen of sweat covered him from head to toe.

"I moved for a million reasons. I was young. Bit of a rolling stone."

"Uh-huh. Is Erin's death what made you become a cop?"

Seamus ran his tongue over his teeth and pondered Harry's question for a moment before answering.

"It could be that injustice made me want to help others."

"Plus you get to play with guns. Right?"

Seamus smirked. "Is that why you became a police officer, Harry? To play with guns?"

"How'd you know…" Harry's face twisted tight for a moment and then released. "Oh, that's right, you were at the meeting. I probably mentioned I was an experienced cold case officer."

"Couple times."

Seamus tried to smile but knew by the look on Harry's face his attempt at levity had appeared more like a sneer. He was tired of this buffoon and his clumsy interrogation style. Even Irish charm needed some morsel to feed it.

"No, I was always about the puzzles," said Harry, rocking back and forth, toe to heel. "I never had any interest in the violence. Just the puzzles."

Seamus pulled his hands out of his pockets and crossed his arms across his chest. He knew the posture might appear threatening, but he was trying to hold himself back. The urge to head-butt this man was becoming impossible to resist.

"That's the funny thing about violence, isn't it?" said Seamus. "Sometimes it has an interest in *you*."

Harry nodded vigorously, took his hands out of his own pockets, and rubbed his right bicep with his left hand. After a moment he stretched, bending side to side.

"Yeah… but me, I like the puzzles. Anyway, that's why I'm

trying to help solve what happened to your sister-in-law. I'll be honest with you, I was thinking maybe you had some insight."

"I don't. What insight I had failed me years ago."

Harry ceased his impromptu calisthenics. "But if you told me what you know, maybe I would see something different? Since I'm not so close to the case?"

Seamus shook his head. He based the style of his head shake on the way his friend, officer Johnny Lima, had reacted back in the day when Seamus asked him if his partner had survived a shooting in the Overtown section of Miami. It was a slow headshake, full of regret. Remembering Johnny and mimicking the sadness of that response kept him from wanting to grab Harry by the throat.

"I don't know anything that can help you. I'm sorry. But if something jogs my memory, I'll be sure to find you."

"Great. Do you want me to jot down my phone number?"

"I won't have any trouble finding you. I know where you live."

Harry jerked back his head. "You do?"

Seamus held his arms out to his sides, palms up, unlocking the grin he'd been struggling to find.

"Of course, I do. Pineapple Port."

"Oh, right." Harry offered a weak chuckle. "Well, it was nice to see you again."

Harry thrust out a hand to shake and Seamus took it.

"Good strong handshake you have there," said Harry, wincing.

"Nice to talk to you, Harry. Good luck with your cold case."

"Thanks."

They remained standing until Harry offered a quick nod and headed back toward the community center.

Seamus watched him scurry away.

"Eejit," he muttered.

CHAPTER TWENTY-TWO

Like all big dogs, Abby thought she was a lap dog. Charlotte's legs were going numb and Abby's elbows poked painfully into the meat of her thighs, but she didn't make the wheaten hop down. *Never take a loving dog for granted,* was her philosophy. They don't live long enough to do that.

Though, it might not hurt to maybe shift an elbow to the left...

She scratched around Abby's ears pondering her dilemma. Pool aerobics was half an hour away and she had to make a decision. Should she warn Jackie that Seamus made the perfect suspect for Erin's murder? All the elements were there: lust, jealousy, money, revenge... everything but a shred of proof.

And what if Jackie told Seamus? Seamus would want to kill her. If he *did* kill her, he probably killed Erin as well and Charlotte would have cracked the case. Of course, adopting the self-sacrifice style of sleuthing meant a short detective career.

Career. Hm. There was that word.

How would she feel if she'd met a man and someone told him that she was a murderer? She'd be angry. Whether she was a killer or not, she'd be angry.

Wait. I couldn't be some sort of detective, could I?

Declan would also be angry to hear she was running around telling people his uncle was a killer. Declan, who had been nothing but kind to her as he mourned the discovery of his mother's body. They'd had so much fun at sushi...

She smiled at the memory.

There were plenty of good reasons *not* to warn Jackie. There was only one reason *to* warn her, but it was a doozy.

She could end up dead.

Charlotte stopped scratching the dog and rubbed her eyes. Abby thrust her nose behind her arm and flipped it away from her face, demanding further attention.

"You're pushing it now."

She had to get ready for water aerobics and fought to extract herself from beneath the dog. Before heading down the hall she picked up the chalk and wrote *Detective?* on the chalkboard. A smile crept to her lips until she remembered not only did she have to talk to Jackie, but she had to meet Gladys' grandson, Brad, for lunch.

She huffed and put the chalk on the counter.

Worst. Day. Ever.

Charlotte was late for aerobics. She waded into the pool and took her usual place beside Mariska and Darla as they swung their legs back and forth in unison. On her way in, she'd nodded to Jackie. The woman was beaming. They could throw her back in the pool at night to save electricity on the lights.

"You're late," said Darla.

"I know. I can't decide what to do about Jackie and Seamus. It made me drag my feet."

"I almost didn't come myself," said Mariska, placing a hand on her belly. "I think I had too many sausages at breakfast."

"Well you had *six*," said Darla.

"They were tiny."

Charlotte scanned the pool. She felt eyes on her and located them in Harry's head. He motioned to her to come to him.

"I'll be right back," she said to the ladies and half-walked, half-aerobicized toward Harry at the back of the pool.

"What's up?" she asked, arriving beside him.

"I think you might have something with that Seamus theory," he whispered, making little circles under the water with his left foot.

"Why do you say that?"

"I just talked to him."

"You *what*? You told him what I said?"

"No, of course not. I never mentioned you. But I think I tricked him into making a mistake."

"Really…" Charlotte didn't know whether to be relieved she had a real reason to warn Jackie or to be upset the killer was Declan's uncle.

"I asked him if Erin's death was what made him move to Miami, and he said 'maybe' followed by some hoo-ha about it inspiring him to help others, blah, blah, blah."

"So?"

"Erin wasn't *dead* then. She was *missing*. I asked if Erin's *death* inspired him to move."

"Only the killer would have known she was dead…"

"Right. I thought it was pretty clever of me."

Charlotte tilted her head from side to side, thinking. "It's not exactly bulletproof though, is it?"

Harry shrugged. "You have to start somewhere."

"Anything else?"

"He seemed pretty standoffish. Threatening, even."

"He threatened you?"

"Not exactly. It was more his body language, some of the things he said. He said violence would find me, in so many words."

"Violence will find you? What is he, a dark fortune cookie?"

Charlotte glanced toward Jackie. The poor woman's face was going to crack if she didn't stop smiling. She hadn't shown this much enthusiasm for water aerobics since… well, since *never*. How was she going to tell her that her new boyfriend might be a killer?

"Seamus got into a fight with Declan when I was over there…" Charlotte mused aloud.

Harry stopped swirling. "A fistfight?"

"No, they were just yelling…"

As she replayed the events in her mind, she remembered how angry Declan had been.

Maybe being a killer was in his blood...

Suddenly, she felt sick. She stopped moving her legs to the beat.

"He didn't admit to dating the dead girl," said Harry. "But I had to be careful there. I didn't want to tip him that I received my information from you."

"Well, it was Mariska, but thank you," mumbled Charlotte putting her hand on her stomach. "I think I'm going to go."

"Are you going to warn Jackie? You should tell Frank to look into Seamus, just in case."

Charlotte grimaced as another wave of anxiety pains washed across her.

"I don't know. Yes, probably. Not now. I have to go. I have..." Charlotte closed her eyes and took a deep breath. "I have a date."

"Oh yeah? Good for you. Go get 'em, girl."

Charlotte's lip snarled and she turned and waded out of the pool.

Charlotte's date arrived at the sound of Abby's barking. He had knocked much too loudly. Abby's barking triggered Katie next door, which set off Miss Izzy across the street until a symphony of dogs rang through the streets.

Charlotte took a quick look in the bathroom mirror. She still looked half asleep. She'd been so upset over the dilemma of talking to Jackie and the idea that Declan's uncle might be a killer that she'd thrown herself into bed and taken a nap. She'd barely woken up in time to get a shower and get dressed.

Mustering what little enthusiasm she could, she pushed Abby aside with her leg and answered the door.

"Charlotte?" said a sandy-haired man wearing a polo, khaki shorts, and a braided leather belt. He was handsome in a predictable way, not too pretty, not too rugged. She could tell by the way he thrust out his chest that he knew exactly how good-looking he was.

"You must be Brad." She used all her strength to pull Abby back and away from the door. "Come on in. She won't hurt you.

Are you okay with dogs? Can I let her go?"

Brad took a step inside. "Oh, sure, yeah, no problem."

Abby bound forward, sniffing and circling Brad's legs like a squiggling fur tornado. Charlotte scowled as she watched him raise his arms above his head and submit to the torrent of attention. His motion was the international symbol for *not a dog lover*. Dog lovers bent over and petted a happy dog, scratched them behind the ears, or maybe even squatted and sat on a heel, the better to receive sloppy kisses. People afraid, uncomfortable, or unimpressed by dogs raised their hands to avoid accidentally touching them.

"You're as pretty as my grandmother said you were," he said, hands still high above his head as if she had him at gunpoint.

Awkward.

"Thank you, but you know grandmothers," she said, trying to keep it light. "They like to exaggerate."

"No, *really*. You're gorgeous."

As Brad's frat-boy gaze swept down her body, Charlotte felt the urge to cover up. She'd worn a summer dress, but as his leer settled on her breasts, she regretted her choice. *Had she been dressing to impress?* Maybe. Everyone liked to be admired... and Brad was cute, but his aggressive attention made her uneasy and his reaction to Abby was already one *huge* strike against any chance they had of hitting it off.

"Thank you," she said, crossing her arms against her chest.

Brad glanced around the house.

"Looks like you're quite a reader. Brains and beauty, eh?"

Charlotte tried to force a smile but she knew it looked more like she'd just smelled something rotten.

"Let me grab my bag."

Abby realized there would be no pets from Brad and wandered to the sofa. She hopped up and flopped down her head.

"I thought we could grab lunch if that's okay?" said Charlotte.

"That's perfect," he said, looking at his phone. He quickly typed a text and then slipped it back into his pocket. "I'll drive, you just tell me where to go."

"I'll be back in a bit, Ab."

Abby raised her eyes and then looked away, sulking.

"She understands you?" he asked as they walked to the car.

"Of course."

What a person-without-a-dog thing to say.

"So she knows you'll be back in a bit?"

"I always am."

"What does she do while you're gone?"

"Reads. The books are mostly hers."

"Seriously?"

Charlotte looked at him.

Brad chuckled as he slipped into the driver's side of his black Mercedes-Benz CLS.

"No, I know," he said. "Funny. Door's open."

Charlotte sighed and opened the passenger side of the car.

Charlotte navigated Brad to Pickles, a casual restaurant in the heart of downtown. Pickles seemed like a good choice because it wasn't too expensive and it was a notch above a diner. She assumed Brad intended to pay and thought it would be rude to take him to the most expensive place in town. As he asked her to take a moment to admire his car's oversized wheels and black rims, she began to regret the decision. A nice bottle of wine and a dozen oysters might have been just the thing.

The window seats were taken, so they sat at a table in the center of the tiled-floor dining area. The restaurant was homey, and she could tell Brad wasn't impressed. He did everything but wipe the seat before sitting down.

"You eat here a lot?" he asked.

"It isn't much to look at, but the food is good."

Brad raised his eyebrows. "I guess I'll have to take your word for it. Don't know if it would have been my first choice without your suggestion."

Let it slide. Be nice. It will all be over soon.

"So... you're visiting your grandmother?"

"Yep, that time of year. Gotta put in the family time."

Charming.

"Where do you live when you're not here?"

"Atlanta. I'm a mortgage broker there. Big firm. I'm one of the top guys."

"I've heard good things about Atlanta…"

"It's a blast. I love it. So much to do…" Brad looked around the restaurant and surveyed the people eating there. "Little more sophisticated than this place, if you know what I mean."

"Mmm."

Charlotte's mind began to drift. She was still trying to think of the best way to warn Jackie without getting herself killed in the process, either by Seamus for ratting him out or by Jackie for crushing her dreams. She shouldn't be sitting here with Brad, she should be out saving her friend. She also wondered what the special was. They had a delicious Monte Cristo sandwich with pepper jelly but it wasn't on the regular menu. What made it a Monte Cristo? Did they eat them in *The Count of Monte Cristo*?

"Do you know where the sandwich Monte Cristo got its name?" she asked Brad before she realized it.

Brad looked at her as if she were crazy. "Because it is a Monte Cristo sandwich?"

Right. Duh.

"So what is there to do around here?" he asked. "Besides Google sandwich names."

Charlotte looked at her purse where her phone sat.

I'd rather be Googling sandwich names…

Determined to be nice she smiled and shrugged. "The usual things I guess. Actually—"

"You should come to Atlanta," he said, cutting her short. "I could show you around. Take you to some *real* restaurants. *Serious* food. We could hit the clubs… my boys would love you, I'm sure."

"You have sons?"

"No my boyz, with a zee, you know, my crowd."

"Oh. Gotcha."

"You could stay at my place, I have four bedrooms. *You* could pick the one you want to stay in…"

Brad reached out and quickly stroked the back of Charlotte's upper arm with his fingers, his million-watt smile pointed at her like a gun.

She flinched, but before he could react to her repulsion, his phone rang.

"Just a sec…" he said, glancing at the screen. "I have to take this. Big client."

He stood and walked to the corner of the restaurant where he spoke in a voice loud enough for everyone to hear.

Charlotte put her elbow on the table and plopped her chin in her hand, staring out the front window. She couldn't imagine what she was going to do with this guy for the rest of the day. She wasn't going to be anywhere alone with him, that was for sure. He was much too confident, and in her experience, confidence rebuffed tended to turn into anger.

A man walked by the window and Charlotte straightened as he looked inside. His eyes flashed as his gaze met hers.

Declan.

He looked away and passed by without slowing. Charlotte felt a wave of disappointment. She felt sure he'd seen her.

Why wouldn't he stop?

Declan appeared again in the window, this time walking the opposite way. He stood tall, but with every step his head grew lower, until it disappeared behind the opaque partition of the window, making it appear to her as if he walked down a flight of stairs. She giggled as the top of his head disappeared.

"Sorry about that," said Brad, returning. "Big client. Two million-dollar property. That's about average for me—"

Charlotte kept her eyes trained on the window and Declan's head popped into view, jutting forward from the side of the window, the rest of his body still hidden so it looked like a floating head. Declan grinned, but as his gaze drifted from Charlotte to Brad his smile faded. His head withdrew before he walked by in his original direction without looking into the restaurant again.

"Who was that?" asked Brad.

"A friend of mine," said Charlotte, staring at the corner of the window where she last saw Declan.

"Dork much?" Brad chuckled to himself. "Anyway, I was thinking. There's nothing to see around here, right? Not really. Why don't I grab us a bottle or two of booze and we go back to your house and just get to know each other? I make a mean buttery nipple. Do you have butterscotch schnapps? The girls go *crazy* for those at home. You'll *love* it. I'll bring all the supplies, it's just that if I see one more tiki bar I'm going to vomit, you know? It would be nice to just chill without my grandmother around. Especially with a pretty girl like you."

Charlotte turned and looked at Brad.

"Really? Does that work on anyone?"

"What?"

"Buttery nipples?"

"Oh *excuse me*," said Brad, his demeanor shifting from cloying to annoyance so quickly Charlotte thought he'd drop a transmission to the floor. "I suppose you'd be more comfortable going to Hooters for some beers like your usual date, trailer park girl?"

Charlotte stood, her face burning with anger.

"There isn't even a Hooters around here," she said through gritted teeth.

She paused, sure that wasn't the comeback she'd had in mind, before spinning on her heel and storming toward the door.

"Your loss," called Brad.

CHAPTER TWENTY-THREE

Declan fumbled with his keys but found his front door unlocked.

"Hey, Laddie, how was your day?" asked Seamus as he walked in. Seamus had his feet on the sofa table watching baseball on TV. A crumpled bag of potato chips sat resting against his foot, shaking as Seamus bobbed his toes to a beat unheard to all but him.

"Dreamy," said Declan, throwing a white plastic bag on the kitchen counter.

"Do I detect a note of sarcasm? Whatcha got there?"

"Sandwiches for dinner. I hope you like Italian subs."

"I do. Grand. So what's wrong?"

"Nothing. Work was slow."

Declan cracked himself a beer. He noticed the empty bottle on the sofa table and grabbed another from the refrigerator for his uncle.

"That doesn't look like *work* cranky," said Seamus, accepting the beer with a nod as Declan flopped down on the opposite side of the sectional. "That looks like *girl* cranky."

"Maybe," he mumbled.

"Come on, tell Uncle Seamus everything."

Declan rolled his eyes.

"I saw Charlotte in town. She was with some guy in a restaurant."

"Maybe it was her brother."

"She doesn't have a brother," said Declan taking a swig. "At least I don't think so… I guess I don't know, but I don't think so."

"So was he bigger than you?"

"I'm not going to *fight* him for her. I'm not challenging him to a duel for crying out loud."

"Okay, okay… that was just my first thought. Give me a second."

"It doesn't matter. It's just… I thought maybe… I don't know."

"Well, let me ask you this, boyo, have you asked her out?"

"No. Not exactly. We got some sushi…"

"Well, there's your first mistake. Taking a woman to eat raw fish. What's wrong with you?"

"It was *her* idea. We had a good time."

"So why didn't you arrange a second time?"

"I don't know, it… I didn't think it was a date exactly, she just had information about Mom and we happened to be hungry."

"Can't you happen to be hungry *again*? I can be hungry three or four times a day."

"Yeah, I don't know…"

"How are you supposed to win a race if you don't even step to the line?"

"It's not a race."

"You know what I mean. You should ask her out. Why not?"

"It's just strange. Dating the girl who found your mother in her backyard."

"People have met in stranger ways."

"Really?"

Seamus considered. "Maybe not. That *is* a good one."

"Exactly. Enough about me. How was your day?"

"Oh, things are going quite well on my lady front."

Declan grimaced. "There has got to be a better way to word that."

"Hey," Seamus put down his beer and leaned his elbows on his knees. "What do you know about this Harry guy?"

"Harry? The guy from the crime meeting?"

"Yeah. The blowhard who found the bullet."

Declan shrugged. "No more than you do. Why?"

"He seemed interested in me today. Asking me some strange questions."

"Like what?"

Seamus sat back. "Nothing. No worries. He's just an odd one."

Declan was about to ask his uncle to explain when his phone rang. He fished it out of his pocket and answered.

"Declan?"

Charlotte.

"Hey..." He scrambled for something to say but every sentence he contrived started with *I saw you with that guy today...*

"I need to talk to you," she said. Her voice sounded uncharacteristically tight.

"Shoot."

"Um... Not on the phone. Could you come over?"

"Now?"

"If you could. Now would be great."

"I guess..."

"And could you do me a favor? Could you pick me up on the way? I'm at Gina's coffee shop downtown."

Declan pictured Gina's in his head and scowled.

"Down the block from where I just saw you?"

"Mm-hm."

"Are you okay?"

"I'm fine. Long story. Well, short stupid story, but I'll tell you when I see you."

"Okay... I'll be there in a few minutes."

Declan hung up to find his uncle staring at him.

"So?"

"It was Charlotte. She wants me to come over. I guess she has more news."

"See? You're in like Flynn. Don't mess it up."

Declan smiled and then sobered when he saw his uncle notice.

"Well, your sandwich is here. Go ahead and eat. You don't

have to wait for me."

"Oh, I won't," said Seamus.

Declan grabbed his keys and headed for the door.

"Fancy meeting you here," said Declan as he approached Charlotte's table. She was already standing, ready to go.

"I can't tell you how much I appreciate this," said Charlotte as they walked to his car. She was wearing another summer dress. Declan decided he liked that look on her.

"What happened?"

Charlotte threw up her hands and flopped them back down to her sides.

"I was set up with the grandson of one of the Pineapple Portians. He was an ass and I walked out on him, but that left me with no ride home. Charity isn't exactly a hotbed of taxi service, and if I called Mariska, word would get back to his grandmother and the whole thing would be a mess."

Declan shot a glance toward Pickles searching for the man he'd seen with Charlotte. "Are you okay? He didn't hurt you or anything?"

"Oh, god, no, nothing like that. He just decided very early on that I was a poor little trailer park girl unable to resist his big-city charm."

"It's not a trailer park. They're modular homes."

"Exactly." Charlotte laughed and met Declan's gaze as they slipped into the car. He noticed the laugh lines on either side of her mouth, long lines that traveled from the apple of her cheeks to just below her lips. He liked them. *How had he not noticed them before?*

Charlotte looked away. Declan thought she may have blushed, but the light was dying and he doubted his eyes.

"To your house?" he asked.

"Please. I appreciate this. I had something to tell you anyway or I wouldn't have bothered you."

"No bother."

I'm thrilled you had a terrible time with that guy. Which

surprises me.

They rode in silence for a few minutes. He heard a soft snorting noise from his right and glanced over to see Charlotte grinning and shaking her head.

"What's so funny?"

"He wanted to make me a buttery nipple."

"He what?"

"Brad. He said he wanted to go back to my place so he could make me a buttery nipple."

Declan's mouth hung open. He laughed.

"This guy you've never met before said the words *buttery nipple* to you?"

Charlotte laughed harder, nodding her head as she covered her mouth and snorted another laugh. The sound of her hysterics made Declan laugh harder.

"Class act," he said.

"You have no idea," said Charlotte, trying to catch her breath. She lowered her voice to mimic her date.

"Just talking to a big client… should be worth two million…"

She began giggling again, this time a high-pitched peal that made her eyes water.

"I'm sorry," she said. "It's not that funny. It's just—"

"The stress of it gave you the giggles," said Declan.

Charlotte turned to him.

"Yes. How did you know that?"

He shrugged.

I just feel like I know you.

"Where do these people come from?" he asked, changing the subject. Charlotte's infectious laughter and his glee at Brad's douchebaggery had filled him with giddiness.

"Atlanta, apparently."

"You should have said something. I could have come in and saved you."

Charlotte looked at him, her eyes glistening with laugh-tears.

"You'd have done that?"

"In a second."

Charlotte smiled. "That's sweet."

"It is, isn't it?"

Charlotte slapped him lightly on the shoulder and wiped her eyes.

Declan pulled into Pineapple Port and slowly made his way over the speedbumps to Charlotte's house.

"So I'm allowed in?" he asked as they stepped out of the car.

"Yes. Though the decor hasn't changed much, I'm warning you now."

"Don't go changin'."

Charlotte opened the door and Abby rushed to do her meet and greet. Declan gave her a good head scratching and stepped inside. When he looked up Charlotte was staring at him, smiling.

"What?" he asked.

"Nothing. How come you don't have a dog? You seem to like them."

"Oh, I love dogs. Mine just died, two months ago. Arnie. He was originally my grandmother's but she died when he was still pretty young. It's still hard for me to think about getting another right now."

"Oh no. What kind was he?"

Declan stood and retrieved his wallet from his back pocket. He pulled out a photo of a monkey-faced dog with large eyes.

Charlotte grinned. "Such a cutie. Brussels Griffon?"

"Yes. How did you know?"

"I stitch them."

"What?"

"I'll explain in a bit. Can I get you something to drink?"

"Um, sure. Do you have a beer?"

Charlotte nodded and moved toward the kitchen. Declan followed her but stopped to study the black wall covered with chalk scribbles between the living room and the kitchen. He hadn't noticed it last time, but then, there'd been some distractions.

He touched it.

Chalkboard paint.

"I suppose a chalkboard wall doesn't help make the place less dorm-like," said Charlotte, opening the beers.

"I guess it's kinda hip," he said. His gaze fell upon his address scrawled on the wall. There was a loopy circle drawn around it.

Is that a heart around my address?

Declan glanced at Charlotte and then moved to take a place on the sofa. She joined him and handed him his beer. He tried hard not to stare at the stacks of books scattered around the room. The urge to find them a shelf made his face twitch.

"So did you have more information?" he asked.

Charlotte nodded slowly and took a sip from her beer. She looked uneasy. She'd been forthcoming, if not excited, to share other news with him so he couldn't help but be intrigued about this new information.

She took a deep breath and began.

"Mariska, Darla, and I put your case through the *Dateline* filter..."

"The *Dateline* filter?"

"Do you watch *Dateline*?"

"No. I mean, yes, sometimes. Here and there."

"If you watched any at all, you'll know nine times out of ten it's the husband."

"I think I do recall that trend."

"There has to be a motive, and it is always money, sex, drugs, or all of the above."

"Sure. Or rock and roll, but that's less common."

Charlotte smiled. "Ha. Right. So anyway, following those general guidelines, the husband theory is out, because your father was already dead."

"Right..."

"So that takes us to the boyfriend."

"George."

"Right, maybe, but what if it wasn't George?"

"They found love letters..."

"But his guns didn't match the ballistics."

"He probably ditched the gun he used. I mean, that only

makes sense. Don't they always throw the gun in a pond, too?"

"Yes... But let's say for the sake of argument, George is cleared."

"Is he? Is that what you have to tell me?"

"No. I know it's hard for you to understand... but we've all known George for years. Decades. He's not the killing type."

"Did you think he was the having-an-affair-with-his-young-secretary type?"

"No. Fair point. But if you knew his *wife*... let's just say that is easier to imagine."

Declan took a sip of his beer. He felt agitated. He had a hard time grappling with the fact that George's guns had come back clean. In his mind, George had to be the killer, but he could see the wheels of justice were going to roll slowly. He wanted this all behind him. He wanted his mother's killer found. Removing the most likely suspect from the list would mean little to no hope of identifying the killer, and he didn't want to think about that.

"So where are you going with this?" he asked, trying his best not to take his simmering anxiety out on Charlotte.

"We know George wasn't her only boyfriend."

Declan's hand stopped in mid-air, his beer inches from his lips. He lowered the bottle.

"You're not trying to imply Seamus had something to do with this? Is that why we had to meet here? Or did you just need a ride home?"

Charlotte blanched.

"I'm sorry. I didn't mean that the way it sounded. You're right. Tell me what you know."

"I..." Charlotte fidgeted and rubbed her right temple with her fingers. "Seamus had motive on every level. He was your mother's boyfriend. He was no doubt jealous of the other man who may or may not have been George. If he adopted you after her death, he stood to receive her insurance money."

Declan put down his beer.

"You're kidding, right? He's a *cop*."

"Cops make mistakes. And he wasn't a cop yet. Maybe that's

why he became one, to do good to make up for—"

Declan stood. "Or maybe he became a cop to help people in situations like he found himself in when his girlfriend went missing."

"That could very well be." Charlotte also stood. "And I'm not saying Seamus did it, I'm just saying it isn't totally out of the realm of possibility. Maybe just keep it in mind—"

"Seriously? You know how long you've known George? Well, I've known Seamus longer than that. *He didn't do it.*"

"He probably didn't. It's just—"

"It's just what?"

"He's dating my friend Jackie…"

"And you're afraid he's going to *kill* her?"

"I—" Charlotte clenched a fist. "I don't know. But it seems irresponsible to not mention it to her…"

Declan gritted his teeth and whirled toward the door. "You're way off base with this one. I've got to go."

"Declan, please, I didn't mean to upset you. I want to find your mother's killer as—"

Declan paused, his hand resting on the doorknob. He turned to Charlotte.

"As much as I do? No, Charlotte, I don't think you do."

"I'm sorry, that was a stupid thing to say. I—"

Declan opened the door. He took one step onto the landing and nearly crashed into a man walking up the short flight of cement steps. The sandy-haired man juggled a bottle of liquor, nearly dropping it to the ground. Declan glared at him and then looked at the bottle. It was Butterscotch Schnapps.

Brad.

"Your buttery nipple is here," he called out, pushing past the man.

"What the hell, dude," said Brad, grabbing the railing to steady himself as Declan passed.

Declan saw Charlotte arrive at the doorway as he flopped into his car and turned the ignition. She wrestled to lock the dog inside and stood on the porch, staring at him. He put the car in reverse and then paused, wondering if it was safe to leave her with the creep who had been so rude to her earlier. He stared at Brad. Brad was staring at Charlotte, his eyes sweeping down her body. Brad turned and looked at him.

Did he just smirk at me?

"Dammit," he said, punching the steering wheel with the side of his fist. He slammed the car back into park and got out.

"You," he said pointing at Brad. "Go. Get. *Now*."

"Who the hell are you?" asked Brad, his attention now focused on Declan. "I think that's up to her," he added, throwing a free thumb in Charlotte's direction.

"Go," said Charlotte.

"Hey, easy girl. I was just trying to say sorry things didn't work out so smoothly today," said Brad. "I didn't know your *boyfriend* was here. But you're obviously over him. Why don't we just go inside and let everyone cool off."

Brad moved as if to enter the house and Charlotte thrust her arm across the doorway to block him. His lip snarled.

Declan saw white. He strode forward and grabbed Brad by his shirt, yanking him from the stairs and pulling him to the driveway. He wanted to put himself between Brad and Charlotte.

"Go. Before I turn that bottle into a butterscotch enema."

Brad caught his balance against the house. He stared angrily at Declan, but after sizing him up, he shook his head and scoffed.

"Screw you both," he spat, turning to walk away. As he moved, he threw the bottle of schnapps and it exploded to the ground, splashing his Teva sandals with sticky liquid.

Declan took a few steps toward Brad and the man picked up the pace, pausing only to flash his middle finger from the middle of the road.

Declan looked at the sweet pool of liquor at his feet.

"Sorry about that," he said.

"A butterscotch enema?" asked Charlotte.

Declan began to smile and then squelched it. He couldn't stop thinking about what she had suggested.

How well do I know Seamus?

"You good?" he asked. "Do you want help with the glass?"

"I'm fine. But Declan, please—"

He waved her off.

"I have to go. Be careful. Leave the booze for now and go inside."

He returned to his car. He lowered the window and stuck out his head.

"And lock your door," he called to her.

He pulled away as Charlotte stood on her small porch, her arms crossed against her chest, watching him go.

CHAPTER TWENTY-FOUR

Declan slammed the door to his house a little too loudly. Seamus popped his head around the corner.

"You okay? Starting to think entering a house like a grizzly bear on meth is your signature entrance."

Declan sighed.

"I'm fine."

Seamus disappeared again in the direction of the guest room. Declan stared where his uncle's head had been for a full minute, and then followed him to the back of the house. He looked into Seamus' room and found him packing towels into a small gym bag. Next to the bag was a dingy pair of tighty-whities underwear, an empty sports bottle, black lifting gloves, and a .38 special revolver.

Declan's gaze settled on the revolver, though he could feel the dingy underwear screaming for attention.

"I'm not sure what to mention first. That those underwear should be burned or that there is a revolver on your bed."

"They're my lucky underwear," said Seamus, picking them up and thrusting his finger through a hole in the cheek. "I was wearing them the day I was shot in the bum, instead of the spine or the head." He wiggled his finger back and forth so Declan could appreciate the luckiness of the briefs.

"Please don't do that."

"And the gun," said Seamus, pulling the underwear off his finger and picking up the revolver. "It's the gun I used to bring down the man who put the hole in the underwear."

Declan watched Seamus brandish the weapon, Charlotte's voice echoing in his head.

He's the perfect suspect.

The gun had a silver barrel and pearl handle.

"That doesn't look regulation."

"Oh, it isn't. I brought it with me to Miami. Always kept it near. See this?"

Seamus stepped forward and Declan took a half step back.

"You afraid of guns?"

"No. I— You just caught me off-guard."

Seamus shrugged and pointed just above the grip. "Look at the scrollwork there, see it?"

"Looks like an 'S.'"

"It is. 'S' for Seamus. The moment I saw it at the pawnshop, I knew it was my gun."

"Was that before or after mom disappeared?"

Seamus pulled his head back like a turtle and stared with his jaw set.

"After. What's that got to do with anything?"

Declan shook his head. "It doesn't. I don't know. Everything comes back to her lately."

Seamus switched the gun to his left hand and patted him on the shoulder. "I know, boyo, this is all terrible. Hey, maybe sometime soon we can go to the range and do a little shooting. I'll teach you a thing or two."

Seamus opened a drawer and put the gun inside.

"So what's with the bag?"

"I'm going to go for an evening swim with Jackie."

"Shouldn't you take your lucky underwear?"

"I don't need luck when it comes to the ladies."

Seamus grinned and walked passed Declan, who followed him to the front door. Seamus tipped an invisible cap as he left.

Declan traced his upper lip with the tip of his tongue, staring at the closed front door. He heard the sound of Seamus' car roaring to life and saw it through the sidelight window as his uncle pulled away. He waited a moment longer, whirled, and pounded toward Seamus' bedroom.

Declan opened the drawer where Seamus had thrust his gun and was surprised to find it still there. It was so *real*. A tiny part of him thought the gun would disappear before he could get to it—as if it never existed.

He reached to grab it and then stopped.

Should I worry about fingerprints?

The technicians would find Seamus' prints all over it, of course. He'd just watched the man grip the handle. Prints weren't the goal. Now that he knew Seamus had a gun, he could ask Sherriff Frank to test the ballistics against the bullet found with his mother's bones. When it came back negative it wouldn't *prove* his uncle's innocence, but it might help.

He thought about asking his uncle to submit it, voluntarily, but worried. What if he said no? How well did he know the man? They'd only spoken a handful of times in fifteen years.

What if Charlotte was right?

She'd made a compelling argument. No, he hadn't wanted to hear it, but it was a good argument nonetheless.

Declan looked for something to use to pick up the weapon. He turned and spotted the graying underwear still on the bed.

No.

Choosing a tube sock nestled in the drawer beside the weapon, he gingerly lifted it, the weight driving home the reality of the situation. He carried it to the kitchen, where he dropped it into a gallon Ziploc bag. He grabbed a magazine off the table and slipped the bag between the pages. Tucking the entire package under his arm he headed out the door.

Twenty minutes later, Declan stood on Sheriff Frank's doorstep. The gun, and any secrets it held, were out of his hands.

His stomach roiled and he took a deep breath to calm his nerves. The guilt of handing his uncle's gun to Frank paled only in comparison to his desperate need to find his mother's killer. It was too late to second-guess his decision to turn in the weapon, but now the urge to confess to his uncle chewed at his guts like a hungry rat.

A rat. That's what I am now, right?

He tried taking another deep breath.

Whoever said breathing exercises calmed the nerves had less important things to worry about.

Looking to the left he saw Charlotte in her driveway, resting her face against her hand, staring with her one uncovered eye where he knew a broken bottle of butterscotch liquor lay smashed. In her other hand, she held a hose. She stood that way until he reached her house. She looked up and jumped at the sight of him.

"You're back."

"I am. I see you hung on my every word and locked yourself safely in the house."

"I had to pick up the glass," she said, motioning toward a lumpy trash bag sitting against the side of the house. "Just finished hosing the gunk into the grass. The ants are going to think they've died and gone to ant heaven."

"And wake up with terrible little ant hangovers."

"I can only hope I made the right decision. Believe it or not, this is the first time I've experienced a butterscotch schnapps attack."

"Really? That *is* surprising. I figured you trailer park girls were swimming in the stuff."

Charlotte chuckled. "So what brings you back to my neck of the swamp? I thought you were mad at me."

"I'm not mad. I'm agitated. Not at you, with your suspicions."

"Did you ever leave? You weren't watching me from behind the bushes, protecting me from evil, were you?"

"No, I thought about what you said and you're right, the circumstantial case against Seamus is… *compelling*. I'm sorry for the way I reacted."

"Oh don't apologize. *I'm* sorry. I wasn't trying to upset you at all. I just—"

Declan watched as Charlotte's gaze shifted from his eyes and focused behind him. He turned and flexed, expecting to find

Brad bolting up the driveway toward him, brandishing a bottle of Goldschläger.

"Hey, Charlotte," said a man at the foot of the driveway.

Declan didn't recognize him. He wasn't Brad. He was older and taller, a bit pudgy around the middle.

Charlotte gasped and he turned to see what face accompanied such a noise. *Elation? Shock? Horror?* He studied her expression and settled on *surprise...* with a touch of something else. *Concern?*

"Junior? Is that you?" she asked, her eyes darting in Declan's direction.

The man waved.

"Yep. Came by to support Dad through this bullshit. Mom's a mess, as you can imagine."

"Right. Of course, um..." Charlotte looked at Declan and he could see she was at a loss for words. He turned to introduce himself, but before he could take a step, Charlotte found her voice and blurted her next sentence like a warning.

"Junior, this is Declan. He's the son of the woman I found."

Charlotte's tone made Declan pause. Junior's face went ashen and he heard the man's last comment replay in his head.

Came by to support Dad through this bullshit...

Declan swallowed. Junior began to raise a hand as if to shake, but thought better of it and let his hand fall. He nodded to Declan.

"I'm sorry about your mother, but I can promise you my father isn't responsible," he said.

Declan offered a stiff nod of his own. He couldn't imagine the appropriate response.

"I haven't seen you in forever," said Charlotte, clearing her throat. "Are you staying long?"

"No," Junior wiped the sweat from his brow and took a step backward into the street. "You know I hate this place."

"You escaped young."

"You're still here, I see."

"Oh, well, you know. The closer I get to retirement the more it seems senseless to leave."

Junior smiled. "What are you, twenty-five now?"

"Twenty-six."

"Ancient. I remember when you were a little kid running around. Get back to me when you turn forty."

"You had a kid last I heard?"

"Yep, two. Just had another girl last April."

"Still living in Philadelphia?"

"Boston now. Got a new job up there."

"Oh, well, good for you."

"You married?" his gaze shifted from Charlotte to Declan and back again.

"Me? No. Got a dog though, if that counts."

"Sounds good to me. Believe me. Two kids are a handful."

"No doubt."

"Well, good to see you, Char."

Junior waved again and with a last nod toward Declan, continued his neighborhood walk.

"Good to see you. Have a safe trip back."

Junior nodded without turning.

Declan turned and met eyes with Charlotte.

"George's son," he said.

Charlotte nodded. "Junior. I hope it wasn't rude to call him that; it's all anyone ever called him around here."

"Probably half the reason he wanted to leave."

"I'm sure now he goes by—"

Charlotte stopped and looked toward Junior's retreating form, her lips still poised to say the word that came a moment later.

"George."

"Hence the 'Junior,' right?" said Declan, wondering where that beautifully complex mind of hers had gone this time. "What's wrong?"

"I'm doing math in my head," mumbled Charlotte. "I hate math."

"Can't say I'm a fan."

"Your mother was in her early thirties when she went missing. She was young for George Senior, but George *Junior* might have been a more logical match as a boyfriend."

Declan scowled and looked down the street, a small part of him yearning to run after the man. He wanted to grab all the possible suspects and throw them into a building until someone confessed. The building he'd require to achieve this just kept getting bigger and bigger.

"You think *that* guy killed my mother? You think my mother dated *him*?"

"George, Junior had access to the foot of his father's orange tree."

"What?"

"The love letters were signed *George*. It could have been either one of them. He probably wouldn't have signed them Junior if he was trying to be more grown-up, especially dating an older woman."

"You've got to be kidding me. You just got done telling me all signs point to my uncle, and now you're saying it might be *that* guy?"

"I don't know. We have to consider the possibility."

Declan ran both hands through his hair and stared into the sky.

"Oh Charlotte," he said with a groan.

"What? What's wrong?"

"I wish you'd come up with this theory about an hour earlier."

CHAPTER TWENTY-FIVE

"You *what*?" asked Charlotte, her voice rising toward a screech. Declan had asked her to step inside and they stood in her living room. Abby sat nestled in the corner of the sofa, staring at them from beneath heavy lids.

"I gave Seamus' gun to Frank for ballistics testing."

"What gun? His police gun?"

"No, he had a gun out on his bed when I went home. He said he bought it here, years ago."

"To kill your mother?"

"Yes. Of course. He said, 'What's that Declan? Oh, that old thing? That's just the gun I bought to kill your mother.'"

"I'm sorry. That was a stupid question. But really... maybe it wasn't that weird since you came home to find him with a gun lying around willy-nilly on the bed."

"Willy-nilly? Charlotte, you *have* to start hanging out with people your age."

"What did he say?"

"He said he got it at the pawnshop shortly after Mom went missing. It used to be his, you know, the pawnshop."

"He gave the shop to you?"

"He sold it to his partner, Bonehead. He came over from Ireland with Seamus and my father. Seamus sold his half of the shop at a rock-bottom price, with the understanding that if Bone died, he'd leave it to me in his will. The guy didn't have any kids, so he was fine with that. He died young. Cancer."

"Bonehead?"

Declan pointed to his head. "He had a lumpy skull. Liked to hit things with it."

"Things?"

"Other people, mostly. It's an Irish thing."

Charlotte closed her eyes and raised her eyebrows, shaking her head. She had a headache. She needed an aspirin. She spotted two sitting on the counter where Al had emptied his pockets.

That'll do.

She popped them into her mouth and poured a glass of water to wash them down.

"Okaaay… Did your uncle say why he took the gun?"

"Maybe to protect himself… maybe to kill the person who killed Mom, I don't know. I didn't get into a whole conversation about it."

"Why not?"

"I think before I even realized my intentions, I was trying to play it cool in hopes he'd leave the gun behind. He was getting ready to go swimming with Jackie and he'd put the gun in a drawer."

"With Jackie." Charlotte flopped on the sofa next to the wheaten, who lifted her head in annoyance and then collapsed back down on the pillow.

"Tell me he didn't take the gun with him to see Jackie."

"No, that's what I'm trying to tell you. He left the gun and I started thinking about what you said—about him being the perfect suspect. Next thing I know I'm taking the gun to Frank for testing. I felt like a robot on cruise control."

"Holy moly. It was the right thing to do but maybe you should have asked him? It seems kind of sneaky. I'm sort of impressed and horrified at the same time."

"Join the club."

Declan sat on the wooden folding chair that was making a poor attempt to fill a corner of the room. He couldn't decide if he felt the need to sit or if he just felt sorry for it.

"He's going to be mad," said Charlotte, tilting her head back on the cushion and staring at the ceiling.

"I know. But I was afraid he'd say no and the gun would go missing. I had to know; I couldn't miss my chance... but I feel terrible."

He wobbled back and forth, testing the strength of the rickety chair.

"Can I please bring you some furniture from the shop? This is ridiculous."

"You can sit over here. I can kick Abby off the sofa."

"No. She's the only other person in the room who could be less comfortable than me on this thing."

Charlotte looked up and smiled. "You called her a person."

Declan shrugged and tapped his knuckle against his lips, thinking.

"I should tell him now."

"Who? Seamus? Tell him you just gave his gun to Frank?"

"Yes. It would make me feel a little less dirty and I could judge his reaction. See if he looks worried."

"He'll probably be mad, innocent or not, so I'm not sure how good a gauge that would be."

Charlotte sat up straight. "But you said he was swimming with Jackie. We can go to the pool, you can tell him what you did, and I can check on Jackie. Two birds, one trip."

"It pains me that you think he could hurt Jackie."

Charlotte pulled down the corner of her mouth but remained silent. Declan thought for a moment and then slapped his hands on his thighs.

"Fine. Let's go."

Declan headed for his car but Charlotte waved him toward her golf cart. Everyone in Pineapple Port had a golf cart, and Charlotte's was cherry red with *Sweet Charlotte* painted on the side in gold script. Declan had never noticed the detailing before and stopped to study it.

"I know. It's awful. Mariska had it detailed for me as a birthday gift one year. Don't even say it."

"I wasn't going to say anything," said Declan, sitting in the passenger seat. "I think it's *sweet*, Charlotte."

Charlotte punched his thigh and he grinned.

With Charlotte's foot pressing the pedal to the floor, it took two minutes to reach the pool. They heard the sound of laughter as they approached. Declan saw his uncle and Jackie in the center of the pool. Seamus picked her up and whirled her around in the water.

Charlotte and Declan paused and watched them frolic until the waterlogged couple ended up locked in an embrace, kissing.

"Oh god. I'll never unsee that," said Declan, covering his eyes.

Charlotte went ahead and he followed, averting his gaze as they approached. He didn't see anyone else in the pool area.

"Seamus," he called.

Seamus removed his lips from Jackie's and turned toward the voice.

"Declan. What are you doing here?"

"I need to talk to you. Can you come over to the edge?"

"Can't it wait?"

"No."

Seamus looked at Jackie, shrugged, and began wading toward the edge. Charlotte patted Declan on the shoulder and whispered *good luck* before splitting off to walk toward Jackie.

"What is it?" asked Seamus. "I'm kind of busy here. It's not her fault. I'm irresistible."

"I have to tell you something."

Seamus stared, silent. Declan swallowed and squat down so he could lower his voice.

"I... um... you know that gun you had on the bed?"

"What about it?"

Declan took a deep breath and decided to confess the way one might rip off a Band-Aid; quickly and cleanly.

"I gave it to Frank."

"Frank? Frank who?"

"The Sheriff."

"Why?"

"Because it was brought to my attention that when it comes to suspects in Mom's murder, you fit perfectly. You had motive, access, and possibly the weapon."

Seamus' eyes grew wide and his lip curled into a snarl. He reached up and grabbed Declan by the lapels with both hands, yanking him forward. Declan scrambled to catch himself but fell face-first into the water. He scrambled to find his feet and pushed away from his uncle, feeling no resistance. He stood and wiped off his face, sputtering, ready for the next attack.

Seamus stood facing him, breathing heavily. From the corner of his eye, he saw Charlotte running toward them. He heard Jackie calling Seamus' name as she waded toward their end of the pool.

"Why would you do that?" barked Seamus.

"I had to know."

Seamus took a step forward and Declan raised his fists.

The large smile on Seamus' face took a moment to register. Declan lowered his hands a few inches.

"Why are you smiling? You're messing with my head. Cut it out."

"I'm smiling because I would have had to know, too."

"You're not mad?"

"No. Not really. It's always a little annoying when someone suspects you killed their mother. Particularly, when that woman also happened to be the love of your life... but it showed courage."

"To sneak behind your back?"

"True enough, I wish you'd just asked me. I would have given you the bleedin' gun. But it took courage to search for answers you might not want to know."

Declan's shoulders unbunched. He took a deep breath.

"You are a puzzle," he said.

"Being unpredictable keeps you alive," said Seamus, slapping the water.

"So we don't have anything to worry about?"

Seamus shook his head and then stopped and knit his brow. "Well, now that you mention it... that might not be *entirely* true."

"Why?"

"The gun is unregistered and the serial numbers have been rubbed away."

"Seriously? Did you do that?"

"I refuse to answer on the grounds that it may have definitely been me."

"You said you got it at the pawnshop. The gun had to be registered."

"Oh I'm sure it was when it came in, but once I appropriated it for my use…"

"And what was your idea there?"

"I had my reasons. But those reasons had nothing to do with your mother."

"Frank was going to run the test himself. Maybe he won't even ask about it. I didn't tell him it was your gun."

"Really? Trying to protect your old uncle?"

"No. I just thought I might want to kill you myself if it came back positive."

"Fair enough."

Seamus lunged forward, grabbing him by the neck, and they wrestled to push each other underwater. Once they'd tested each other's strength, they separated, both trying to clear the water from their eyes and noses. Declan found Charlotte staring at him from the side of the pool. She was squatting, dragging her fingertips along the pavement.

"Boys are so stupid," she said.

"You said it," said Jackie. "What are you two going on about?"

"So, who gave you this cockamamie idea about me?" asked Seamus, ignoring Jackie's question and looking hard at Charlotte, his eyebrows raised.

"*Dateline*," she admitted. "But I guess everything is going to be okay?"

"Right as rain," said Seamus, wading over to Jackie and putting his arm around her. He was about to walk back toward the center of the pool when he turned.

"Oh, hey, Charlotte. Did you find some pills at your house? Al said he might have left some there by accident. When he emptied his pockets?"

"He did—I just took them. I had a little headache. Did he want them back?"

Seamus looked at Jackie and then back at Charlotte.

"Uh… no. Don't worry about it."

CHAPTER TWENTY-SIX

"When do you think Frank will have the results?" asked Charlotte as they pulled into her driveway. Declan sat next to her, his wet polo sticking to his shapely chest like a wet suit. It was not an unpleasant effect.

"He said he'd rush it. He left right after I gave it to him, but I don't know how long it takes to get the results."

Declan stepped out of the golf cart and looked at his car. He scowled, and Charlotte realized he didn't want to get his car wet.

"Why don't you stay for dinner?" she asked.

"I can't. I mean, I'm all wet."

"Like you're going to ruin my expensive furniture?"

Declan snickered. "I guess I'm safe there. Though, I might warp your fine wooden folding chair."

"Haha. I have things you could wear. I have a whole shed full of clothing for stitching out back. I could grab some sweat shorts and a tee."

"For stitching? That's right; you were going to tell me about that."

Charlotte motioned for Declan to follow and she led him through a gate into her fenced back yard. The moment they entered, they came face to face with the grave.

"Oh—" said Charlotte, stopping so quickly Declan bumped into the back of her. "I didn't think—"

"Don't worry about it," said Declan, touching her shoulder and speaking softly. "I've already seen it. It's okay."

At the feel of his touch, a shiver ran down her spine. She hadn't been ready. It felt good. She wanted his hands on her.

Run your hand from my shoulder down my arm. Touch my neck.

"This your shed?" he asked, walking toward the building in the corner of her lot.

Charlotte mourned the loss of his touch, before snapping to and realizing she was standing in front of his mother's previous resting place.

Oh my god. I just got hot-to-trot in front of his mother's grave. What is wrong with me?

She followed Declan toward the shed.

"Yep, that's the sweatshop," she said, a little too perkily. She cleared her throat and tried to find a more appropriate pitch.

She wanted to touch him. She wanted to run up and tackle him. *Why do I want to touch him?* She could barely fight the urge.

"I have a fair amount of odds and ends stock. I'm sure I can find you something," she said.

Charlotte spun open the Masterlock. The ridges of the knob felt good against her fingertips. She opened the doors to the spacious shed. She flicked on the light.

"Electricity and everything."

"Look at that thing. It's huge," said Declan, admiring the embroidery machine. Resting on its metal stand, it stood over five feet tall.

"It only has one head, but it's all I can handle, really," said Charlotte as she slid out a large cardboard box of clothes. She paused.

I did not just say that.

"Who needs more than one head, really," said Declan.

Charlotte glanced at him to find him lightly touching the various knobs of the machine. She felt giggly.

Should I point out he's fingering my knobs?

She snorted a laugh.

"What?" asked Declan.

"Nothing. Sneeze. Dusty. Here."

She stood, holding a pair of men's sweat shorts. The fabric

felt softer than usual. This was a really good pair. She squeezed the cotton between her fingers, stroking it with her thumbs.

"I knew I had a pair. Black, extra-large. Will that work?"

"That's perfect, thank you. I'll pay you for them."

Declan reached out to take the shorts. They tugged back and forth for a moment.

I can't let go of these shorts. They are so soft.

"Can I have them?" he asked.

She reluctantly released them, her fingers still rubbing against each other as her hands dropped to her sides.

"The tees are inside. Red okay?"

"Perfect. Then I'll match your golf cart."

"Haha."

Declan nodded toward the machine. "So you sew things on that?"

"*Embroider*," she said, holding up a golf headcover with the face of a Golden Retriever stitched on the side. "I don't *sew*."

This golf headcover is so fuzzy. I never noticed before...

"And you sell them here?"

"What? Oh, yes. Here and online. I'm a satellite office for friends of mine up north. Mariska's son has an online store, Doodlesport.com."

"Doodlesport? Is that an embroidery term?"

"No, it's a dog. They named it after their Labradoodle."

"Oh. Cool."

She brushed past Declan and felt a shiver again. With a furtive glance toward the open grave, she broke into a trot and opened the backdoor.

"Hold on," said Declan.

Charlotte turned to find him pulling his shirt over his head. His hands stretched above his head and she could see the muscles dance across his ribs, the grooves above his hips leading down to where his wet shorts clung to—

Oh holy hell.

Charlotte turned back toward the house, standing rigid as if someone held a gun to her back.

Well, in a manner of speaking...

"Maybe I can keep from getting everything wet if I leave this outside?" said Declan.

She closed her eyes.

I think you're a little late, buddy.

She turned, slowly, because she couldn't decide on the appropriate expression and was afraid she'd look like a cartoon wolf.

She decided on "passively disinterested," but as she froze her expression into place, she felt more as if she radiated "maniacal mannequin."

Declan held his shirt in his hand. He had the chest of a Greek god.

No—an Irish god. Are there Irish gods? There must be. Celtic, right? I'll have to look that up. I want to touch it. No. Shut up, Charlotte. What is wrong with you?

Charlotte admired the 'V' shape of Declan's torso. His shoulders were broad and muscular, but his waist was thin, though not disproportionately so. It was a classic swimmer's body. He had a smattering of dark hair on his broad chest, but it looked as though he trimmed it.

"Do you swim?" she heard herself ask.

"Do I swim?"

Are you blushing? How adorable is that?

He shifted the shirt he'd been holding out to his side in front of him, blocking her view of his midsection.

Dammit.

"I do."

"At the beach? Do you surf?"

"No, it's too far to go every day. I have a current pool in the backyard. The kind with the jets that let you swim in place? It was my big splurge. I don't love jogging."

"We certainly have that in common. You... uh... you just have that 'V' thing, you know, that surfers and swimmers get."

Declan shrugged. "Thanks, I guess."

"Your chest looks shaved. I thought maybe that was for speed?"

Why can't I stop talking?

Declan looked down at his chest. "I don't compete. It's just a little man-scaping, I guess. My last girlfriend said when it started to curl it was 'gross' and I got in the habit."

"Gross? What, is she afraid of actual men?"

"I caught her with another man, so I don't think fear of men was the problem."

"Oh. Sorry."

Wait. Did he say last girlfriend?

"You said last girlfriend. You mean the girlfriend before your current one?"

"There is no current one."

"But I thought you said you were good? At the shop?"

"What? Oh—I meant good with being set up with other people's grandkids. Not good, as in I have a girlfriend. Hey, can we stop talking about my grooming habits and love life and go in now? These shorts are starting to chafe."

"Sorry. There's an outdoor shower right here if you want to slip into the sweat shorts before you come in. We can leave your clothes out here to dry or I can throw them in the dryer."

"I'll just drape them over the shower. That works."

Declan threw his shirt over the wooden-slat wall of the shower and stepped inside.

Charlotte felt the urge. She fought it, valiantly, for a microsecond, and then spun and burst into the house.

One of the kitchen windows overlooked the shower. She ran to it and leaned over the counter. Slowly, she raised her head until her eyes were high enough to peek down. He had his back to her. The window was high enough that there was no reason Declan would look up and notice her, but it gave her a bird's eye view of *him.*

Declan's shorts fell to the ground with a heavy wet slap she could hear from inside.

Boxer briefs. Nice.

He fumbled with the new sweat shorts a moment, removing the tag. He paused. He seemed to be trying to decide whether to leave on his underwear. His thumbs hung in the waistband, toying with sliding them down.

Tease.

Declan nodded his head side to side and made his decision. He stepped out of his boxer briefs. Charlotte could see the flash of his white tush, glowing against the slightly darker skin of his sinewy back.

Mesmerized by the moon, she nearly didn't see him start to turn toward her. She ducked as if under fire, slamming her elbow into the edge of her stove, sending pain vibrating through her funny bone. She howled and slid to the floor, gripping her arm with her right hand.

A moment later, Declan burst through the back door.

"Are you okay?" he said, reaching her with one long stride.

Charlotte looked up at him, wincing in pain, waiting for the tingling sensation to subside. He wore sweat shorts and nothing else.

"Hit my funny bone," she muttered.

"How the heck did you do that?" he asked. As he did, he looked out the window. With his height, Charlotte knew he could see the view into the outdoor shower.

Whoops.

He squinted at her.

"I was over there," she said, pointing to the other side of the room. "And swung it back into the handle of the refrigerator."

"How did you end up on the floor over *here*?"

"I ran. You know, when you hurt yourself and you bolt? I ran and slid to the floor in pain when I'd run as far as I could. Which was here. In front of the stove."

"You could have just turned and kept running."

"That would have been *weird*."

She touched his leg. The hair felt brilliant beneath her fingertips.

He must have the best leg hair ever.

Declan grabbed the hand not stroking his leg and helped her to her feet.

Awww. She stared at his legs. She wanted to sit on the floor and touch them again.

Would that be weird? That would be weird.

She patted him twice in rapid succession on his right pec.

Bouncy.

"All better now, thanks," she said and moved away from the window toward the island counter to separate herself from the urge to play his pecs like bongos. She opened the refrigerator and stared inside, suddenly struck by how empty it was. It looked like her apartment. She grimaced and shut the door before Declan could see.

"I have a frozen pizza?" she said, opening the freezer side.

Declan walked over and stood behind her. She tried to box him out and prevent him from seeing. There was nothing inside except a pizza, a pint of mint chocolate chip ice cream, a bottle of vodka, and a bag of peas.

She reached in and pulled the lid from the ice cream. She grabbed a rugged chunk of it with her fingers and slipped it into her mouth.

Heaven.

She knew why she ate it. It wasn't for the taste. She couldn't believe she was about to act on the scenario running through her head, but she was going to do it.

I have to.

She replaced the lid and felt his fingers touch her hip as he leaned to peer inside.

You came to me.

Fool. You're mine now.

"That bag of peas looks outnumbered by junk food," he said.

He has no idea what's about to hit him.

Charlotte shut the door and turned. She looked into Declan's eyes and he stared back, silent.

"I have to do this," she said.

Charlotte placed her hands on Declan's chest and paused, feeling the rise and fall of his breathing, steady, but picking up pace. Emboldened by his acceptance, she slid her hands to his shoulders and lifted her chin, willing him to make his lips available to her.

He slipped his arms around her waist and leaned forward into her kiss. For a moment, she couldn't decide what felt better;

the kiss, or his willingness to follow her lead. He pulled his mouth from hers and kissed her neck, his teeth touching her skin with every other nibble.

She made her decision. The kissing was better. *Hands down.*

She tilted back her head and groaned quietly, the electricity of anticipation filling her chest and taking the fast train downward. He felt *amazing.* He leaned back against her kitchen island and pulled her closer.

Declan's lips returned to hers. Tongues touched, and the corner of her mouth found the chance to curl into a smile. Her world tasted like mint chocolate chip ice cream. She hoped he appreciated her makeshift breath mint.

Someone's knocking on my front door.

She wanted the idea clamoring through her brain to be a metaphor, but as the banging began a second time, she recognized her thought as literal.

She *did* hear someone at the door.

"No. No, no, *no.* You've got to be kidding me," she mumbled, barely removing her lips from Declan's. "Ignore it."

"I know you're in there," called a voice, accompanied by a third string of knocks.

I know that voice. Only one person in the neighborhood said "know" with two syllables.

"It's Darla," she said, resting her head on Declan's chest. She rubbed her cheek back and forth across his chest hair.

"You said to ignore her," he said, cupping the back of her head, his lips now resting on her hair.

"She has a key."

Declan sighed. "You better get it. She sounds determined."

"You have no idea."

Running her palms across Declan's muscular back, she forgot what they'd been talking about. She kissed his chest before the sound of her door opening threw her back into the present. She spun and saw Darla freeze as she looked up from Abby's bouncy greeting and spotted them in the kitchen.

"Oh—oh—I'm so sorry. You never—you—I was worried…"

Charlotte's back was to Declan, but her right hand moved to

pet the soft cotton of his shorts along his outer thigh. It was soothing.

"It's okay Darla, what do you need?" It was hard to find the breath to make the words. Her heart was racing.

She moved to take a step forward but felt a tug on her shorts. Declan had hooked his finger into an unused belt loop and pulled her back into position. The tug of the fabric against her hips made her long for missed opportunities.

"You have to stand in front of me," he whispered his tone, urgent.

"Why—" Charlotte took a step back and felt something against her butt. Something *hard*.

"Soft shorts," she whispered over her shoulder. "No restraint."

"I hope you mean the fabric."

"I don't," she said, reaching behind her back to feel for him. Declan made a little "aagh" noise of horror and spun away from behind her. He walked around the island and stood behind it, his elbows leaning on the tiles.

"Hi Darla," he said, waving. "My clothes were wet, we're waiting for them to dry."

"I can see that. Really. I'm at a loss for words."

"Darla," said Charlotte. "Since when are you such a prude?"

"Oh Char, I don't mean you two and what you'd call hanky-panky..."

"I don't think we would call it that. We're not a hundred and four."

"*You* might," said Declan in her ear.

Charlotte shot him a glare and they smirked at each other.

"You two are adorable," said Darla. "I don't care what you're up to. I invented that stuff. I've been hotter and heavier than that in an air-conditioned Kentucky laundromat at one o'clock in the afternoon."

"Please don't go there."

"Sorry. Anyway, what I'm trying to say is y'all can do whatever you like. Hell, if I were your age I'd—" Darla threw a hand out toward Declan. "Well, I don't want to give you any advanced ideas you might not be ready for. It's the fact that it is *Declan* here that has me flustered."

"She expected someone else?" he mumbled. Charlotte slapped the island behind her without turning. The sensation in her hand was like a pleasure firecracker.

What the hell?

"What do you mean?" she asked Darla.

"I came with news. Frank just got back. The test was positive on that gun you gave him, Declan. He needs to know where it came from."

Charlotte turned as Declan rose from his elbows and stood straight. Charlotte didn't worry about what Darla could see now. If finding out your uncle killed your mother wasn't a boner-killer, she didn't know what was.

CHAPTER TWENTY-SEVEN

"Seamus!"

Declan burst through the door of his home. Seamus wasn't at the pool and Charlotte had confirmed that he wasn't at Jackie's. When he arrived home and saw his uncle's car in the driveway, the mixture of dread and relief left him frozen in his seat for a full minute.

"Out here," called Seamus' voice.

Declan spotted him standing next to the lap pool, still wearing his trunks. He strode across the living room and slid open the door to join him in the backyard.

"What are you doing?" asked Declan.

"Well, I'm already damp and I'm lookin' at this contraption of yours. You're in good shape. I'm wondering if I could master it."

"Seamus, we need to talk."

"Oh, don't worry about it, boyo. I forgive you. I told you that."

"No, you don't understand. It matched."

"What matched?"

"Your gun and the bullet they found. Ballistics was a match."

Declan had never seen his uncle lose his cool. The man's face went pale as death.

"You're joking with me?"

"I wouldn't joke about this."

Seamus' legs buckled under him and Declan reached to keep

him from tumbling into the shallow pool. His uncle squatted on his heel, steadying himself with his fingertips on the ground.

"Tell me..." said Declan, trying to keep his voice as steady as the situation would allow.

"Tell you what? That I killed Erin? Are you mad?"

"Then how? How could a gun you've had in your possession for the last fifteen years match?"

"I feel sick..."

"Then tell me."

"I don't feel sick because I'm guilty, *eejit*." Seamus screamed, tapping the side of his head with his non-steadying hand. "Use your head."

"Seamus, I'm doing everything I can not to choke you right now. Do not push me."

"I'm sorry. Help me up, son."

Declan clenched his jaw and pulled Seamus to his feet. His uncle wiped his hands over his face several times as if trying to awake from a dream.

"What is it?"

"If I was the murderer, do you think I'd be standing here looking at your pool after you told me you gave my gun to the police? I'd be in the Maldives by now."

"Why the Maldives?"

"Non-extradition country."

"Should I ask how you know that?"

"Oh lord, they're going to look into me now..."

"Who?"

"The police."

"So? You're an ex-cop. That would only help you."

"I'm not an ex-cop."

"What?"

"I'm a CI. Well, a quasi-CI. Off the books."

"A confidential informant?"

Seamus looked at him. "Really? How many times are we going to cover what CI stands for?"

"I know what it *means*, but what are you talking about? All this time you weren't a police officer? What about the pictures you sent me over the years with you in uniform."

"Wearing the Santa hats? The boys gave me a suit to wear to make cards for you. My friends were officers. When I left here, I was a mess. I got in a bunch of trouble. Eventually, I got caught, but they had bigger fish to fry than me. I made a deal, and I did good. I'm a talented thief and a better liar, but my greatest gift is my gab. After that, whenever they wanted information about anyone, they'd slip me into that person's life. I could do things they couldn't."

"You made a *living* doing this?"

"I didn't need much. Got a lot of free drinks out of it, too. And I did some finding on the side."

"Finding?"

"Private eye stuff. Private cases. Off the books. Everything off the books. This might come as a shock to you, but the police don't always do things by the book."

Declan felt short of breath. He stepped back to take a seat on a patio chair.

"How am I supposed to believe anything you say after you just told me you were a professional liar?"

"Don't you see?" Seamus put his hands on his hips and threw back his head to stare at the sky. "I took the gun from the pawnshop. Someone sold it there a week after Erin's death."

"You took the gun after Mom's death…"

"I've been carrying around the gun that took her from me. I had the answer in my possession for almost *two decades.* My lucky gun. I might be the worst illegally operating CI slash private investigator that ever lived."

"Why would they sell the gun to your pawnshop? Was it a message? A final kick in the teeth?"

"I don't know," said Seamus. "But we need the old records. When are they coming?"

"Who?"

"The police. When are they coming for me? Are they here now?"

"No. I was at Charlotte's when Frank's wife came to tell her the news, but they agreed to give me a little time. I wanted to talk to you first. Charlotte knows it's yours, of course, but Darla doesn't, so she can't tell Frank. But Frank isn't a complete idiot. He'll put two and two together."

"How do you know Charlotte won't go right to Frank?"

"She won't."

"Are you sure?"

Declan flashed back to the memory of their kiss. When he left, she'd barely been able to stop touching him. He'd felt the same.

"Reasonably."

"Do you still have the old pawnshop records?"

"Yes. They're in the back of the store in boxes."

"Good. Take your car. I'll take mine and park it somewhere in a lot near the shop. They'll come here first looking for me, and if my car is gone they'll assume I made a run for it. It might buy us some time."

Seamus slapped Declan on the shoulder as he passed. He paused only long enough to grab his keys and then headed for the door. Declan found his keys and was almost to the door when it opened again, nearly hitting him.

"Whoa."

Seamus stuck his head in the door.

"If I didn't make it clear, I didn't kill Erin. You know that, right?" he asked.

Declan paused and then nodded. Seamus bear-hugged him and disappeared again closing the door behind him. Before Declan could grab the doorknob, Seamus opened the door and popped his head inside once more. He had to bob backward to save his nose.

"Are you trying to kill *me*?"

Seamus touched his shoulder to be sure he had his attention.

"Just an FYI, your girlfriend's on ecstasy."

"What?"

Seamus closed the door and was gone.

CHAPTER TWENTY-EIGHT

Charlotte sat across from Frank at Darla's kitchen table, staring at a photograph of Seamus' gun.

"It can't be," she mumbled, slowly stroking the cloth placemat, her head resting on her fist. It didn't feel as good as she thought it would. She didn't know a placemat could be so depressing.

"Charlotte, you have to tell me who the gun belongs to or I'm going to have to arrest Declan," said Frank.

"Why would you bring him in? He's the one who gave you the gun."

"He's interfering with an investigation by hiding the owner of the gun. So are you, at this point."

"Oh Frank, stop it," snapped Darla. "You're not going to arrest Charlotte."

"Darla, you stay out of this."

"Stop it," said Charlotte, sitting back in her chair. "I don't want you two fighting over me."

"Oh, we don't need you to fight, Sug. It only has to be a day that ends in *y*."

Frank scowled.

"Now look. The gun must be his uncle's. I'm going to go to his house now."

"He asked for a little bit of time," said Charlotte, her voice cracking into a whine she hadn't heard since she was a child. The last time she'd talked to Frank this way she was in the eighth grade and he was threatening to take away her skateboard for nearly knocking over Mrs. Taylor. Being raised by a community meant oodles of substitute moms, but it also meant multiple disciplinarians; some carrying more weight than others. Frank had been high on the list.

"It's been three hours. For all I know, he's spent all this time helping his uncle escape."

"He wouldn't do that."

"How well do you know him?"

"Pretty well, I'd say," mumbled Darla.

"What does that mean?" asked Frank.

Charlotte glared at Darla, who winked and turned to grab a cup of coffee. There was a short knock at the door and Mariska walked in with a bowl in her hands. Bob followed close on her heels with a platter wrapped in plastic.

"I brought pierogis," said Mariska, setting the bowl down on the kitchen island.

Charlotte smiled. Darla must have called Mariska to help distract Frank, who loved pierogis. The two of them were geniuses at manipulating men.

"What do you have there, Bob?" asked Frank.

"Meat tubes."

"Kielbasa," corrected Mariska, taking the platter from him. Bob shrugged.

Frank stood to get in line for food and then turned and looked at Darla.

"This is a setup."

Darla refused to acknowledge him, opting to plow ahead making a plate of food for her suspicious husband.

"I'm not going to forget what we're doing here," added Frank. "Charlotte, tell me who the gun belongs to, or I'm going to pick up Declan and his uncle right now."

"Right after you eat," said Darla.

"Fine."

"I have a new theory about the murder," said Charlotte moving toward the food. Frank couldn't make her talk if her mouth was full. She looked down into the bowl and saw the potato-filled dumplings floating in a sea of melted butter. Her stomach growled.

"Potato and cheese?" she asked.

Mariska nodded, already pulling a plate for her from Darla's cabinets. The two women knew each other's kitchens as if they were their own.

"I have some fabulous kielbasa, too. Sit down. I'll bring it to you."

"Hi, Bob," she said, sitting back down in her chair.

"Hey," said Bob from Frank's comfy chair. "I'm glad you were all hungry. If she asked me if I could finish that bowl one more time I was going to have to move out."

"Oh you shush," said Mariska, kicking the side of the chair as she passed it to put down Charlotte's plate.

Charlotte cut a pierogi in half with her fork and gobbled it down.

"I'll bite. What's your new theory?" asked Frank, sitting with his plate of Polish heaven.

"What if the love letters they found under George's orange tree aren't by George senior, but George junior?"

Mariska's mouth fell open.

"He's just a boy."

"He's in his forties now," said Bob.

Mariska shook her head. "Where do the years go?"

"He caught me outside and said hi; said he was back in town to support his parents. But maybe he's back in town to make sure he isn't about to get in trouble himself?"

"Maybe. If he was guilty he'd be better off halfway to Mexico," said Frank, thoughtfully swirling a piece of kielbasa in a pool of mustard.

"Maybe coming to the scene of the crime isn't the best move, or maybe that's the best way to keep control of things," suggested Charlotte.

"We found out about the letters from an anonymous phone call. Why would he set his father up for the murder after all these years? And how could he be sure we wouldn't know the letters were his?"

"Maybe he didn't make the phone call and his father took the blame to protect him. Maybe he's here to thank him and help."

"This just keeps getting worse and worse," said Mariska, trying to sneak a second piece of sausage onto Charlotte's plate. Charlotte fought it off with her fork and then gave in as it found a home among the dumplings.

"All I know is Mariska and Darla aren't keeping any secrets," mumbled Bob. "If those two were in charge of keeping the enigma code in World War II, the Germans wouldn't have lasted a day."

Mariska glared at him and Bob returned to flipping through Frank's television channels without further comment.

"Did I see Declan's car in your driveway a little bit ago?" asked Mariska.

Charlotte rolled her eyes. She hadn't done a thing in her entire life that Mariska didn't see, judge, and comment upon.

"Yes. Twice. First time, I shared my theory on Seamus and he was none too happy. Then Brad showed up and what a mess."

"Bingo," said Frank. "I knew it was Seamus."

"Declan was jealous?" asked Mariska.

Charlotte stared at Frank a moment, cognizant that she'd slipped. Frank definitely knew the gun belonged to Seamus now. She decided not to make it worse and turned to Mariska.

"When I say it was a mess, I mean that literally. Brad brought me some cheesy cocktail ingredient to make up for being a bore earlier and, long story short, Declan ran him off. His revenge was to throw the bottle on my driveway."

Charlotte made an explosion noise and threw up her hands.

"I am going to talk to Gladys about that ass," said Darla, throwing a fork in the sink with a clatter.

Usually, Mariska would reprimand her friend for her language, but instead, she stood, grinning at Charlotte. It was unnerving.

"What?"

Mariska's smile grew broader. "Declan was jealous."

"He was just being a gentleman. He—"

Charlotte's cell phone rang and she stopped in mid-thought,

scrambling to grab it.

"Hello?"

"It's Declan."

"I know. What's going on?"

"Darla, did you get that pepper jelly recipe from Penny?"

Charlotte looked up from her phone. She could barely hear with Mariska talking in the background.

"I'm sorry, what did you say? I'm here with everyone. Did you talk to—" Charlotte shot a furtive glance at Frank and then decided there was no point in hiding the owner of the gun anymore. "Did you talk to Seamus?"

"I did; it wasn't him. We—"

"I did. I got the recipe and I found out what we did wrong with the last batch. Turns out you have to—"

Charlotte huffed. "For the love of Ball canning jars, will you two hush?"

"Sorry," mumbled Darla.

"I'm sorry, can you say that again?" she asked Declan.

"We traced the gun to the original owner. Seamus said he took the gun from the pawnshop, but he never bothered to see who'd sold it. We went to the shop and found the old bill of sale. You'll never guess whose gun it is."

"We don't have to use pectin at all," whispered Darla as she picked up Charlotte's plate.

"We don't?" replied Mariska in the same volume ten whisper.

"Aah," said Charlotte, sticking her finger in her opposite ear. "Who?"

Charlotte's jaw fell slack.

"Come here," she said. "Frank's going to come get you if you don't show up, so just come here and bring the paperwork."

Charlotte hung up and took a moment to stare at Darla and Mariska as she shook her head.

"What?" asked Darla. "Oh. Like *you* knew you could make jelly without pectin."

Charlotte put down her phone and turned to Frank. As she did, there was a knock on the door.

"Could this place be any louder?" asked Charlotte.

"Was that Declan? Is he coming here?" asked Frank.

"You're all crazy," mumbled Bob from his chair. "Are there any pierogis left? You didn't eat them all, did you?"

Charlotte locked eyes with Frank, trying desperately to block out the commotion.

"Declan confronted his uncle about the ballistics test."

"So it *was* Seamus' gun."

"Yes. But he didn't do it."

"That's something for the lawyers to sort out," said Frank, waving dismissively.

"No, that's what I'm trying to tell you. Seamus used to own the pawnshop before Declan. He took the gun from there shortly after Erin went missing. He didn't know who sold it to them, he just liked the gun. So he and Declan went to the shop and dug up the old pawn records."

"And?"

"And it was *George*. George Sambrooke sold the gun to the pawnshop ten days after Erin went missing."

Frank looked at the picture of the gun on the table beside him. He planted a stubby finger on it.

"'S' for 'Sambrooke.'"

Charlotte leaned forward to look at the photo and saw a swirly 'S' engraved into the gun just above the grips.

"Sambrooke?" said a voice.

Charlotte looked up and saw Penny standing beside Frank, two jars of pepper jelly in her hand. She looked down at the photo. Charlotte watched as the color in her face packed up and headed out of town.

"Why do you have a picture of my gun?" she asked.

A jar of jelly slipped from her left hand and bounced on the carpet, rolling to a stop against Charlotte's toes.

CHAPTER TWENTY-NINE

"You're telling me this is *your* gun?" asked Frank.

Penny nodded, almost imperceptibly. She looked as though she might fall, so Charlotte leaped up and put a chair behind her. Penny sat and touched the photo as if she was seeing a ghost.

Frank put his hand on Penny's. "This is important. Are you positive this is your gun?"

"George bought it for me."

"Penny, we need to go down the station. I need George…" Frank glanced at Charlotte. "Both Georges, to come in, too."

"Why?"

"Penny, we need to do this at the station."

There was another knock at the door and Darla left to answer.

"Should I go home and get my crowbar?" asked Bob.

"What are you talking about?" asked Mariska.

"So we can squeeze some more people in here?"

"Oh, shut up."

Declan and Seamus entered. Seamus walked a direct line to Frank and handed him the paperwork.

Frank took it.

"I'll do anything you want me to. I had no idea the gun killed Erin."

"What?" said Penny, her voice cracking.

"Penny, I need you to stay calm," said Frank, putting his hand on her shoulder. She jerked away from him and stood, the chair toppling behind her.

"That gun has only been fired once. Once. I shot at George. Not really—I was just trying to scare him. But I didn't kill anyone."

"Penny, I told you, we need to get you to the station—"

"What do you mean you shot at George?" asked Darla.

"Darla, dammit—" said Frank, but he was cut short by Penny.

"He was having an affair. He was sleeping with that girl."

"What girl?" asked Seamus.

"Erin."

"Penny!" roared Frank.

"It didn't even come close to hitting him. It went into the closet. You can still see the mark. He took the gun away from me and I never saw it again."

"Penny, don't say another word," said Frank in his most stern voice. Charlotte shivered at the sound of it. "Is George at the house?"

Penny stared at him, shaking, her eyes wild.

"Penny, is George at the house?"

"You said not to say another word," screeched Penny.

"You can answer my question."

"No. He and Junior went fishing."

"Where?"

"Out of Tampa."

"When will they be back?"

"Tomorrow afternoon."

"Okay. Penny, I'm going to ask you to come with me so we can do this properly." Frank turned to Declan and Seamus. "I want you two to come as well."

Seamus and Declan both nodded.

Declan looked at Charlotte and she bit at her lip, unable to do anything else.

"Call me if you need anything," she said.

Declan answered with a tight smile. He paused, and then leaned down and kissed her on the lips. He held the kiss for five seconds and then with one last look, turned to leave.

"Oh my," said Mariska.

"That was kind of romantic, huh?" said Darla to her.

Charlotte smiled. She tried not to, but it was hopeless.

Frank ushered Penny out of the house with Seamus and Declan on his heels.

Mariska, Darla, Bob, and Charlotte remained in stunned silence as the door closed behind them.

"So..." said Bob after a moment. "Was that a *no* on the extra pierogis?"

Mariska sighed.

"So are you thinking what I'm thinking?" asked Charlotte.

"That Frank's bourbon has been left unattended?" asked Bob rising from his chair and shuffling toward Darla's lanai. "I'll hide it. It will make him crazy."

"That George is guilty as sin?" answered Darla, watching with little interest as Bob headed for her husband's liquor cabinet.

Charlotte shook her head. "We have to go to Penny's house."

"What are you talking about?" asked Mariska.

"Penny said she shot into the closet and you can still see the mark. We should go look for it."

"Frank will figure it all out," said Darla, returning to her dishes.

"But what if she gets word to George and warns him? What if there is evidence that goes missing by the time Frank can get George into the station?"

"The police have to do things by the numbers," said Mariska.

Darla turned. "But we don't."

"Exactly," said Charlotte. "If Penny calls George and tips him off, who knows what will go missing by the time Frank gets there."

"But how will we get in?" asked Mariska.

"The door is probably open," said Charlotte.

"And if it isn't," said Darla, slipping into the office off the kitchen. She returned with a small case. "I've got my lock picks."

"Your lock picks," said Charlotte, ogling Darla. "Who *are* you?"

"Her second husband was a thief," said Mariska.

"I learned all sorts of fun things."

"I'm going home," said Bob, Frank's bourbon under his arm. "You broads are nuts."

Charlotte sat on Penny's back step. She had agreed to meet Mariska and Darla there in fifteen minutes.

"Hey."

Charlotte jumped at the sound of Darla's voice. She was clothed in black. Charlotte could barely see anything but the parts of Darla's face that weren't covered with camouflage.

"What is on your face?"

"It's dark blush. Can you see me?"

Charlotte stepped closer. In the dim light of the half-moon, she saw a tinge of red on the dark powder covering Darla's face.

"You look like a baboon's butt. Why did you have such dark blush? Were you trying out for Bride of Frankenstein?"

Darla shrugged. "It was a phase."

"Hey," said another voice. They turned and found Mariska wearing dark slacks and a black sweater with a giant goldfish in the center of it.

"Girl, I can see that goldfish from a block away!" said Darla.

"It's the only black, long-sleeve thing I had."

"Well turn it inside out."

Mariska muttered 'fine' and began pulling the sweater over her head. She didn't get far before she froze with her hands above her head, her arms bound by the same sweater that now covered her face.

"What are you doing?" asked Charlotte.

"It's caught on my earring," said Mariska. "I'm trapped."

"Oh for crying out loud…"

Charlotte and Darla jostled to free Mariska's ear from the knitting. They managed to get the sweater back down.

"The fish is fine," said Charlotte. "Leave it. We're not Seal Team Six."

"Goldfish Team Three," said Mariska.

Darla snorted a laugh.

Charlotte sighed and tried the doorknob. Many of the

residents didn't bother to lock their homes, but no such luck with Penny.

"It's locked."

"Ooh—goody," said Darla, pulling her lock-picking pack from a navy fanny pack around her middle. "I need some light."

Charlotte put her phone on flashlight mode and covered it as best she could, concentrating the beam on the back doorknob. Little transpired without notice in Pineapple Port, and she wanted to get inside as quickly as possible.

The door swung open.

"Still got it," said Darla.

The three went inside and shut the door behind them.

"Which closet did she shoot?" asked Mariska.

"She didn't say. I guess we'll have to check them all."

Charlotte switched on a light.

"What are you doing?" asked Darla, ducking behind the kitchen island.

"She has blinds on all the windows, and if you were her neighbor, what would you find more suspicious: the lights on like usual, or a flashlight beam moving all over the darkened house?"

"Flashlight," said Mariska. She grinned. "I love trivia."

They moved from door to door, searching for some sign of a bullet hole. Charlotte went upstairs to begin her search, and after checking Junior's old room with no luck, began running her hand along the door of Penny's walk-in closet. She stepped inside and pulled a string hanging from a bulb to illuminate the ten-by-ten room. Her gaze fell upon a patch mark in the wall, about a foot from the carpet, left unpainted. She touched it and then looked at the outside wall. Slightly higher, she found a second patched area, concealed by paint. They had patched the wall but only painted the outside.

"Anything Char?" called Darla from just outside the master bedroom.

"Yes, I found it."

"Really?"

Darla scampered over and Charlotte pointed out the holes.

Mariska joined them a moment later and studied the marks as well.

"So she wasn't lying. She did shoot the closet," said Darla.

"In a jealous rage," added Charlotte. "She might have done George's defense some damage with that statement. Or her *own*."

"You don't think Penny could have killed her," said Mariska.

Charlotte shrugged and pointed at the higher location of the outer patch. "It looks like the bullet went down... so the bullet must have..."

She pulled back the carpet inside the closet to look for the bullet's final resting place. Several of the floorboards possessed a slightly different grain.

"Looks like they replaced the floorboards," she said.

"Why three?" asked Mariska peering into the closet.

"What's that?"

"Why three? It looks like they replaced three floorboards. The bullet couldn't have hit three of them, could it?"

"I wouldn't think so," said Charlotte, considering the possibilities. "Maybe a couple broke when they tried to pull them up?"

The familiar "whoop whoop" of a siren blared outside and the three of them jumped.

"It's the cops," said Darla.

"It's probably Frank," said Mariska.

"That's worse. We have to hide."

"Where?"

"The window seat," said Charlotte, pointing to a long bank of cushions beneath Penny's bedroom windows. She ran over to it and opened it. "Nearly empty."

"I can't get in there," said Mariska. "That's like trying to shove a ham into a can of beans."

"I can," said Darla. She ran over to the window seat and climbed inside.

Charlotte turned off the closet light.

"Get in the far corner of the closet over behind where the robes are hanging."

Mariska scurried inside the closet.

Charlotte ran to the window seat just as Darla was about to close it.

"Move over."

"Move over?" screeched Darla. "Are you crazy?"

"This was my idea."

"And I appreciate that, but there is no room to move over."

Charlotte snapped her gaze to the bedroom door. Someone was already in the house.

"Take a deep breath," she said.

"What?"

Charlotte clambered into the window seat, resting the lid on her back so it would close as she lowered herself onto Darla.

"We're like low-rent vampires," whispered Darla. "And your breath smells like kielbasa."

"You just had coffee, this is no picnic for me," Charlotte hissed back.

"If you're in here come out," called a man's voice.

"It's Frank," said Darla.

"Shhh."

They heard footsteps heading for the bedroom, and then nothing as Frank hit the carpet.

There was the squawk of a walkie-talkie.

"This is Frank. I don't see anyone at the Sambrookes'. The back door was open but no sign of forced entry."

"10-4 Sherriff," said a woman's crackling voice.

Charlotte held her breath waiting for Frank to leave.

That's when she heard the unmistakable sound of someone expelling gas.

Mariska.

"Oh she *didn't*," whispered Darla.

"Come out of there," said Frank. "Come out with your hands up."

"Don't shoot," said Charlotte.

"What the hell?" said Frank. "Charlotte?"

Charlotte rose out of the window seat in time to see Mariska walk out of the closet with her hands in the air. Mariska looked at her.

"Kielbasa," she said, moving a hand to her stomach. "Sorry."

Frank grit his teeth as he strapped his gun back in its holster.

"I could have killed you two," he said.

Charlotte stepped out of the window box and glanced at Darla, lying at the bottom, shaking her head, her eyes wide. She closed the lid.

"I'm sorry, Frank. We wanted to check out Penny's story before George got back," said Charlotte.

"What do you mean before George got back?"

"We thought if Penny tipped him off he might try and hide evidence and we wanted to confirm her story about shooting the closet. Look."

Charlotte walked to the closet.

"Mariska you can put your hands down now."

Mariska put down her hands and moved out of the way so Frank could follow Charlotte.

"You can barely see the patch mark from the outside, but it is clear on the inside and under here..." Charlotte pulled up the carpet. "You can see the floorboards are different. They've been replaced."

"Three of them," said Mariska. "We think that is strange."

Frank walked back out of the closet and stood with his hands on his hips.

"If this does turn out to be important to the case, it might be unusable if people find out we were snooping around without a warrant. I need you two to get out of here right now."

"I'm sorry," said Charlotte.

"I'm sorry, Frank," said Mariska as they moved to leave.

"You too, Darla," said Frank.

Charlotte and Mariska froze and looked at each other. Nothing happened.

"Darla. *Now.* I'm not playing with you."

The window seat creaked open and Darla sat up.

"How'd you know?" she asked, climbing out.

"There are few sure things in this world," said Frank, presenting a hand to help Darla out of the box. "But one of them is if two of you are up to something, the third isn't far behind."

CHAPTER THIRTY

Walking home from Penny's, Charlotte was so lost in her thoughts she didn't hear Harry come up from behind her.

"Hey Charlotte," said Harry. "I hear Seamus had a scare tonight."

Charlotte jumped, startled by his voice.

"What do you mean?"

"You don't have to pretend with me. I'm a cop, remember?"

"Ex-cop."

"Once a cop always a cop."

"How did you hear?"

"Seamus called Jackie and Jackie told me. I was with her in the clubhouse when he called."

"Oh. So you know about the gun."

Harry nodded. "George's gun. I'm glad things aren't getting off track. It seems pretty clear George did it, as much as I hate to say it. Finding the bullet cracked the case wide open."

"I guess. Penny says she only fired it once."

"*She* did? Penny fired it?"

"That's what she said. She said she shot at George to scare him. He took it away and that was the last she saw of it."

"Why would she shoot a gun in her own house?"

"Jealousy. Turns out George was having an affair with Erin, and Penny was trying to scare him."

"Really..." Harry wiped his brow with the back of his hand. The evening was muggy. "Well, I guess after that he used the gun to kill Erin. Must have felt he had to get rid of her if Penny was that upset."

"Seems a little extreme."

"I know extreme. You wouldn't believe some of the things I've seen…"

Charlotte struggled to find something to say before Harry launched into another cold case story.

"The weird thing was the floorboards—"

She stopped. She wanted to bounce what she knew about the floorboards off Harry. His cold case experience might give him some insight. Unfortunately, telling him about them would mean admitting they broke into Penny's home, and she had to keep that under wraps.

"What's that?" he asked.

"Nothing."

Harry stared at her a moment in silence.

"Is Penny home? Did they pick up George yet?" he asked.

"Last I heard Penny is still at the station. George and Junior are out fishing, unreachable until tomorrow."

"Hm. Hopefully, they aren't trying to get away."

"I don't think so. He doesn't know the gun's been found. He probably thinks it's long gone. Dumb luck that Seamus ended up with it, all these years."

"Dumb luck has taken down more than one killer. Dumb luck and *me*."

"I keep thinking it *has* to be someone else."

Harry shrugged. "I hope so. But I doubt it considering the evidence. I'll see you later."

He strode off into the darkness.

"See ya."

Charlotte went home and checked her phone for messages. She hoped Declan would call when he had the chance, but it was getting late.

Charlotte awoke to the sound of Abby barking and someone knocking on her door. She looked at the clock. It was seven-thirty a.m. She'd fallen asleep on her sofa, rolling the facts of the case over and over in her mind. She stretched and plodded the few steps to the door.

"We're going to take an apple cake to Penny," said Mariska, holding what she could only assume was the aforementioned apple cake beneath tin foil. Darla stood behind her.

"Did you get in trouble?"

Darla rolled her eyes. "Oh, you know how they bluster. Just had to sit it out and now everything is fine. Though I didn't mention we were going back to Penny's before he left this morning. Didn't want to upset the apple cake, if you know what I mean."

"Are you sure she's back? Or up? She must be exhausted from the stress alone."

Mariska clucked a string of tsk noises. "She's back. She called me, upset. I told her I'd bring her a cake. She's terrified about what they're going to do to George when he gets home but she can't reach him. He's not answering his phone."

Charlotte remembered Harry's warning that George might be making a run for it. Maybe he was right.

"I guess you want me to come with you? Can you give me a second?"

The ladies made themselves a pot of coffee while Charlotte showered and hopped into a clean pair of shorts and a v-neck tee. She'd stitched the tee herself; it featured a soft-coated wheaten face embroidered on the chest with *Abby* underneath it.

"Oh that is so adorable," said Mariska as she rejoined the ladies.

The three of them walked the block and a half to Penny's house. When she answered the door, Charlotte saw the dark circles beneath her eyes. For all Penny's pushy behavior, she always looked ready to tackle the world. It made Charlotte sad to see her so broken. Her maid, Maria, stood behind her, a concerned look on her face, no doubt worried that Penny had beaten her to the door. Penny didn't reprimand her. That was a bad sign.

"We brought you cake," said Mariska, holding out the plate.

Penny nodded toward it and Maria scurried forward to grab it.

"Can I get you some coffee? Some of the cake?" asked Penny.

"I'd love some," said Mariska. She loved her cooking, and rightfully so.

George strode up behind them, a cooler in his arms.

"Hello ladies," he said.

"George."

Penny wrestled the cooler out of her husband's grasp, put it on the floor, and hugged him. George stood still, his arms at his sides, his face a mask of confusion.

"We caught a huge tarpon, but I didn't expect this. What's gotten into you?" he asked, peeling Penny's arms from him.

Penny's eyes began to well with tears. Charlotte had never before seen any emotion in Penny other than smug satisfaction. It made her uncomfortable to watch.

"They found my gun," said Penny.

"What gun?"

"*My* gun. The one you bought me. The one I nearly killed you with."

George shot a look at the three other ladies.

"What are you talking about?"

"They know I tried to shoot you. But you need to tell me what happened."

"Penny, I don't know what you're talking about. I sold that gun eons ago."

"They have it," said Penny, stamping her foot. "And the bullet matches. Frank's coming to get you."

"Matches what?" George looked at Darla. "Is Frank here?"

"No. But he wants you. You and Junior."

"Junior headed for home when we left the boat. What do you mean by *the bullet matches*? What bullet? Matches what?"

"My gun. They found it and they matched it to the bullet that killed Erin Bingham."

"That's impossible," said George, meeting eyes with everyone in the room in quick succession. "The gun's never been used."

"Except by Penny," said Charlotte.

"Yes. Except by Penny. Apparently, she told you about that. She scared the crap out of me and I took it away. I had no use for it so I sold it to the pawnshop. I'd bought it in a pawnshop in Tampa and it was the first idea that came to mind."

"You bought it from a pawnshop?" echoed Penny, her lip curling. "But you had it engraved for me?"

"No, it just happened to have an 'S' on it. I was in there looking for golf clubs and saw the 'S' and… anyway, I sold it."

Penny scowled. "Why didn't you just go to CVS and get me a cheap teddy bear?"

"Honey, you *really* have to work on your priorities," said Darla.

"Can I ask you about the floorboards?" asked Charlotte.

"What floorboards?" snapped George.

"In your closet. The ones that were replaced."

"Replaced? I don't know what you're talking about."

"Can we go upstairs?"

"This is insane," said George, gritting his teeth. He found everyone staring at him and relented.

"Fine."

He stormed up the stairs toward the bedroom with everyone in tow.

George reached the closet and threw out his hands.

"Here we are. What can I do for you?"

Charlotte glanced at Mariska and Darla and then took the lead.

"When Penny shot at you, where were you?"

"I was standing about where you are," said George. "We'd been arguing. I came upstairs and Penny came into the room with the gun. She was very upset. She didn't mean for it to go off. But it did, missed me, and went into the wall."

"Here?" said Charlotte, pointing to the rough patch beneath the paint that she'd noticed the night before.

"Yes."

"The inside isn't painted, so you can see where the bullet exited," said Charlotte, stepping into the closet and turning on the light. She crouched down to pull up the carpet as George stuck his head inside.

"Mr. Sambrooke, do you want me to put the fish in the refrigerator?" asked Maria, stepping into the room. George ignored her.

"Under here, three floorboards were—" Charlotte pulled up the rug and froze, cutting her sentence short.

"Were what?" asked George.

"Blood," said Charlotte, in an exhaled whisper.

"What?"

George squatted beside Charlotte and inspected the floorboards.

"Is that blood?" he asked in an aghast whisper.

Charlotte stared at the floorboards, doubting her eyes. The night before the three slightly different floorboards had been there. Now, boards that matched the rest of the floor were there, dark with a deep red-brown stain.

Darla and Mariska clamored to push their heads into the closet.

"Oh my," said Darla. "But last ni—"

Charlotte pounded her fist into Darla's toe.

"Ouch," she cried, stepping back out of the closet.

Charlotte glared at her until she caught her eye.

"Darla, you have to call Frank."

"Did you kill her and put her in the closet?" asked Mariska, staring at the stains.

"We didn't kill anyone," said George, straightening. "This is the first time I've ever seen this."

Penny moved away and sat on the bed. As she did, Maria moved forward, walking slowly, focused on the closet. George watched her and stepped out of her way as she approached, such was her determination. She looked down and saw the floorboards. As she did, she gasped and covered her mouth.

"Maria, what's wrong with you?" asked Penny.

"The girl," said Maria.

"What girl?"

"Ms. Erin. She came to see Mr. George."

"Who? When?"

"A long time ago," said Maria. "She came to see Mr. George. She said it was very important. I told her to wait in the office. But—" Maria looked from George to Penny and back again.

"Maybe I should not say."

"Maria, don't be afraid," said George. "Tell us. What happened?"

"I was asking her if she wanted something to drink, and you both came home. Mrs. George was screaming. I—I knew it was about the girl. I… I knew."

"You knew I was having an affair with Erin," said George, his voice tired. He refused to look at Penny, who stared holes through him. "Go on."

"She said, 'What do I do?' and I said, 'Hide' but there was nowhere to hide in the office, so I pointed to the bedroom. Here she could hide under the bed or in the closet or in the window seat like the children used to."

Charlotte and Darla exchanged a look.

"Mrs. George, you were so upset. Mr. George ran after you. I forgot about the girl until I saw her opening the front door. She ran out of the house."

"Was she okay?"

"I don't know. Yes… She ran out of the door."

"Did you ever see her again?" asked Darla.

"No. Right after that Mr. George, you took the gun and drove away. Mrs. George, you went out on the patio with the bottle."

"The bottle?" asked Charlotte.

"The almonds," said Maria.

"Amaretto," said Penny. "I used to be quite fond of it."

"So Erin ran out of the house…" said Charlotte. "Was she hiding in the closet? Maria, this is important. Was she hiding in the closet?"

Maria paled and looked at the bloodstained floorboards. "As I left the room, yes, I saw her run into the closet."

Darla and Mariska gasped in unison.

"*You* shot Erin," said Penny.

Penny grabbed the post of her bed to steady herself.

"That's impossible…" she mumbled.

George looked pale. "I never saw her. I didn't know she was here… Penny?"

Penny shook her head.

"But who buried her?" asked Mariska.

All eyes turned to George.

"It wasn't me," he said. "I took the gun and drove to PJs to have a few beers. Then I went and stayed at my brother's for a night… maybe two. I left the gun in the glove compartment and sold it back to the pawnshop a few days later."

"Oh PJs," said Darla. "I forgot about that place."

"They made the best Stingers," said Mariska.

"Didn't they? I liked—" Darla caught sight of Charlotte's hard stare and stopped. "It was a nice little bar," she mumbled.

"Maria, did it look like the girl was bleeding?"

Maria shook her head and shrugged. "She went very fast. She didn't talk."

"But the stain?" Charlotte looked at Penny. "You must have seen the blood? Replaced the carpet?"

"We had hardwoods then," said George. "We installed the carpet years later."

Penny nodded.

"What about when you patched the wall? You had to have seen the blood on the floor."

"I didn't patch it," said George. "By the time I came back, it was fixed."

"I did it," said Penny, her voice nearly a whisper.

"You patched it?" asked George.

Penny nodded. "I had my drink and then I had it patched. I was so upset. I couldn't bear the idea of looking at the hole in the wall…"

"You had someone do it? So you didn't do it yourself?"

Penny huffed a mirthless laugh. "Of course not. I told him George was cleaning the gun and it went off. I was mortified."

"Him? Who?"

Penny stood. "I need a drink," she said. "I feel sick. My nerves… I need a drink. I couldn't have killed her. It was an accident..."

"Penny, this is important," said Charlotte. "Who patched it for you? Who saw the blood if it wasn't you and George?"

Penny shuffled down the hall toward the stairs, clutching her stomach with one hand and waving the other above her head as she went.

"Harry, of course," she said. "He did all our handiwork."

CHAPTER THIRTY-ONE

Frank and Darla came to Mariska's house while the technicians removed the bloody flooring for DNA testing. Charlotte was already there.

"You have to go pick up Harry," said Charlotte. "I mentioned seeing the floorboards before I could stop myself. Who else could replace the old floorboards but the guy who cleaned up the mess?"

"Let's think about this a second," said Frank, taking a sip of bourbon. "Why would Harry get involved?"

"Harry was George's foreman and all-around right-hand man back then, right? He would have been the guy at the building site. The guy who found Erin's body."

"But why would he bury her? Why wouldn't he just call the police?"

"He knew George was having an affair with her. Or maybe he saw the bullet hole and the blood and found her body the next day. He put two and two together and buried her to protect George. To protect his job."

"Maybe. But why try so hard to find the bullet *now*? The bullet that is the most damaging piece of evidence against George? He could have buried George years earlier." He realized what he said and winced. "Figuratively."

"*Did* he find it?" asked Charlotte. "Or did he already have it? Wasn't it strange that the professionals didn't find it? Isn't it weird he bought a metal detector? And wouldn't a guy who kept bloody floorboards probably keep a bullet if he could?"

"It was stuck in the floorboards?" said Darla.

"Oh my god," said Charlotte.

All eyes trained on her.

"What?"

"The bullet chipped her rib. It couldn't have been in the floorboards."

Frank's jaw fell slack.

"Oh no... he didn't..."

"What?" asked Darla.

"If he found the body... There was a chip in her rib where the bullet lodged. A chip with scratch marks around it. He didn't find the bullet. *He dug it out of her.*"

"Charlotte," said Mariska, horrified.

"He pulled it out of her before burying her for insurance. So he'd have some way to attach the crime to George in the future."

"That is disgusting," said Darla.

"Do you think Harry has been blackmailing George all these years?" asked Frank, thinking aloud.

"That happens on *Dateline* a lot," said Darla.

"This is crazy," said Frank. "You're sucking me into your craziness. Why would Harry bury the body, let alone dig a bullet out of it? George had to have done it. He's unaccounted for. He said after the blow-up with Penny he went to his brother's house, but his brother died of cancer years ago and can't corroborate his story."

"But Al can," said Charlotte. "He saw Erin on the side of the road wearing a red belt. Only, it *wasn't* a belt. She was bleeding out. Running for help and home, bleeding from a bullet in her gut. She was embarrassed for Penny to find her and thought she could make it."

Frank shook his head. "It's too much. You're saying Harry finds her body, knows she was sleeping with George, and figures *he* shot her? And then what? He buries her to protect George? Protect his job? And why protect him all these years only to throw him under the bus now? And if he was the anonymous tip about the love letters, how did he know about them?"

"He was the only one who knew I saw the clean floorboards. Who else could have replaced them?"

"Penny?" said Darla. "She slept there last night."

"So you're sure you told Harry about the floorboards last night?" asked Frank.

Charlotte nodded, recalling their conversation. She gasped.

"What?"

"I told him Penny shot at George and he said, 'Why would she shoot a gun in her own house.' Only I never said she shot at him in the house. I was doing everything I could to be sure he didn't know we were *in* the house before I slipped up with the floorboards."

"Hm. At the very least, I need to question him," said Frank.

"No. We have to get him to confess. We don't have anything to prove any of these theories."

Frank rubbed his hands over his head.

"I don't know, Charlotte. I don't know. We should turn over what we know and let the big boys find the truth."

He stood. "Harry isn't going anywhere and it's getting late in the day. I'm going to sleep on this. Darla?"

"I'll come home in a bit," said Darla.

"You and the gossip," he muttered. He waved goodbye and shuffled out the door looking tired and annoyed.

The moment he left Darla looked at Charlotte.

"What are we going to do?"

Charlotte chewed on her fingernail, deep in thought.

"We need to get into Harry's."

"How?" asked Mariska. She looked at Darla who was already poised to speak. "I know you can break in Darla, but what if he's home?"

"I know he takes a walk every night. There has to be a pattern." Charlotte looked at Darla. "This sounds like a job for Tilly."

Tilly was the biggest busybody in the neighborhood, and that was saying something.

"I'm on it."

Darla fished in her purse for her phone while Charlotte

mulled her plan.

"Tilly," said Darla. "What time does Harry walk and what's the pattern and time?... Harry Wagner, right... Okay... Left or right?... Okay... Time? Got it. What's that? I don't know what you're talking about... You live on the other side of the neighborhood, how could you... never mind. Okay, well, I'll let her know. Thanks. Bye."

"What was that?" asked Charlotte.

"She saw us breaking into Penny's."

Mariska scowled. "But she lives—"

"I know," said Darla. "I don't know how the old bat could have seen us sneakin' into Penny's. I think she's a witch."

Charlotte put her hands on her cheeks. "That means we're in The Book."

Tilly's obsessive-compulsive personality had spawned a mythical book of charts that everyone in Pineapple Port had heard about, but no one had ever seen. In the book, she logged every movement in the neighborhood. If it happened in Pineapple Port, chances were good that Tilly logged it in The Book.

"What did she say about Harry?"

"He leaves at seven p.m. during the summer, six after daylight savings time. He always goes to the right. He does the main loop three times and it takes him exactly thirty minutes unless he stops to talk to someone."

"Good," said Charlotte. "If he stays on the main loop, that means he doesn't pass his house again. Darla, I need you and your lock picks. Mariska, you stand post at the end of Harry's street so if he comes back early or it takes us longer than we hoped, you can chat him up and stall."

"Got it." Mariska looked down her hallway. "Do you think I should bring Bob for protection?"

They all looked down the hall. They could hear Bob snoring.

"You'll be fine," said Charlotte. "But if he has a shovel, *run.*"

CHAPTER THIRTY-TWO

Charlotte and Darla hustled through Harry's yard to get to his back door. It was still too light to spend time picking the front lock beneath the watchful eye of the Pineapple Portians. Especially since Tilly apparently had a crystal ball.

Darla unzipped her fanny pack, retrieved her lock picks, and went to work.

"Can you teach me how to do that?" asked Charlotte, watching with interest.

"Sure Sugar, as long as you promise to always use your powers for good."

Charlotte held up her hand. "I promise. I'll use my powers for good and for breaking into your houses when I run out of chocolate."

"That works. My definition of 'good' is pretty loose so you should be safe. I once broke into my neighbor's house to steal her peach jelly recipe."

"Shame on you."

"Well, the she-devil wouldn't give it to me after I asked nicely, *and* I gave her my shoofly pie recipe."

"Oh, well then, she got what she deserved. You didn't say it was a shoofly infraction."

"Exactly."

Charlotte heard a pop and the door opened.

"Tada," said Darla, shoving her picks into her pack.

"You need to get a utility belt, like Batman. The fanny pack just isn't as cool."

Darla grinned. "It's a diversion. It tricks people into thinking I'm less cool than I am."

They crept into the house, listening for signs of life. A low buzz combined with a steady percolating caught both their attentions. They turned in unison to see a large saltwater fish tank happily bubbling against the far wall of the living room. A yellow tang and a blue dory gawked at them from behind their glass prison.

"I didn't know he had fish," said Darla.

"Me neither. But then, people tend to shut down when you try to tell them what a cute thing your fish did that day."

Darla barked a sharp laugh. "Like boring the pants off someone ever stopped him."

Charlotte looked down the hallway. The layout of Harry's house was similar to Mariska's with a large combination kitchen/living area and a hall that led to the bathroom and bedrooms.

"I don't think he'd hide anything in his living room or kitchen. Let's go down there."

Charlotte could see the back bedrooms and the bathroom doors were open, but the first door on the right, the one that Mariska used as an office in her home, was locked.

"I'm guessing in here."

Darla pulled out her tools and got to work.

"It's also the only door with a key lock," she mumbled. A moment later, the door eased open.

The room inside looked like a cross-section of a police station. Even the floor had cheap linoleum tile instead of the carpet that ran through the rest of the hallway and bedrooms. There were binders and papers piled everywhere, and a phone with twenty unused extensions.

"Has he been working as a cold case detective from his home?" asked Darla.

"Maybe he consults?"

A two-drawer file cabinet sat next to a sturdy metal desk. Cardboard tabs labeled the drawers as *Solved* and *Unsolved*.

Charlotte opened the *Unsolved* drawer to find it full. She flipped through the tabbed folders.

"Jessica Hampton... Anthony Vera... These are the cases he brags about *solving*," she said, recognizing the names from Harry's endless tales of heroics. "They're all in the *Unsolved* drawer."

"He's been lying?"

"Unless he switched the labels on his drawers."

Charlotte pulled open the *Solved* drawer. There was only one folder hanging in it, labeled *Erin Bingham*. She looked over her shoulder at Darla before extracting the file and laying it open on the desk, careful not to disturb the mess around her. Inside were a few yellowed newspaper clippings about Erin's disappearance held together with a paper clip and a lined piece of paper with a sketch of a home and lot.

"That's my house," said Charlotte, noting her address scribbled in the corner.

The drawing of her backyard had an X where she'd discovered Erin's body.

"I don't think this is new. I think he made this drawing a long time ago."

Darla squinted at the paper.

"How can you tell?"

"It's done with a Bic pen model 3452, which they discontinued in two thousand two."

"Really?"

Charlotte smirked. "No, but wouldn't that be cool if I knew that?"

"Ha. That would be very cool."

"It just looks old. Maybe he did it to remember where he buried the body."

Another sheet of paper, clipped to photocopies of what appeared to be the love letters found at George's house, had the words 'orange tree' written in red ink.

The back of the folder held a plastic baggie. This wasn't the Ziploc she'd lent Harry at her home, this was an *official* evidence bag. Charlotte pulled it out and held it to the dying light filtering through the partially closed blinds. There was no mistaking what she held.

Darla stopped flipping through a pile of binders she'd found stacked against the wall and moved to the window, drawn by the contents of the bag.

"Is that *hair*?" she asked. "And blood?"

Behind a clump of dark hair tied with a string, a small swatch of white cloth stained reddish-brown sat, small and terrifying.

"It must be Erin's. It looks like there are nail clippings, too."

"Oh gross. Why?"

"In case he needed them?"

"For what?"

"For making sure George was arrested. See the scratchy little bubble in the bag? I bet the bullet used to be in here. He kept it waiting for the day he'd have everything he needed to finally solve the case. Namely, the body."

Darla covered her face with her hand. "This is so awful."

"This means he *had* to have buried the body. Where else would he have gotten her hair and nails? And she was already bleeding when he found her; he took a piece of her shirt."

Darla shook her head

"No. This is nutty fruitcake with a big dollop of cuckoo cream on top. Why didn't he just turn George in if he had all this evidence? Why would he *bury a girl*?"

"Maybe he found Erin, suspected George, and wanted more time to think about what he should do before he sent his boss to jail?"

Charlotte recalled the conversation she'd had with Harry on the day he'd found the bullet.

"He mentioned the request for a larger patio took him by surprise. Maybe they laid the cement over her and he lost his chance to go back? He said the extra work was a pain, but maybe he was angry about the cement for a whole other reason."

Darla stared at her, shaking her head.

"Baby girl, you had me up until the part *where he buried her*. There's no point in a sane person's life where you think, *well, I'll just bury this body for now.*"

"Yeah. I'm having trouble with that part, too."

Darla's gaze roamed over Harry's office, inspiring Charlotte to do the same. They ended up staring at a cheap particleboard shelf filled with books about forensics and cold cases. There was a boxed DVD set of the television show *Cold Case* and tiny figurines of police officers mixed with a single Sherlock Holmes. The bookend was a realistic human skull.

"I'm starting to get the shivers," said Darla, staring at the skull. "Please don't tell me that is real."

"Please don't ask me to check. I've had my share of skulls this year."

Charlotte looked back at the opened *Solved* drawer, devoid of files.

"Darla," she said.

Darla jumped. "What? What is it?"

Charlotte looked at her. "What if he was never going to turn in George?"

"Whaddya mean?"

"What if he wanted to solve a *cold case*? He *failed* in Chicago. When Erin fell in his lap, maybe he saw a chance to stack the deck in his favor."

Darla turned back to the bookcase.

"You might be right," she said.

Charlotte placed the hanging folder back in the drawer. As she did, she spotted a small megaphone tucked in the back. She grabbed it and held it aloft for Darla to see.

"I guess he likes to talk people off ledges, too," said Darla.

Charlotte squeezed the trigger.

"Hey Darla, we should get out of here."

Her voice sounded low and creepy.

Darla's eyes grew wide. "The anonymous phone call. That's the voice I heard when I answered Frank's phone; the call that told him about the orange tree."

"Shoot. My fingerprints are all over it," said Charlotte, rubbing the handle on her shirt.

"Now you're wiping off *his* fingerprints."

"They're going to find it in his file cabinet, shouldn't that be enough?"

Holding it with her shirt, she dropped the megaphone back into place and pushed the drawer shut.

"Why didn't we wear gloves?" she asked, rubbing down the handles of the file cabinet.

"I didn't think for a second we'd *find* anything. Certainly not locks of hair and some kind of sicko museum to cold cases."

"Look." Charlotte pointed to floorboards propped between the file cabinet and bookshelf. "There are the clean floorboards. He *did* swap them out."

"The crazy thing is this almost makes sense to me now," said Darla. "I don't know what that says about me."

Charlotte nodded. "I think we have it. Penny shot at George to scare him, accidentally hitting Erin who was hiding in the closet. When the coast was clear, Erin ran for home, but she was hurt worse than she thought. She ended up collapsing near my future home, possibly trying to avoid Al's car. Harry found her, maybe on his way back from patching the hole, maybe just before. Either way, he thought he had a case to solve."

"If he fixed the closet first, he would have seen the blood in the closet. Wouldn't he have said something to Penny?"

"Maybe he thought there was a fight and was embarrassed to say anything. Even patching a bullet hole, the blood was in a strange spot. You wouldn't assume a murder took place. You'd think maybe Penny punched George in the nose or someone cut their hand trying to fix the wall and then gave up."

"And then he found Erin and he knew their history..."

"Exactly. He realized the blood in the closet was hers, and hid her body so he could be the one to solve her case. He assumed *George* had murdered her, so he went back and swapped out the floorboards to have proof of Erin being there."

"But why wouldn't he think Penny killed her? She was the woman scorned."

"Would you call someone to patch your wall with blood in the closet if you'd just killed a girl there?"

"Probably not."

"And George was gone, mad at Penny. Harry probably thought he was laying low."

Darla sighed. "All this when that poor girl was trying to end it with George and do the right thing. What terrible luck."

Charlotte grimaced. "Let's get out of here. We have to tell Frank."

Darla took one step outside the room and screamed, which in turn made Charlotte scream. She caught her breath, still shaking, and stumbled forward, pushing her way into the hallway past Darla who stood frozen, staring toward the kitchen.

Charlotte saw the figure at the end of the hall. It took everything she had not to scream again.

"Harry," she said.

"I'll tell you what's terrible luck..." he said.

"Now Harry, don't do anything stupid," said Charlotte, holding up her hands as she visually searched him for weapons. He appeared unarmed. As her eyes adjusted to the dim light of the hallway, she saw he was pale as a boiled potato, beads of sweat covering his brow.

"Not *your* bad luck," he said, his voice hoarse. "Mine."

"What?" said Charlotte. She felt like she was clinging to the wing of a jet; no one was moving and yet everything was moving too fast.

"I was wrong again?" said Harry, putting his hand on the wall to steady himself. "Penny shot her?"

"Yes," she said, the world beginning to focus. "Harry, Erin was hiding in the closet. When Penny shot at George, the bullet went into the closet and hit her. Penny and George took their argument to another room and she ran out."

"Then you found her," said Darla, trying to push forward.

"Stay back," said Charlotte throwing out an arm.

"The hell I will," said Darla. "I've lived my life. You get behind *me*."

The two of them began to wrestle, both vying for human shield status.

"Stop it," barked Harry. "I'm not going to hurt either of you."

He turned and shuffled into his living room, flopping into his La-Z-Boy and breathing heavily.

The girls followed him.

"Are you okay?" asked Charlotte.

Harry's eyes opened and focused on her. "Cancer."

Charlotte remembered Harry's makeshift belt. She'd suspected as much.

"Harry, we need to get you to a doctor," said Charlotte. "You don't look well."

"Or maybe we'll just bury you in a yard for safekeeping," muttered Darla.

Charlotte shot her a look. "Call 911."

Darla found Harry's phone and dialed.

"I deserve that," he said, "I wanted to solve one case... I saw the blood. Thought George shot her..."

"But you buried her," said Charlotte. "How could you do such a thing?"

"She was already dead. Nothing could change that."

Harry clenched his fists.

"Harry?"

"Hurts," he hissed, straining against the pain.

"Just take it easy. Someone will be here soon."

Harry looked at her with his milky blue eyes.

"I'm sorry—"

"Harry, please relax. I'm not the one who can forgive you. What you did was a horrible thing. You kept her family in the dark for years."

"Tell them I'm sorry," he said, his voice a whisper.

"You're going to confess everything now, right?" she asked.

He nodded, grimacing with the pain. "If I can... I... I give up."

Harry's eyes closed and Charlotte heard the sound of sirens in the distance.

"They're almost here, Harry."

Harry didn't move.

CHAPTER THIRTY-THREE

"Hey Frank," said Darla. She was on her cell standing in Harry's front yard as they loaded him into the ambulance. "You wouldn't believe what happened."

"Darla!" said Charlotte. If Darla told Frank they broke into Harry's house, all the evidence they'd found could be inadmissible.

Darla waved her away.

"I was walking with Charlotte when we saw Harry just about collapsing as he went into his house. We helped him inside and they're taking him away in an ambulance now."

Nice.

"He doesn't look good. But I'll tell you what looks worse..."

Darla told Frank that while they were waiting for the ambulance they stumbled onto Harry's fake police station. The replaced floorboards were in plain view but, she'd let Frank come and inspect the rest of it.

"Who knows what you'll find," said Darla before disconnecting.

When she hung up Charlotte caught her eye.

"Did he buy it?" she asked.

"Not a word. But it's enough for plausible deniability. He's on his way over."

Terrified that Frank would forbid her from sharing all her new information with Declan, Charlotte put herself halfway down the street by the time he arrived at Harry's house. Mariska and Darla joined her and they walked home together.

"I never saw Harry," Mariska said. "I'm so sorry. I swear I kept guard the whole time."

"I think he stopped his walk early," said Charlotte. "He didn't look good. He probably took a shortcut home."

They told Mariska about what they'd found, and she gasped at every morsel of information. By the time they reached the bit about the bloody shirt, Charlotte was worried they might need a second ambulance for her.

Charlotte went home and called Declan. She tingled with excitement knowing she was a phone call away from giving Declan the closure he needed.

Case solved.

It wasn't until she began the story that she realized how horrific it was. Being accidentally shot by a jealous wife while hiding in the closet of a married lover wasn't the most glamorous way to die. Being buried by an obsessive-compulsive cold case detective was adding insult to injury.

Charlotte heard her voice relaying the details as if it didn't belong to her. Who was this girl telling Declan all this painful information? Why would she want to do that?

"So no one did it," said Declan when she was done.

"What?" She felt relieved that he was still on the phone and hadn't decided to kill the messenger. "I said it was *Penny*, remember? And then Harry buried her hoping to solve the case."

"No, I know," said Declan, his voice monotone. "But no one did it. Penny shot her by accident. What Harry did afterward is disgusting, but she was already dead. There's no real villain. No one for me to blame except maybe..."

Charlotte waited, but as the silence stretched, she realized who he had in mind.

Erin.

Erin and George had cheated on Penny, and she'd paid the ultimate price.

"I'm going to go," said Declan. "I have to tell Seamus."

"I'm so sorry," said Charlotte.

"It's not your fault. Thank you for letting me know. Thank you for your help."

"I—"

Charlotte fell silent. Nothing made anything better.

The phone disconnected.

A day went by, then two. Was she supposed to call Declan, or give him his space? She began scoring the days on her chalkboard, like a prisoner whiling away her sentence.

On day three, she broke down and called him, but the phone went to voice mail.

She understood Declan's need to be alone. Being accidentally shot by a jealous wife while hiding in the closet of a married lover wasn't the most glamorous way for his mother to die. He had a lot to process. He had every right to his space.

But she didn't have to like it.

On day four, she bought a shelf and neatly arranged the pile of books on her living room floor. She thought, *build it and he will come.*

He didn't.

It had taken her three hours to assemble the shelf and he never showed. Apparently, *Field of Dreams* and IKEA had little in common.

On day five, Harry passed away. It didn't help that there would be no earthly justice for his part in Erin's disappearance. The doctors said he died of complications from bone cancer, but Charlotte suspected he'd succumbed to a broken heart. Even after doing unspeakable things to ensure his success, he couldn't solve a murder. At eighty years old, he'd blown his last shot at cold case glory.

Harry lived long enough to confess everything to the police, including how he stole George's trash for weeks in hopes of finding more evidence against him. He discovered George and Erin's love letters, which he buried beneath George's favorite orange tree. For Harry, the letters confirmed George's guilt. He never dreamed Penny might have pulled the trigger, or that

Erin's death could have been an accident.

He planned to plant evidence until the police found it impossible *not* to arrest George. Along the way, he also intended to claim responsibility for the identification and capture of Erin's killer.

His last words were, "I moved the file..."

The nurses didn't know what it meant, but Charlotte did. Harry had prematurely moved Erin's file from *Unsolved* to *Solved*. Maybe he thought he'd jinxed the case by moving it from cabinet to cabinet before his suspect's conviction.

Or maybe, in the last moments of his life, he relived the fleeting joy he'd felt moving that file to the *solved* drawer.

On day eight, Charlotte returned to Harry's home when his son arrived to run an estate sale. She hoped Declan would show, but he didn't.

When it was clear the pawnbroker wouldn't appear, she bought Harry's forty-gallon fish tank for twenty dollars. The yellow tang alone was worth that. She thought adding the tank to her living room could be a first step toward "décor." What was more Florida décor than a fish tank?

By day nine, Charlotte had to wonder if Declan's absence meant more than a need for alone time. She couldn't enter her kitchen without remembering the way she'd spied on him in the shower. The way she'd pounced on him like she'd been lost in the desert and he was a tall drink of water.

Mortifying.

He was probably *terrified* to see her again.

So embarrassing.

They seemed to get along so well and then...

Shameful.

Every time she recalled petting his leg hair her face burned and her stomach flipped like a small-time crook. Only a complete *psycho* would do something like that.

What had come over her?

She needed to embroider a scarlet 'N' on all her shirts for

'*Nymphomaniac.*'

Was he *so* irresistible?

Well, yes.

But still… Why? Why? *Why?*

On day ten, she was considering the pros and cons of Googling the proper way to commit hara-kiri when there was a knock on the door. She peeked through the window.

Seamus.

She flung open the door.

"Is he okay?" she blurted, her heart swelling with hope.

This explained everything. Declan was in a terrible accident and slipped into a coma. He's in a wheelchair and that's why he can't meet me on top of the Empire State Building…

"Whoa. Hello, Charlotte."

Seamus held up his hands as if protecting himself.

"Hello. What's wrong with Declan?"

"Declan? Nothing."

"Oh," Charlotte's heart and face fell.

So this wasn't An Affair to Remember. Bummer.

Seamus tilted his head. "Did you *want* something to happen to him?"

"Huh? No. Of course not. It just would have been—never mind. What's up?"

"First, thank you for all your help with Erin. I haven't had a chance to thank you."

"I didn't do anything, but you're welcome."

"Second, I need you to do me a favor."

"What?"

"Go to the pawnshop."

"Is Declan there?"

"Yes. That's the point."

"But… he hasn't called or returned a message… I don't think…"

"Just take my word for it and go. He's thinking of you, I promise."

Charlotte grimaced.

"Did he ask?"

"In a fashion."

"I don't know…"

"I'll give you twenty bucks," said Seamus.

"You don't have to pay me."

"Then go."

"Fine. Now?"

"Yes, now."

"Fine."

"Good."

Charlotte closed the door and went to her room to get ready. She would have taken more care with her appearance, but through her bedroom window, she spotted Seamus waiting for her in the driveway. She reached for a summer dress and then changed her mind, opting for a less form-fitting polo and shorts outfit. She would have worn a goat-hair turtleneck and a solid gold chastity belt if they'd been handy. She didn't want to scare him away again.

Sweetness and light. Humility. Decorum.

"I'll drop you off," said Seamus when she left the house.

She looked at his truck. It felt strange to drive off with him. Just a few days earlier, she'd thought he was a murderer.

"I can borrow Mariska's car," she said.

He shook his head. "I'll drop you off."

"Fine."

Charlotte allowed Seamus to chauffeur her to the store. Though she begged, he refused to offer any further hints as to what she would find there.

Seamus pulled up to the door of the Hock o' Bell and stopped the vehicle.

"Get out," he said.

"Yeesh, fine. You are the rudest kidnapper."

She got out of the car and stood in front of the entrance. She wondered if Seamus would give her a moment to vomit.

"Go *in*," he said.

"I am."

"Now."

"I am."

"Open the door."

"Fine."

Charlotte shoved the door and it opened to the familiar tinkling bell.

She stepped inside and froze.

This is a bad idea.

She was about to turn and leave when she heard him.

"Hello. Welcome to—"

She turned toward the voice.

"Charlotte?"

"Hi."

"Hi."

Declan stared at her for a moment before speaking, just in time to stop her from babbling.

"What are you doing here?" he asked.

"I'm not entirely sure."

She turned to motion to Seamus, but he and his car were gone.

Figures.

"Um, so how are you?" she asked beginning to stroll around the shop. It was too uncomfortable to stand and stare at him. She wanted to hug him and tell him how sorry she was for his loss *and* her behavior, but she couldn't touch him. It was like being a monkey in a cage and someone had left the bananas just out of reach.

Bananas? What is wrong with you?

She squinted, trying to think of a better simile, and stubbed her pinky toe on a dresser.

"You okay?" he asked.

"Fine," she said through gritted teeth, keeping her face turned from his.

"Well, to answer your question, I'm good," he said. "I think I've come to terms with everything. I realized not much has changed. Either way, Mom's gone, but now I know what happened to her. That's better than *not* knowing."

Charlotte nodded, still avoiding his eyes.

"Good. I'm glad. If there's anything I can do…"

Something touched her shoulder and she turned to find Declan standing behind her, a tiny smile on his lips.

"You're walking away from me and I need you to stay right here," he said.

"Why?"

"Because there are two things you can do for me."

"What?"

Declan touched the side of her face with his hand, his thumb tracing her cheekbone. Both Charlotte's natural urge to deflect affection and her desire to appear less aggressive failed her. She leaned into his touch.

Maybe Mariska's hug therapy is working after all…

"I want you to go to dinner with me," he said, looking into her eyes.

"I think I can do that."

He leaned down and kissed her on the lips.

"I missed you," he whispered in her ear, his rough cheek brushing hers.

She led his mouth back to hers and kissed him again.

"I missed you, too. You didn't call back…"

"I know. It wasn't that I wasn't thinking about you. I was in a weird place. I wasn't sure I was ready… but seeing you here now… I can't think of anything I want more."

He gave her a peck on the forehead and then straightened, putting one arm around her shoulders.

"Which brings me to thing number two," he announced, waving his hand toward the corner of the store. "Voilà."

She looked, finding only more furniture and knick-knacks.

"What?"

"See this corner? This is proof I've been thinking of you. This is all for you. I mean, if you want it. I busied myself decorating your house… without your house."

"Really?" Charlotte said, scanning over the sofa set, tables, and lamps.

"It's totally up to you. I'm not pushing it on you. It just made me happy."

"You could have just called…"

"I suppose. This seemed easier at the time."

Charlotte smiled. "Thank you. I was going to ask you to help me pick out a few things. You have good taste… I mean, Abby will *love* sleeping on that sofa. I'll pay you for it all though."

She walked into the diorama of her living room.

"Except this lamp," she added. "Not a fan of the lamp."

"Yeah… I was on the fence with that myself. Good call."

"And seriously, let me pay for it."

"No, really, it's no big deal. Anyway, you've already done enough for me."

"What have I done to deserve a room's worth of furnishing? It's like I won a game show."

"You broke into Harry's house to prove what he did."

Charlotte closed her eyes and shook her head. "Try not to say that in public."

"It was *that* important to you to find my mother's killer. You did that for me."

"It was important. It kept me up at night. But it wasn't totally selfless," said Charlotte.

"What do you mean?"

She crossed her arms across her chest and took a deep breath.

"Before this all started, I felt lost. I didn't have… I dunno… a *calling*. I always thought my purpose would come to me, but as year after year went by, I had less faith."

"And now?"

"I want to keep trying to help people. I think I want to be some sort of private eye. Maybe your uncle could tutor me?"

Declan laughed. "Tutor you in what? Bad jokes?"

"Bad-assery. Detective stuff."

"The next time something interesting happens in Pineapple Port, you'll probably be fifty."

"That's true." Charlotte shrugged. "I'm still ironing out the details."

"Sheriff Charlotte," said Declan.

"I was thinking more like Charlotte's House of Snoopery," she said.

"That's terrible."

"I know, isn't it? But it's kind of cute. It would look good on a t-shirt."

Declan looked as if he was trying not to laugh.

"You'd better not be laughing at me," she said, slapping his chest.

Bouncy.

No. Bad Charlotte. Focus...

"I'm serious," she added. "This stuff made me feel *alive*."

"I'm not laughing at you. I'm just remembering... I think I know one reason why you felt so *alive*."

"What are you talking about?"

"Remember when we were in your kitchen?"

Charlotte blushed so hard she thought her eyebrows would burst into flames.

Oh no. Here it comes.

"I've been meaning to talk to you about that. I don't know what got into me—"

"I do," he said. "You were on ecstasy."

Charlotte laughed.

"Very funny."

"No, seriously. The pills you took. The ones Al left on your counter?"

"The aspirin?"

"Not aspirin. X. Al told Seamus he left ecstasy at your house."

"*Al?* Seventy-something, five-foot-nothing, Al?"

Declan nodded. "Apparently, there's some kind of underground club in Pineapple Port where the old folks get crazy..."

Charlotte couldn't find a way to close her gaping mouth. She remembered the feel of fabric between her fingertips. The gorgeous roughness of the cement around the pool...

"So you're saying *that's* why I felt so—"

Declan smiled. "Well, I like to think I had *something* to do with it."

Charlotte scoffed and turned to hide her smirk.

"Hey... if you're going to be like that I won't tell you what the divot above your lip is called."

"Oh," she said, turning. "I forgot to look that up. What is it?"

"A philtrum."

"Ew. That's not a very pretty word. Philtrum."

"Well, it has another name."

"What?"

He walked toward her and tapped her philtrum with his finger.

"Cupid's bow."

As he said the words, he leaned in to kiss her again. She reached up and pulled him closer to her.

When their lips parted, he smirked.

"I'm going to admit it. That was a little corny," he said. "I mean, it *is* called Cupid's bow, but still... corny. It sounded cooler when I planned it."

She nodded. "I wasn't going to say anything but... yeah. Not as corny as admitting you planned it but..."

Grinning, she hugged him and looked over her new furniture as he held her in his arms.

Decorating the house is going to be fun.

~~ THE END ~~

WANT SOME MORE? FREE PREVIEW!

If you liked this book, read on for a preview of the next Pineapple Port Mystery AND the Shee McQueen Mystery-Thriller Series (which shares characters with the Pineapple Port world!)

THANK YOU!

Thank you for reading! If you enjoyed this book, please swing back to Amazon and leave me a review — even short reviews help authors like me find new fans!

GET A FREE STORY

Find out about Amy's latest releases and get a free story by joining her newsletter!   http://www.AmyVansant.com

ABOUT THE AUTHOR

USA Today and Wall Street Journal bestselling author Amy Vansant has written over 20 books, including the fun, thrilling Shee McQueen series, the rollicking, twisty Pineapple Port Mysteries, and the action-packed Kilty urban fantasies. Throw in a couple romances and a YA fantasy for her nieces...

Amy specializes in fun, exciting reads with plenty of laughs and action -- she tried to write serious books, but they always ended up full of jokes, so she gave up.

Amy lives in Jupiter, Florida with her muse/husband a goony Bordoodle named Archer.

BOOKS BY AMY VANSANT

Pineapple Port Mysteries
Funny, clean & full of unforgettable characters
Shee McQueen Mystery-Thrillers
Action-packed, fun romantic mystery-thrillers
Kilty Urban Fantasy/Romantic Suspense
Action-packed romantic suspense/urban fantasy
Slightly Romantic Comedies
Classic romantic romps
The Magicatory
Middle-grade fantasy

FREE PREVIEW

PINEAPPLE

MYSTERY BOX

A Pineapple Port Mystery: Book Two – By
Amy Vansant

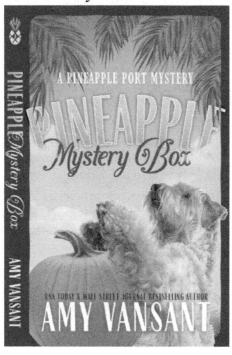

CHAPTER ONE

He didn't mean to kill her.

Well, he *did*, of course, but not that way. Not with a knife and not so soon. Now there was *ooze* all over his hand. The blood slipped down the back of the blade like a kid at a water park. His lip curled with disgust.

What a mess.

He'd spent a week researching sleeping medicines. *A week.* He hadn't spent that long studying for his GED exam. He'd spent *hours* driving to three different counties to buy the pills. *Real* sleeping pills, not capsules. Capsules would have been easier, crack them open and pour—but something in his gut told him she'd be able to taste whatever came out of a capsule. It must taste terrible or why stuff it in a gel cap?

He was half way home from the drug store before he realized he'd forgotten to wear the ball cap with the blond mullet flowing from the back to hide his mug from the cameras. *Idiot.* He pulled over and pictured his face on all those videos, like watching a tiny episode of *Dateline* in his head. After stressing for a good five minutes, he decided that returning *with* the mullet cap to buy new pills didn't make any sense.

He'd hit the gas. Nothing to do but hope he reached South America before the cops pieced together the mystery of Bobbi Marie's death. If his plan worked, the cops wouldn't even begin work on the outer edge of the puzzle. If his plan only *half* worked, he'd still be long gone before they completed the edges, started the center, and realized the picture was of him.

When *he* committed a crime it was like a puzzle of the *sky*. Sky puzzles were the hardest to solve. All blue, maybe some wispy clouds...

Yep.

I'm a sky puzzle.

Back at his apartment, he'd mashed his cache of sleeping pills with a mortar and pestle usually reserved for crushing mint leaves to make mojitos. Girls *loved* mojitos. His original plan had been to run to Mexico but he'd decided that was too predictable. *Everyone* ran to Mexico. And Brazilian girls probably liked mojitos, too. He'd started watching the Spanish television channels to learn the language. He'd be good either way.

After smashing half a sandwich bag of light blue powder, he rinsed his tools. Reaching to return the mortar to the cabinet, he paused, staring at the stone bowl. He'd crushed sleeping powder into every pore of the thing. Could he still take it to South America with him? He knew he'd knock the South American girls' socks off with his mojito recipe, but he didn't want to knock them—or himself—out. Did they have mortars and pestles in South America?

Dang. I should have done more research on South America.

He drove to a nearby strip mall, threw the bowl into a dumpster with a reverberating clang, and stopped at a store to buy a new set. This time he wore the mullet cap. It felt good to get some use out of it.

Back at home, he stirred the entire bag of sleeping powder into a pot of milk on the stove. He tasted it several times, adding a bit more milk here and a dash of sugar there until he found it drinkable. Bobbi would never notice a thing.

Sleepy-milk in a thermos, he drove to the old lady's apartment at *Casa Siesta*, letting himself in with the key he'd had cut while she napped one afternoon. She'd never noticed that he let himself in *or* that the woman assigned to her assisted living apartment had stopped visiting. He'd told the lazy nurse that he'd be taking over daily visits and she'd been more than happy to check Bobbi off her list.

"Hola! Ready for your warm milk, Bobbi?" He liked to practice his Spanish when he could.

Bobbi Marie glowered at him from her threadbare yellow sitting chair. She was a willful old broad, but her mind had been on vacation since he met her. She still puttered around the apartment and fed her ratty old cat, but the comfy chair absorbed most of her time. A small stroke had made it difficult for her to talk, so she barked everything in short staccato sentences that made him jump.

He was doing them both a favor by putting her out of her misery. Anyway, if anyone came around asking questions, the last thing he needed was her barking his name at the cops. If she even knew his name. He wasn't sure she knew her *own* name anymore. She only seemed to remember the dumbest things.

His eye fell on Friskie, napping in the window. The tabby's patchy fur looked worse than Bobbi's chair. The only thing *friskie* about that cat was its bladder.

I should send the cat with her. A nice bowl of sleepy milk for kitty...

"I'm practicing Spanish," he said, setting Bobbi's mail on her sofa table. "Thinking of moving to Brazil."

"Porch geese."

"What's that?"

"Porch geese. Not spansch."

He looked at the woman and noticed her misbuttoned dressing gown. It drove him crazy when she did that. "What are you moaning about now?"

She huffed and then barked again. "Brazil."

"What about Brazil?"

"Speak Port-chu-*geez*."

"Portuguese? Wait... You're saying they speak Portuguese in Brazil? Not Spanish?"

She nodded with one hard jerk of her head.

"Woman, you're crazy. You can't even button your dang housecoat. It's *South America*. Of course they speak Spanish. It's right next to Mexico, land of mojitos."

"Cuba."

"Right. Now they speak Cuban. Whatever."

Tucking the thermos under his arm, he patted her on the knee as he passed on his way to the kitchen. It had been a long four months, trying to get the information he needed out of the old cow. He'd threatened, cajoled, and finally discovered that adding a bit of booze to her milk loosened her tongue. Unfortunately, the only thing he was sure of was that his father had given Bobbi a *box*. The old man mentioned it in the last conversation they'd had before he died. He didn't know how big or what it looked like, but it had to be worth a fortune. He *knew* it. Why else would Pop give it to her to hide?

His father had bragged about the box, then went and got himself shivved by another inmate before he'd had a chance to share any details about his treasure chest.

Pop never did have any luck.

By the time he found his grandmother Bobbi, she'd lost her mind and didn't seem to know what was in the box or what she did with it.

Some days she remembered leaving it at the old house. Other days she thought she sold it or gave it to someone.

That theory just about made him sick to his stomach. The idea that someone else might have the goods his father had worked so hard to steal...

Once Bobbi claimed Indiana Jones stole the box. That's when he gave up trying to get a straight answer out of her.

"Tea."

He was unscrewing the thermos when she said it.

"What?"

"Tea."

"What about tea?"

"*Tea.*"

He poked his head out of the kitchen.

"You want tea?"

She grunted.

"But you *always* have warm milk."

"Tea after church."

"After—"

She turned her head away from him and crossed her arms against her chest.

He rubbed his temple with one hand. The crazy old bird thought it was Sunday. Probably thought it was nineteen seventy-six, too, because she hadn't been to church in all the time he'd known her.

He looked at the thermos, sitting there with all his hard work inside. He yawned.

What a day for her to switch to tea.

"Do you want milk in your tea?"

"Yes."

Fine. At least he could put his sleepy milk in the tea. Maybe it would be enough. If not, he'd just have to keep slipping it into everything he could until it did the job.

Yawning again, he reached into the kitchen cabinet and found a box of tea still sealed in plastic wrap. He picked at the edge of the box with his short fingernail. Frustrated, he pulled a long knife from the butcher's block and stabbed at it until it tore open.

He opened another cabinet in search of a teacup but found none. He opened another and another, finding nothing but yellowed Tupperware containers warped by the microwave and enough cat food to keep a pride of lions alive for a year. He whirled and stormed back into the front room.

"Dang it, Bobbi, where do you keep—"

Oh...

His face was inches from Bobbi's.

She'd gotten out of her chair and they'd almost run smack into each other. Only the knife in his hand—the knife he hadn't realized he was holding—kept her from hitting him.

He looked down and watched as a rivulet of blood rode the blade from where the tip pierced her midsection.

Her height had done her in. A shorter gal would have taken it in the ribs. The knife might have bounced off the bone. But Bobbi was nearly six feet tall.

He considered pulling out the weapon, but it was too late

now.

Instead, he *pushed*.

Bobbi Marie barely made a sound. Just sucked in a little wind. Her face fell slack as the knife in his hand reached the wooden hilt. He froze and they stood that way, eyes locked on each other. He could feel her lean against the blade and his wrist trembled with the strain of holding her weight. Her legs buckled and he withdrew. She fell to the ground in a curled clump.

Standing over her, he watched the blood drip from the knife to the floor. He sidled past her and sat in the chair where she'd been only a moment before.

He didn't mean to kill her.

Well, he *had*, of course, but not that way. Not with a knife.

His eyelids felt like they weighed a thousand pounds. In a situation like this, having just stabbed a woman to death, he felt as if he should be more *awake*. Wired, even. Instead, he wanted to sleep. Let his mind rest for a bit.

He closed his lids.

Maybe he'd taste-tested a little too much of the sleepy milk.

A moment later he was snoring.

Get *Pineapple Mystery Box* on Amazon!

ANOTHER FREE PREVIEW!

THE GIRL WHO WANTS

A Shee McQueen Mystery-Thriller by Amy Vansant

CHAPTER ONE

Three Weeks Ago, Nashua, New Hampshire.

Shee realized her mistake the moment her feet left the grass.

He's enormous.

She'd watched him drop from the side window of the house. He landed four feet from where she stood, and still, her brain refused to register the warning signs. The nose, big and lumpy as breadfruit, the forehead some beach town could use as a jetty if they buried him to his neck...

His knees bent to absorb his weight and *her* brain thought, *got you.*

Her brain couldn't be bothered with simple math: *Giant, plus Shee, equals Pain.*

Instead, she jumped to tackle him, dangling airborne as his knees straightened and the *pet the rabbit* bastard stood to his full height.

Crap.

The math added up pretty quickly after that.

Hovering like Superman mid-flight, there wasn't much she could do to change her disastrous trajectory. She'd *felt* like a superhero when she left the ground. Now, she felt more like a Canada goose staring into the propellers of Captain Sully's Airbus A320.

She might take down the plane, but it was going to *hurt.*

Frankenjerk turned toward her at the same moment she plowed into him. She clamped her arms around his waist like a little girl hugging a redwood. Lurch returned the embrace, twisting her to the ground. Her back hit the dirt and air burst from her lungs like a double shotgun blast.

Ow.

Wheezing, she punched upward, striking Beardless Hagrid in the throat.

That didn't go over well.

Grabbing her shoulder with one hand, Dickasaurus flipped her on her stomach like a sausage link, slipped his hand under her chin and pressed his forearm against her windpipe.

The only air she'd gulped before he cut her supply stank of damp armpit. He'd tucked her cranium in his arm crotch, much like the famous noggin-less horseman once held his severed head. Fireworks exploded in the dark behind her eyes.

That's when a thought occurred to her.

I haven't been home in fifteen years.

What if she died in Gigantor's armpit? Would her father even know?

Has it really been that long?

Flopping like a landed fish, she forced her assailant to adjust his hold and sucked a breath as she flipped on her back. Spittle glistened on his lips, his brow furrowed as if she'd asked him to read a paragraph of big-boy words.

His nostrils flared like the Holland Tunnel.

There's an idea.

Making a V with her fingers, Shee thrust upward, stabbing into his nose, straining to reach his tiny brain.

Goliath roared. Jerking back, he grabbed her arm to unplug her fingers from his nose socket. She whipped away her limb before he had a good grip, fearing he'd snap her bones with his Godzilla paws.

Kneeling before her, he clamped both hands over his face, cursing as blood seeped from behind his fingers.

Shee's gaze didn't linger on that mess. Her focus fell to his crotch, hovering a foot above her feet, protected by nothing but a thin pair of oversized sweatpants.

Scrambled eggs, sir?

She kicked.

He howled.

Shee scuttled back like a crab, found her feet and snatched her gun from her side. The gun she should have pulled *before* trying to tackle the Empire State Building.

"Move a muscle and I'll aerate you," she said. She always liked that line.

The golem growled, but remained on the ground like a good dog, cradling his family jewels.

Shee's partner in this manhunt, a local cop easier on the eyes than he was useful, rounded the corner and drew his own weapon.

She smiled and holstered the gun he'd lent her. Unknowingly.

"Glad you could make it."

Her portion of the operation accomplished, she headed toward the car as more officers swarmed the scene.

"Shee, where are you going?" called the cop.

She stopped and turned.

"Home, I think."

His gaze dropped to her hip.

"Is that my gun?"

Get *The Girl Who Wants* on

Amazon!

Made in the USA
Las Vegas, NV
06 November 2022

58872032R00154